A SECOND CHANCE AT LOVE

Paul held Holly a bit more closely than propriety allowed, but she did not resist him as they whirled across the dance floor. He knew that she was caught up in the memory of that time long ago, before the fates had conspired against them, and he intended to use that memory to his advantage. Her lips were parted slightly and Paul fought the urge to kiss them. He had kissed them that night, five Seasons ago, and found them sweetly passionate and giving. Was it possible for them to renew their first taste of love and forget the delusions of the intervening years? Paul was not certain, but his future happiness, and Holly's as well, demanded that he make the attempt.

It seemed as if they had been waltzing for only the space of a heartbeat, but the melody was drawing to an end. They were approaching the balcony and the doors were open. This was the moment Paul had longed for through four insufferable Seasons, and he did not hesitate. Before his angel could gather herself enough to resist, he whirled her out, onto the balcony, and claimed her lips with his own. . . .

Books by Kathryn Kirkwood

A MATCH FOR MELISSA
A SEASON FOR SAMANTHA
A HUSBAND FOR HOLLY

Published by Zebra Books

A HUSBAND
FOR HOLLY

Kathryn Kirkwood

Zebra Books
Kensington Publishing Corp.
http://www.zebrabooks.com

ZEBRA BOOKS are published by

Kensington Publishing Corp.
850 Third Avenue
New York, NY 10022

First Printing: July, 1999
10 9 8 7 6 5 4 3 2 1

Printed in the United States of America

For Amanda McDaniel—thanks for all the encouragement

One

Lady Holly Bentworth sighed as she bent down to place a battered washbasin under a leaking spot in the Pooles' roof. The floor in the small cottage that belonged to the schoolmaster and his family was littered with every pail, bowl, and pot that the Poole family owned. No sooner had Holly stepped back than several drops of rain splattered on her arm and she looked up to see that the old shingles had sprung yet another leak. She gave a sigh of pure exasperation and moved a workbasket half full of clothing to be mended to another corner, out of harm's way. The Pooles' roof was a disgrace. If the schoolmaster's cottage had been on her brother-in-law's land, the damaged shingles would have been replaced long before the sky had clouded over and the rain had begun to fall. Richard, Viscount Bentworth, might have other failings, but he managed the estate he had inherited from Holly's husband very well. Every one of his tenants, servants, and estate employees had ample food on the table and decent quarters in which to live.

Holly's neighbor was a horse of another color. He seemed to take no interest in the country estate he had inherited from his aunt and had visited Midvale Park only once, immediately after his aunt had died. After a tour of his lands, he had left the estate in his agent's care, and had taken no further interest in the property.

Holly had asked about the new owner and discovered that he was an earl who already possessed vast holdings. Midvale Park was the smallest of his estates, separated from his other holdings by many miles. The lands had been most productive, turning a tidy profit every year under his aunt's careful management, but now, under the management of the earl's agent, Mr. McPherson, they were fast falling into ruin.

Though she had taken an instant dislike to the man, Holly had sought out Mr. McPherson several months ago to tell him about the Pooles' roof. He had promised to bring it to his employer's attention, but no repairs had been made. When the rains had commenced, Holly had spoken to Mr. McPherson a second time and he'd informed her that his hands were tied. The earl knew about his schoolmaster's roof, but he had refused to make any improvements on such a minor and insignificant property. This statement had caused Holly to reach the obvious conclusion. The earl did not give a button about Midvale Park and intended to ignore it in favor of his other holdings.

The deplorable state of the Pooles' roof wasn't the only bone that Holly had to pick with her absentee neighbor. She had made a list of matters that required his immediate attention and planned to present it to him, along with a few choice words of her own, when he showed his face at Midvale Park. She would have posted it to him in London, where Mr. McPherson said he had gone to enjoy the diversions of Town, but the agent had been under orders not to give out his employer's direction. It seemed the earl did not wish to be bothered by communications from his country neighbors.

Holly sighed and picked her way through the obstacle course on the Pooles' floor to a relatively dry spot near the door. It was no wonder that Mr. Poole's mother was so ill. It had rained on and off for the past two weeks and the cottage gave little protection from the elements.

"The tea's ready, Holly." Serena Poole appeared in the doorway, her face wreathed in a smile. She was a thin woman in her early forties with a cheerful disposition and no little intelligence. "It was so good of you to bring it. I can't remember the last time we had real tea! I hope you don't mind, but I saved out a bit for Mother Poole. A nice hot cup is bound to cheer her when she wakes."

"I'll bring more tomorrow." Holly smiled in return. Serena Poole was one of her favorite friends. She had taken on the care of her husband's widowed mother without a second's thought, even though they could ill afford another mouth to feed. It was one of the reasons Holly always brought a basket of food whenever she came to visit.

"Come into the kitchen, Holly. It's a bit warmer there. And when we've finished with our tea, we can put our cups under two more leaks."

Holly laughed and followed Serena into the tiny kitchen. The small enclosure was considerably warmer, and though droplets of rain fell through the shingles to sizzle against the hot surface of the stove, the area below the small wooden table was relatively dry and cozy.

"The poultice you made for Mother Poole's chest has relieved most of her congestion." Serena took a chair across from Holly and smiled as she took a sip of her tea. "I've written it down in my book."

Holly nodded. Serena was on her way to becoming a very competent healer. When she'd expressed an interest in the remedies that Holly had given to some of the tenants on the earl's estate, Holly had begun to teach her what she knew of the healing arts.

"I'm concerned about young Neddy's wound." Serena frowned slightly as she mentioned the name of a neighboring child who had cut his foot on a sharp rock. "I drained the abscess, but he complains that it is still sore to the touch."

Holly nodded. "Save the tea leaves, Serena, and steep them again for Neddy's mother. No doubt she could use a cup, even if it is a second brewing. Then lay the hot leaves against the wound and they will draw out the soreness."

"Of course!" Serena sighed, nodding quickly. "That's the very same remedy you used on Tom Beasley's cut finger. I don't know why I didn't think of it."

Holly smiled. "Perhaps because you had no tea leaves. I'll make certain you have a good supply. Tell me how you treated John Wilburn's bruised eye."

"With a conserve of red roses and rotten apple. It removed the blackness within a day."

"And Mrs. Tomley's dyspepsia?" Holly leaned forward to hear her answer.

"Chamomile tea. I infused two dozen flowers in a pint of boiling water for half an hour. Then I decanted it, sweetened it with honey, and gave her the dose you recommended."

"You will make an excellent healer, Serena." Holly smiled her approval. "I have taught you all I learned from my dear grandmama and you have added knowledge of your own."

A blush rose to Serena's cheeks at the compliment. "Thank you, Holly. I find I'm eager for the gypsies to come again, now that you have introduced me to them. The lady they call Tamara has a great knowledge of herbs and she has promised to train me in their use."

"Then you are no longer afraid of the gypsies?"

"Not in the slightest and I am ashamed that I ever was. They are people, just like us, and their circumstances are even worse than ours."

"That is true, but at least their wagons are dry." Holly frowned slightly. "It's more than you can say for your cottage."

"I take your point, Holly, but I am not forced to travel the countryside, chased from one place to another and wanted in none. It's good of Lord Bentworth to give them leave to camp in your field, just as your husband always did."

"Richard's no fool when it comes to getting the best of a bargain." Holly's lips turned up at the corners. "The gypsies heal his sick cattle, mend his pots and pans, and sharpen his tools for the privilege of staying on his land. They do no harm unless harm is done to them, and much good is accomplished by their presence."

Serena nodded and was about to reply when they heard a weak voice from the bedchamber. Both women rose to their feet and rushed to the small chamber to see their patient sitting up in bed, reaching for the glass of barley water that sat on the side table.

"Good morning, Mother Poole." Serena bent down to place her hand against her mother-in-law's brow. When she straightened up, she was smiling. "Your fever has broken."

Holly did the same and then nodded. "Yes, indeed. You are remarkably improved, Mother Poole. A few days' rest and I have no doubt that you will be as right as rain."

"Oh, please do not make mention of rain!" Mother Poole smiled at both of them. "If this downpour continues for much longer, we shall have to ask my son to build us an ark."

Serena laughed. It was clear she was much relieved that her husband's mother was on the road to regaining her health. "Holly has brought us some tea, Mother Poole. I'll go fetch you a cup."

"Tea?" Mrs. Poole's eyes sparkled as her daughter-in-law left the room and she turned to Holly with a smile. "How very good of you, Holly."

Holly waved off the older woman's gratitude. "It's nothing of consequence. Richard provides very well for us."

"It is only what you deserve, my dear." Mrs. Poole's eyes narrowed. "It is only a pity that his wife is not of a like mind. I remember her from Bath, you know. Her aunt was one of my bosom bows."

"I did not know that." Holly knew that she should not listen to gossip about her sister-in-law, but she was unable to resist the temptation.

"Annabelle Forsythe was regrettably top-lofty, even as a child." Mrs. Poole sat up as Holly plumped the pillows behind her head. "I do blame her father for that. She was the only girl, you see, and the apple of his eye."

Giving in to the lure of a good story, Holly sat down in the chair next to the bed and leaned forward to listen. Mother Poole was much recovered and seemed eager to talk.

"Annabelle's mother died in childbirth and that is the reason my bosom bow took charge of the household. Her brother would have been hard-pressed to handle six boys and a baby girl without her assistance. Poor India gave up her chance at marriage and a family of her own to aid her brother."

"That is, indeed, unfortunate." Holly frowned slightly. "I do hope that she is happy now?"

"You may rest assured that she is, my dear. When her brother's children were grown, India went on to become a companion to a lady who travels all over the world. I daresay it is far more enjoyable than raising her brother's family. Dear India was never so happy as the day her troublesome niece married your husband's brother."

"My sister-in-law was . . . troublesome?"

"Oh, my yes! Dear India despaired that Annabelle should ever make a match. She was quite fetching, you see, and the young swains buzzed like bees around her, currying her favors. This served to elevate her aspirations and she considered herself too good for the sons of country squires. She refused several quite acceptable matches, declaring that she could do better. Over the next few years the offers for her dwindled and her looks were already starting to fade when she made the acquaintance of your husband's brother. I daresay she would have reposed on the shelf if he hadn't asked for her hand in marriage."

"I see." Holly nodded. She had wondered why Lady Annabelle had waited until she was nearly thirty to marry. "Why did she accept Richard? Though he has a kind heart, he is not the most handsome of men."

Mother Poole laughed lightly. "No doubt his newly acquired title had much to do with her decision."

Holly raised her brows, but remained silent. Even though she had suspected as much, it would be disloyal of her to say so. Her husband's brother had always been quite shy around the ladies and she had no doubt that Lady Annabelle had taken full advantage of his inexperience.

Serena came in with the tea and Holly smiled at her gratefully. She did not wish to be drawn into further discussion about Lady

Annabelle, as Mother Poole was a good listener and might catch a hint of how little regard Holly harbored for her sister-in-law.

"I must leave you now." Holly rose to her feet. "My step-daughters and I have agreed to assist Lady Annabelle in the preparations for this evening's dinner party at the manor."

"Are you and your stepdaughters to be counted among the guests?" Mother Poole's eyes were sharp.

Holly shook her head. Though she had been careful not to mention the lack of invitations they had received from the manor, Mother Poole had surmised the truth. "No. I fear that would be quite impossible, as there will be an equal number of ladies and gentlemen. Our presence would add three unescorted females to the mix and serve to throw off Lady Annabelle's count."

"Oh, dear." Serena looked very sympathetic. "It truly isn't right that you and the girls are excluded. Beth and Marcie are of an age when they should be making the acquaintance of other young ladies and gentlemen. How will you ever teach them to take their rightful place in society if Richard's wife will not give them leave to attend her social events?"

Mother Poole spoke up, well aware of the injustice. "Serena is right. Beth and Marcie are the daughters of the former Viscount Bentworth and they should be treated as such. Why don't you speak to your brother-in-law about it? He knows his duty, unlike some others I could name. I am certain he would intercede with his wife."

Holly considered the wisdom of Mother Poole's words. It was true that Beth and Marcie were of an age to make their bow to society, and it was her duty to assure their future. For the past several years, Richard's wife had treated both girls as unpaid servants, calling on them to assist her with tasks that should have been accomplished by her staff. Holly did not mind so much for herself, though she had been relegated to the same fate. But she had noticed that her stepdaughters were beginning to resent their aunt's high-handed treatment of them.

"You will speak to Richard about it?" Serena raised her brows with the question.

"Yes." Holly nodded. "I will do it this very afternoon. But I must go now, so that I can catch him alone, before Lady Annabelle's guests begin to arrive."

After a brief word with Serena, instructing her to notify her immediately if Mother Poole should suffer a relapse, Holly pulled up the hood of her cloak and stepped out into the downpour. Her mare was tethered under a lean-to that sheltered her from the rain, and Holly gained her seat without assistance. She clucked softly to her mare to set her in motion and guided her down the path that led to her brother-in-law's lands, deftly avoiding the brush that threatened to turn the path impassable, and ducking under the low-hanging branches of the trees.

Once she had crossed the wooded area that separated Midvale lands from Bentworth holdings, Holly breathed a sigh of relief. The difference was noticeable, even to the untrained observer. Richard's lands were well kept, while the earl's were not. The brush had been trimmed back from the paths and the dead branches had been removed from the trees and sawed into suitable lengths for firewood. The cluster of tenant cottages in the distance sported fresh paint and solid roofs that kept out the rain. Richard might defer to his wife in all matters that concerned society and the home, but he had the say in managing his lands.

Holly had ridden for less than ten minutes when she glimpsed the manor house through the trees. It was a lovely home, built of red brick, large enough to sport a dozen guest chambers. Bentworth Manor was three stories high with a grand drawing room, a commodious dining chamber, a breakfast room, a large kitchen, a superb library, and a music room on the ground floor. The family quarters took up most of the second story and the third story contained an elegant ballroom. A generous space under the eaves had been set aside to house the servants, and Holly sighed as she caught a glimpse of the lovely rose garden that she had planted. She had been happy when she'd lived in the manor house with her husband and his two daughters.

Instead of turning down the neat gravel drive that led to the entrance of the manor house, Holly guided her mare down the path to the stables. Once she had dismounted and left her mare in the care of one of the grooms, she hurried down the path through the woods that led to the dower house and arrived at the small cottage in short order.

"Mama!" Beth, a brown-haired beauty with lovely sea-green eyes and the elder of William's two daughters, flung open the door and held out her hand for Holly's rain-drenched cloak. "You were gone so long, we were beginning to worry. Has Mother Poole taken a turn for the worse?"

Holly gave her a reassuring smile. "No, Beth. She is much improved. Where is Marcie?"

"I'm here, Mama." Marcie's violet eyes sparkled as she rushed up to embrace her stepmother. "I put on the kettle the moment we saw you coming. I'll make you a cup of tea while you change to a dry gown. I declare! You are wet through and through!"

"Of course I am. It's raining." Holly smiled, reaching out to tuck a lock of curly black hair into the loose knot that Marcie had fashioned at the nape of her neck. "Are you ready to go to the manor?"

Both girls nodded, but Holly noticed that they wore identical frowns. Marcie, who had always been more outspoken, even though she was a year younger, sighed deeply. "We're ready, Mama, though I fail to see why Aunt Annabelle doesn't outfit all three of us in caps and aprons and be done with it."

"Marcie!" Holly choked back a startled laugh.

"Have a caution, Marcie." Beth looked askance at her sister. "It truly is not proper for you to criticize your elders."

Marcie turned to Holly. "But it's true, isn't it, Mama? Aunt Annabelle treats us like extra maids that she can call in whenever she wishes."

"Yes, it's true." Holly nodded. Marcie was right and it would be useless to deny it. "But that may not be the case much longer. I intend to speak to your uncle about it. I shall do so diplomatically, of course. I doubt that it would be wise of me to mention caps and aprons."

Both girls laughed and Holly joined in. Laughter had been their salvation in the nearly two years that had passed since William had died and Richard had brought his bride, Lady Annabelle, to be Mistress of the Manor. It had been difficult for Holly to remove to the dower cottage, but even more so for Beth and Marcie, who had spent their whole lives in luxury at Bentworth Manor. The dower house was small, only two bed-chambers and one large room on the ground floor that served as both dining chamber and sitting room, and it lacked the amenities to which the girls had been accustomed. As they had been able to afford only one maid-of-all-work, the girls had learned to dress themselves, arrange their own hair, and help to prepare meals in the small kitchen. Holly knew that if they had been unable to find humor in their current situation, both Beth and Marcie might have grown into bitter young ladies who would spend the remainder of their days feeling cheated by circumstance.

Once Holly had changed to a dry, serviceable gown and joined the girls in the kitchen, Beth reached out her hand. "Are you certain you wish to approach Uncle Richard, Mama?"

"Yes. It must be done, and the sooner the better. Both you and Marcie are old enough to be included on Lady Annabelle's guest list. I shall remind your uncle of that fact."

"I'm not entirely certain that I wish to be included." Marcie frowned slightly. "Lady Annabelle's guests are all horribly top-lofty. No doubt they'd regard us as poor relations."

Beth smiled wryly. "But we *are* poor relations."

"Indeed, we are." Holly chuckled. "But I daresay you girls have the advantage over most young ladies who live in fine houses."

Marcie turned to her with a puzzled look. "How is that, Mama?"

"If a young gentleman comes to offer for either of you, you may rest assured that he is enamored of your person and not of your fortune."

Two

Holly squared her shoulders as she approached the door to the library, preparing for the worst. Her brother-in-law did not like to be bothered when he was working, but this was the first opportunity she'd had to approach him. Lady Annabelle was closeted with her dresser and Richard's man of business had departed only moments before. She must beard the Lord of the Manor in his den before others claimed his attention.

After a quick pat to her smooth blond hair to make certain that it was in order, Holly raised her hand and knocked lightly. The voice from inside that bid her to enter sounded a bit sharp to her ears, but Holly fixed her lips in a smile and opened the door.

"Holly?" Richard, who was sitting behind his desk with a stack of ledgers opened before him, rose to his feet to greet her. He seemed surprised to see her there, but he gave her a welcoming smile. "Come in, my dear. I thought it was my agent with a list of more repairs to be done."

Holly drew a breath of relief. Perhaps Richard was not in a taking, after all. "I must discuss a matter of some importance with you, Richard. I doubt it will take more than a minute or two of your time."

"I always have time for you, Holly." Richard gestured toward a chair and moved toward the side table. "Would you care for a glass of sherry?"

By the eager expression on his face, Holly surmised that he

wished for a brandy and would not imbibe unless she agreed to join him. "Thank you, Richard. I daresay a glass of sherry would be just the thing."

"Good." Just as Holly had expected, Richard poured her a small glass and then took a generous measure of brandy for himself. When he was seated, he turned toward her with a question in his eyes. "What is it, my dear?"

Holly took a deep breath. "I have need of your advice, Richard, about a matter that concerns me greatly. I know this is an imposition, but you have been so helpful to me in the past."

"I have?" Richard appeared both surprised and gratified, precisely the reaction that Holly had been seeking. "I have tried to do right by you, Holly. After all, you are my brother's widow."

Holly nodded. "And you have been most generous in your support. No brother could have been kinder. I do imagine you have noticed that your nieces are maturing?"

"Yes, Holly." Richard nodded quickly. "And they are both turning into lovely young ladies, due in no small part to your example."

Holly smiled. "Thank you, Richard. I do hope that you and Lady Annabelle have found no cause to complain of their comportment?"

"Never. Their behavior has been more than acceptable. You may be proud of them, Holly."

"I am." Holly nodded. "And I am pleased you regard them so highly. Elizabeth reached the age of eighteen on her last birthday and Marcella is only one year younger. That is why I have need of your advice, Richard. Most young ladies of that age have already made their entrance into society. Do you believe that it is time I allow Beth and Marcie to do the same?"

Richard began to frown. "Perhaps, but I do have a problem in that regard. If my pockets were deeper, I should be delighted to stand them both to a Season in London. Unfortunately—"

"Oh no, Richard! That is not what I meant at all!" Holly interrupted quickly. "You must forgive me, for I've made a perfect muddle of this. I did not intend that you launch them in

London. I merely meant that perhaps you might give your permission for them to attend some local gatherings, where they may practice their social skills."

Richard reached out to pat her hand and Holly noticed that he appeared quite relieved. Thus far, her plan was working to perfection.

"Local gatherings? I see no reason why they should not attend those affairs. As you stated, the girls are both of an age where they should be introduced into our local society."

"Oh thank you, Richard." Holly gave him a guileless smile. "The girls will be so pleased at the interest that you have taken in them. Perhaps they could begin here, at one of your gatherings? I should like them to witness Lady Annabelle's gracious manners, as I am certain they could learn much from her example. And I should like them to compare the attributes of any young gentleman they might meet to those of their own dear uncle."

"You are partially correct, Holly." Richard gave a slight chuckle. "Belle is an excellent hostess and the girls could find no better model for their own social behavior. But as far as comparing their young gentlemen to me, I'm not so certain."

Holly smiled. "But I *am* certain, Richard. The girls hold you in high regard. You are so very like their father, you see. You have the same charm and wit, not to mention intelligence. I have no doubt that William would be grateful to you for setting the example in his stead."

"If you truly believe that I might be of some assistance, I shall be happy to oblige you." Richard looked pleased at this compliment. "I will speak to Belle about this immediately and she will arrange some sort of appropriate entertainment for my nieces. I shall get back to you before this evening is out, you may count on that."

"A dinner party for us?" Beth was delighted when Holly pulled her stepdaughters aside to give them the news.

"You are a wonder, Mama!" Marcie hugged her quickly and then drew back to regard her with some amusement. "However did you trick Aunt Annabelle into arranging a dinner party for us?"

Holly felt a flush of guilty color rise to her cheeks. Leave it to Marcie to catch her out. "It wasn't a trick, not precisely. Your uncle was truly pleased to oblige me."

"And he insisted that Aunt Annabelle go along?" Marcie laughed quite merrily when Holly nodded. "No doubt she'll be in a high dudgeon all night. I do hope she doesn't take her pique out on him."

Holly smiled. "I would not be anxious on your uncle's account. I do believe he can take care of himself. And do not forget, he told me that he was determined to lead both of you out in a dance."

"Oh, dear!" Beth's face fell. "You must go over the steps with us again, Mama. I should not like to embarrass our dear uncle when he has been so kind."

Holly nodded. "Of course. We'll practice until you are confident, Beth. Marcie can be your partner."

"But we must switch places after every dance." Marcie imposed a restriction. "I would not like to get into the habit of assuming the gentleman's position."

Beth nodded quickly. "You are right, Marcie. It would be regarded as a dreadful *faux pas* if either one of us made that error. I should be dreadfully mortified."

"It would not be so grave an error as all that." Holly smiled at both of them fondly. "Do not forget that this is just a small dinner party and the guests will be people you have known all your lives."

Beth nodded. "We know that, Mama, but it is still a party at the manor. And we shall be the guests of honor at Aunt Annabelle's table."

"No doubt our dear aunt will expect us to stay when the others have left, and tidy up her dining room." Marcie gave a small chuckle.

"That was not charitable, Marcie." Beth chided her gently. "We should be grateful for this opportunity."

Marcie sighed, looking properly chastised. "You are right, Beth. And I am grateful. I have never attended a formal dinner party before."

"It will be enjoyable to be surrounded by our friends." Beth began to smile. "And I am very glad that the rector's daughter will be there, as I have been wishing to speak with her again. There's so little time after Sunday services to talk. And you said the squire was coming, Mama. He's ever so jolly and he always has interesting tales to tell about his trips to London."

The girls seemed content with the guest list that Lady Annabelle had hastily contrived and Holly was careful to hide her disappointment. She had hoped that they would be invited to one of their aunt's more elaborate parties, where they would meet the sons and daughters of noblemen. She was certain that Richard had been willing, but Lady Annabelle had no doubt decided that her nieces were too countrified to be included among her elevated guests. Perhaps it was best this way, as Beth and Marcie would be spared the barbs some of Lady Annabelle's high-ranking acquaintances might make about their circumstances.

"What will we wear, Mama?" Beth turned to her. "Do you think that the hem on my best gown can be let down again?"

Beth's question raised Holly's spirits. "You shall both have new gowns for the party. I've set a sum of money aside and we'll walk to the village first thing tomorrow, to consult with Mrs. Percy."

"Oh, Mama! You are so very good to us!" Beth hugged her tightly. "We're so glad Papa married you!"

Holly blinked back the moisture that came to her eyes. William's daughters were very dear to her and she loved them every bit as much as if they'd been her own daughters. "Let's make our escape before your aunt thinks of more tasks for us to do."

"Cook said we should stop by the kitchen before we left."

Beth lowered her voice. "She packed another basket of food for us."

Holly smiled. They had made a friend of Lady Annabelle's cook and she often set aside tidbits from the manor kitchen for them. "We must all remember to thank her for her generosity. Your new gowns will come, in no small part, from the money we have saved from our housekeeping budget."

They had just passed through the door to the servants' hall when Mr. Pelton, the butler at the manor, suddenly appeared in their path. "If I could have a word with you, madam?"

"Of course." Holly nodded quickly. "What is it, Mr. Pelton?"

"This letter arrived for you in the post." The butler handed Holly a bulky envelope. "It looked official and I decided to deliver it to you personally, rather than place it on the hall table with the others."

"Thank you." Holly tucked the letter in her pocket and exchanged a conspiratorial smile with the man who had served her husband so well. Since William's death, she had received three other letters at the manor and they had been opened prior to reaching her hands. When she'd quizzed Mr. Pelton about it, he had confided that his new mistress had slit them open, insisting that any of Holly's business should be known to her.

"What is it, Mama?" Beth's eyes were wide and frightened. "Has someone else died?"

"No, dear. I can assure you that they have not." Holly reached out to take her hand. It was no wonder that Beth was overset, for the three letters Holly had received previously had all contained notices of death. The first had concerned her elderly aunt, who had passed away in her sleep, the second had contained notice of her uncle's demise, and the third had been sent to apprise Holly of a distant cousin's death.

"How can you be so certain, Mama?" Beth's voice trembled slightly. "You have not yet read the letter."

Holly gave her an encouraging smile. "Because there is no one left to die. My family is gone, every one of them."

"Don't say that, Mama!" Marcie began to frown. "We're your family now."

Beth nodded. "Marcie's right. You still have a family as long as you have us."

"That's very true." Holly reached out to them, hugging Beth and then Marcie. "And you are the very best family of all."

Three

"I would say that Cook has outdone herself." Holly popped the last bite into her mouth. "Which treat did you like best?"

Beth considered the question for a moment and then she smiled. "The lobster patties. I fancied them even above the roasted goose."

"I much preferred the smoked salmon." Marcie sighed in bliss as she remembered the taste of the flaky fish. "And I especially adored those little round green things on top."

Holly laughed. "They are called pickled capers and I agree that they set off the salmon very well. Tell me what you thought of the figs?"

"Too sweet." Marcie made a face. "I thought the cherry compote was much better. And the raspberry tart was divine."

Beth looked concerned as she turned to Holly. "Are raspberries very dear when they are out of season?"

"Indeed they are." Holly nodded.

"And the lobster?" Beth began to frown. "Is it costly?"

"Very. I wager to say that the cost of this sumptuous feast could have filled our larder for a year."

Beth sighed. "It seems a waste for just one evening, does it not? Uncle Richard's purse would be much heavier if Aunt Annabelle would plan a simpler menu."

"That is very true, my dear." Holly had no choice but to agree. *And,* a little voice inside her piped up, *if Lady Annabelle would forgo just one or two of her lavish entertainments, Rich-*

ard would well be able to fund Beth and Marcie's Seasons in London!

"Why does she continue to spend in this way?" Beth seemed genuinely puzzled. "She's forever complaining that the estate doesn't provide enough revenues. Perhaps it would, if she made an effort to temper her disbursements."

"But a simple menu wouldn't serve to impress her friends." Marcie entered the discussion. "And you know full well that Aunt Annabelle wants her London acquaintances to think that she married a wealthy gentleman."

Holly winced, reminded of the old adage her uncle had been fond of quoting. *From the mouths of babes.* "You must not criticize your aunt, girls. It is far from kind."

"But it's true." Marcie retorted. "You cannot argue with that, can you, Mama?"

Holly sighed. "No, I cannot. And now let us change the subject before I suffer an attack of indigestion, which would be quite a pity after the excellent banquet we enjoyed. What color do you fancy for your new gown, Beth?"

"I am not certain." Beth responded quickly, accepting Holly's wish to discuss a more pleasing topic. "I am fond of yellow because it is so cheerful, and I have always been partial to brown."

Marcie gazed at her sister appraisingly and then she shook her head. "You should not choose yellow. Your complexion is much too pale. And brown is far too ordinary. You must have something that will set off your coloring to perfection."

"What would you suggest?" Beth deferred to her sister's judgment.

"Green." Marcie nodded emphatically. "You will look lovely in green. It will complement the slight tint of red in your hair and bring out the color of your eyes."

Holly nodded. "I do believe you're right, Marcie. Beth would look lovely in green."

"Then I shall choose green." Beth smiled at them both.

"Excellent." Holly was pleased. "And you, Marcie?"

Marcie frowned. "I should think a deep shade of red, or perhaps a violet. What do you think, Mama?"

"The violet is a perfect choice, especially if Mrs. Percy can find a hue that will complement your eyes."

"And for you, Mama?" Beth wore an eager smile. "What color will you choose?"

Holly drew a deep breath. She would have to take caution with her answer for she had not set aside enough money for three new gowns, and the girls would not accept theirs if they thought that she was depriving herself. "I shall not purchase a new gown at this time. I could not wear it anyway, and it would be a shameless waste of our money."

"But why, Mama?" Beth turned to her in alarm. "You will be attending our party, won't you?"

"I would not miss it for the world, but it is only proper that I remain in mourning until the second anniversary of your father's death. I would not like the rector or his wife to think ill of me."

Marcie looked disappointed, but she nodded. "I fear you're right, Mama. The rector is regrettably Gothic about observing the conventions."

"But we could order a dress for you now." Beth wasn't yet ready to give up the notion.

"No, Beth." Holly remained firm. "Fully half the enjoyment of owning a new dress is donning it the moment that it is completed. It should make me sad to see it hanging in my clothespress before I was allowed the pleasure of wearing it."

Marcie began to object, but Holly interrupted her with a smile. "I do believe you girls are old enough to choose your own style of gown and handle the transaction on your own. I'll need to approve your final choice, of course, but I shall leave the rest to you."

"We're to go to Mrs. Percy alone?" Beth's eyes began to sparkle at this unexpected bonus.

"Yes, indeed." Holly nodded firmly. "And while you are closeted with Mrs. Percy, I'll take tea with her sister. If either of you feel that you need my advice, you have only to come next door."

This prompted another discussion about precisely how the girls should handle their purchases and Holly sat back with a smile. She had successfully diverted their attention from the fact that they could ill afford three new gowns.

It was not until they were about to retire for the night that Beth gave a little gasp of dismay. "Your letter, Mama. You have not opened it."

"You are right, Beth." Holly gave a little laugh. She had intended to read it the moment they arrived home, but she had forgotten all about it in their excitement over the contents of Cook's basket and their discussion of gowns. "Let me fetch it from the pocket of my cloak and we'll read it straightaway."

Holly's fingers were shaking slightly as she opened the bulky envelope. She glanced at the signature and her eyes widened with surprise. "It's from your father's solicitor in London."

"I wonder what Mr. Hempton wants?" Beth leaned closer. "I do hope it's not bad news."

Holly scanned the first few lines and then she turned to the girls with a smile. "It's very *good* news. It seems your father has set aside a generous sum for your Seasons in London, held in trust for you. Before he died, he left detailed instructions with Mr. Hempton."

"Oh, Mama!" Marcie was so shocked she could scarcely speak. "Does this mean that Beth and I are to have our Seasons?"

Holly nodded. "Indeed, it does! Mr. Hempton has rented a town house for us in London and he asks us to take possession of it in three weeks' time."

"Thank you, Papa! I just know that you can see us from heaven and you are as excited as we are." Marcie jumped to her feet, hitched up her skirts, and twirled about the room for a moment of supreme happiness. Then she stopped, frowning slightly, and turned to Holly. "Papa can see us, can't he?"

Holly smiled and nodded, even though she was not convinced. It truly did not matter, so long as Marcie took comfort in the notion.

"But just last Sunday the rector reminded us that we must put aside our . . ." Beth stopped in mid-sentence as Holly gave her hand a warning squeeze. They exchanged a speaking glance and then Beth smiled at her sister. "If anyone can see down from heaven, I am certain it is Papa. But you really must practice your manners, Marcie, and not dance around like a whirling dervish. After all, you are a young lady now."

Marcie thought about it for a moment and then she resumed her seat. "You are right, Beth. I shall try to be the pattern card of a perfectly proper young miss. But debutantes are allowed to be excited on occasion, are they not?"

"Of course they are, dear." Holly smiled at her youngest stepdaughter.

"You will advise us, won't you, Mama?" Beth looked a bit anxious. "We have never set foot in London before and we know nothing of the *ton* or its ways."

Holly nodded quickly. "I shall tell you everything I know. Change takes place very slowly in such elevated circles of society and I doubt that much has altered since my First Season."

"How long has it been since your debut, Mama?" Marcie smiled up at her.

"Five years. I met your father during my First Season and married him before it ended."

"You and Papa made a love match." Marcie sighed softly, a faraway look in her eyes. "I should like to find my true love in London, too."

"Perhaps you will." Holly preferred not to disabuse Marcie of her dreams. Though Holly's marriage to William had begun as a marriage of convenience, it was better to keep that a secret.

"There's more to read, Mama." Beth eyed the bulky envelope. "There appear to be two more letters inside."

Holly nodded and drew out the other two envelopes, her eyes widening as she recognized her deceased husband's hand. One was addressed to her and the other to Beth and Marcie.

"It seems your father has left a letter for you and Marcie." Holly handed one of the letters to Beth. "And one for me, as well. Since he has sealed them, he must have intended them to be private."

"Perhaps our letter contains Papa's instructions to obey Mama and act like young ladies of quality," Beth suggested. "And he wished us to read his words before we made our bows to society."

Marcie shivered slightly. "Perhaps, but it is almost like hearing a voice from . . . from the grave."

"That is simply not true, Marcie." Holly made quick to reassure her youngest stepdaughter. "I remember when your father wrote these letters, and it was long before his death. It is not unusual for a father to write a letter to his daughters, well in advance of a special occasion in their lives."

"You remember when he wrote them?" Marcie's anxious expression disappeared.

"Yes, I do. It was the day that Zeus threw a shoe and deposited your father in the stream. When he returned home, he changed to dry clothing and closeted himself in the library before a roaring fire. The next day he sent a packet to London and I am certain that it contained these very letters."

Beth looked much relieved at Holly's remembrance. "Then it was at least a year before Papa took to his bed. Thank you for telling us, Mama."

"Perhaps our letter contains advice to check our mounts for loose shoes before we ride." Marcie giggled slightly. "Papa was not happy about being drenched."

Holly drew a sigh of relief. Both girls seemed in much better spirits now. "I have been thinking about the gowns you will order from Mrs. Percy. Though she is quite talented for a local seamstress, I do believe you should order only one gown apiece from her. We shall wait until we arrive in London to complete your wardrobes."

"How many gowns shall we need?" Marcie turned to her eagerly.

"Three ball gowns for each of you will do for a start." Holly thought back to her own Season and the extensive wardrobe her elderly aunt had purchased for her. "You will also, each of you, require two walking dresses, a new riding habit, a half-dozen morning dresses for making and receiving calls, and three evening gowns that are suitable for formal dinner parties. I will post a letter to Madame Beauchamp tomorrow, requesting appointments for you."

Beth nodded quickly. "Madame Beauchamp is a modiste?"

"Yes, and she was considered all the crack when I was in London. She made my presentation gown and I shall ask her to make yours, as well. And if I find that she is still in favor, we shall order all of your gowns from her."

"What shall we take with us, Mama?" Beth frowned slightly. "Most of our gowns will not serve in London, will they?"

Holly smiled. "Not by half. Still, there may be a few things we can salvage. I will leave it to you to go through your wardrobes tomorrow and glean out what little will be of use, but we must begin shopping the moment we arrive in Town. There are many items that we must purchase."

"Tell us about them, Mama." Marcie's eyes were gleaming with excitement.

"You will need slippers and gloves to match your new gowns, bonnets, parasols, and other accessories. It is extremely important that both of you look your very best."

"How about you, Mama?" Beth raised her brows. "You will need a new wardrobe also, if you are to be our chaperone."

Holly felt a jolt of surprise at that reminder. "Why yes, I suppose I will. But my clothing will not need to be as elaborate as yours. It is entirely acceptable for a chaperone to possess a limited wardrobe."

"You won't be required to wear mourning, will you, Mama?"

Marcie looked anxious. "Though black looks very well on you, I should like to see you dressed in a pretty color. You are still very young and beautiful, you know."

Holly smiled. "Thank you, dear, but my manner of dress must reflect my status as the widow of a peer."

"But only for the first month." Marcie's lips curved up in a smile. "After that, you can wear whatever you please. It will be very exciting, Mama. I am convinced that once the gentlemen of the *ton* renew their acquaintance with you, you'll be deluged with invitations in your own right."

Holly shook her head. "No, dear. If any invitations arrive for me, I will not accept them. I shall be quite content with making the acquaintance of the other chaperones and conversing with them."

"Why, Mama?" Beth looked puzzled.

"Because these are your Seasons, not mine. I will be there only to assist you as your chaperone and your mother."

"But won't it be nice to wear lively colors again, perhaps even bright red if you like?" Marcie was not willing to give over so easily.

Holly laughed. "Not bright red, dear. It would not suit my complexion. I should think a soft gray would be nice, or perhaps a pale lavender."

As the two girls exchanged speaking glances, Holly almost groaned aloud. If she knew Beth and Marcie, they were hoping to deck her out in the brightest of colors and the loveliest of gowns. She would have to be on her guard around them, for it seemed they would not be satisfied to leave her with the elderly dowagers who served as the other debutantes' chaperones.

"What is it, Mama?" Beth faced her with a completely guileless smile. "Aren't you excited about going to London with us?"

"Of course I am, dear." Holly returned her smile. Perhaps she was mistaken and the girls were not planning on making any mischief.

Marcie reached out to pat Holly's hand. "I am so glad you

are coming with us, Mama. Beth and I are certain that you will have a simply *wonderful* time."

Holly winced. Though she could not fault Marcie's seemingly innocent comment, there was more than a hint of impishness in her eyes. Holly had no doubt that neither of her girls would give her a moment's peace until they were convinced that she was enjoying the Season every bit as enthusiastically as they were.

Four

Holly wore a happy smile as she went through the familiar ritual of readying herself for bed. Though she had not wished to appear so excited as Beth and Marcie over the prospect of their come-outs, she felt positively giddy at the thought of returning to London to spend the Season. It gave her cause to hope that she might change her situation once both of her stepdaughters had made suitable matches, and escape the genteel but undesirable life of a poor relation that was hers at Bentworth Park.

She had made a plan for her future. Serena Poole had given her the notion when she had complimented Holly on her knowledge of the healing arts and had asked for instruction so that she might assist the tenants who resided on Midvale land. If Serena wished to become a healer, perhaps others might have the same desire.

Holly knew that she was uniquely qualified to instruct any who wished to learn. She had learned much from her grandmother and even more from the gypsies who camped on Bentworth land. From the very beginning, when she had been merely a curious child assisting her grandmother, Holly had kept careful notes of the remedies and their ingredients. She had made detailed drawings of the herbs to be gathered and written records of the methods that were used to prepare and cure them. She had trusted nothing to memory and now she had good reason to be glad of that caution. She had referred to these notes when comparing methods with the gypsy healers and then she had added their remedies to her own. Holly now possessed a small trunk of carefully filed and labeled receipts, and each contained the remedy for a specific malady. In their entirety, they made up a textbook of sorts, and Holly intended to use it as such.

Holly's dream was to open a school where she would teach her knowledge to those who wished to become companions to the chronically ill. When her students had completed their training and passed an examination to test their mastery of the subject, she would place advertisements in the London papers to secure positions for them. Perhaps it was an impossible dream, but Holly had hopes of turning her knowledge into a genteel business that would earn her financial independence.

As she sat down in front of her dressing table, Holly stared at her reflection in the mirror. She appeared far too young to be the headmistress of a school and something would have to be done about that. Even with her hair smoothed back and secured in a tight knot at the nape of her neck, she could not have passed for more than her true age of twenty-three. But the opening of her school would have to be postponed until both Beth and Marcie had married and set up their own households, and perhaps she would appear older then. In the meantime, she planned to make inquiries of some of the other widows and dowagers she would meet while she chaperoned her stepdaughters. If the majority of these ladies agreed that there was a need for a service such as hers, she would proceed with her plans.

Once she had brushed her hair, Holly shook it free and slipped off her robe. Then, clad in her warm nightrail, she sat down on the edge of her bed and prepared to read the letter that dear William had written to her.

Beth scanned the letter quickly and then she turned to her sister in shock. "This is a very strange letter, Marcie. Papa begins by urging us to enjoy our Seasons and then he goes on to say that he loves us very dearly."

"What is strange about that?" Marcie approached the edge of the bed, where Beth was sitting, and leaned close, attempting to decipher the words.

"It's the rest of the letter. Papa says that we are now old enough to know precisely why Holly agreed to marry him."

Marcie frowned. "But we already know that. Holly loved Papa. She told me that she did."

"I know that she came to love him eventually, but not when they were first married. Papa says that they were the best of friends, but it seems that Holly's heart was engaged by another gentleman."

"Then why did she marry Papa?" Marcie looked quite overset. "Do not tell me that she married him for his title, for I will refuse to believe it!"

"Of course she did not. Holly is far too honest to do any such thing. She married Papa because he needed her help, and because she wished to be our mama."

Marcie sat down next to her sister, a puzzled expression on her face. "But what happened to the gentleman that Holly loved?"

"It appears that he disappointed her. Papa says that he captured her heart and then callously jilted her!"

"Oh, dear!" Marcie's eyes were wide with astonishment. "It's very fortunate that Holly did not marry him. He must have been a despicable rake."

Beth nodded. "A rake of the first water, according to Papa. This scoundrel made plans to meet Holly at the lily garden in the park, to discuss their future together. She risked all to keep their appointment, but he failed to appear. Holly neither saw nor heard from him again."

"Poor Holly!" Marcie blinked back tears at this sad story. "Was Papa acquainted with this horrible cad?"

"No. And Holly, herself, did not know his identity. He was dressed as a pirate and they met at a grand masquerade ball, where they danced the waltz together. Holly fell hopelessly in love with him that very night, and he assured her that he felt the same. But Papa believes that he was simply diverting himself for a few hours by toying with Holly's affections."

"I hope that I never meet a gentleman like that!" Marcie's eyes blazed with anger at the rogue who had stolen Holly's heart. "How did Papa learn of this?"

"Holly told him. He found her crying, in a friend's garden, during an afternoon musicale. She confided that her heart was broken and she feared she could not go on with her Season, but her aunt was depending upon her to make a good match to save the family's failing finances."

"It is almost like a plot from one of Mrs. Radcliffe's novels," Marcie breathed. "And Papa offered for Holly to save her family from ruin?"

"Yes." Beth nodded, a small smile crossing her face. "Papa was her knight gallant."

"And Holly accepted his offer?"

"Not straightaway. You see, Holly thought she had nothing to offer Papa in return. Though she considered him a very dear friend, she felt she would be doing him a disservice by marrying him without love."

"But Papa must have convinced her." Marcie appeared quite puzzled. "After all, they married."

"He did, but first he had to tell Holly why he needed a wife. There was a very good reason, you see, and we did not know of it."

"What was it?"

Beth swallowed with difficulty and reached over to place an arm around Marcie's shoulders. "Papa married Holly for us, Marcie. Though he did not tell us for fear that we should become overset, the doctors had told him that he had less than two years to live. He did not wish to leave us alone in the world, and he did not judge Uncle Richard capable of assuring us a happy future, for he was a bachelor at the time. Papa writes that the moment he confided this reason to Holly, she accepted his offer and they were married by special license."

"Oh, Beth!" Marcie wiped away the tears that sprang to her eyes. "Poor Papa! And poor, poor Holly!"

Beth hugged Marcie a bit tighter. "It is a very sad story, but it did turn out well in the end. Papa was already more than a little in love with Holly and she learned to love him, too. And there is no doubt that Holly regards us as her very own daughters and loves us to distraction."

"That is true." Marcie nodded, a small smile appearing on her face. "I am glad Papa saw fit to tell us, Beth. I had wondered why he went off to London and married so suddenly, and now I know the reason behind his action. Papa did exactly the right thing for us."

"Yes, he did. I am very grateful that he married Holly and did not leave us in Uncle Richard's care."

Marcie shivered slightly at the thought. "Think of how miserable we should be, living in the manor house under Aunt Annabelle's thumb!"

"There is another page to the letter." Beth turned the sheet of vellum to read the other side. She was silent for a moment, her eyes scanning the words, and then she turned to Marcie with shining eyes. "Oh, Marcie! I do believe Papa was the finest man who ever lived!"

Marcie raised her brows. "Why? What does the letter say?"

"Papa wants us to encourage Holly to enjoy the Season. He says he's put aside enough money to finance *three* Seasons and he wishes for Holly to have one, too. He warns us that she will resist us, and he urges us to use all our wiles to assure that she finds her perfect match."

"Papa wants Holly to marry again?" Marcie's voice was shaking slightly.

"Yes. He says so very plainly. He believes that Holly should cast off her mourning and enjoy every entertainment that the *ton* has to offer. And he wants us to make certain that she meets gentlemen of quality while she is in London, and does not hide behind the skirts of the other chaperones. He cautions us that this will be no easy task. Holly has already suffered one disappointment and she will not give her heart easily to another gentleman. But Papa is determined, and he charges us with the duty of choosing an appropriate husband for Holly if she will not do so for herself!"

An expression of pure astonishment crossed Marcie's face. "Papa wants us to play matchmaker?"

"He not only wishes us to do so, he *charges* us with the duty. It is right here in his letter. And then he goes on to say that if we truly love Holly, we should spare no effort on her behalf."

Marcie's eyes began to gleam with excitement. "What a lark this will be! And we have already begun by insisting that Holly have new gowns. We shall have to take care that she does not choose something dowdy, for she must be the brightest star of the Season."

"Precisely." Beth began to laugh. "We will be superb matchmakers, Marcie. We know Holly better than anyone else, and that will make it much easier for us to select appropriate gentlemen for her to meet."

Marcie nodded, lifting her chin in determination. "We will not fail, Beth. At the end of the Season, dear Mama will marry her perfect match!"

A tear dripped down to stain the page of William's letter and Holly sighed as she read on. Her dear husband had been the kindest of men and infinitely sensible of her feelings. She missed him dreadfully, as he had been the finest gentleman that she had ever known. Even when he had been faced with the specter of his own death, William had taken time to write these encouraging words to her.

Now that our daughters have grown into young ladies, I urge you to take a care for yourself my dear Holly. You must find a new life far away from Bentworth Manor. You are still young and beautiful and you must put aside your mourning and take full advantage of the Season I have funded for the three of you. If you are so fortunate as to find a gentleman to love, you must not hesitate to marry again. It is my greatest desire that you will give your heart to a worthy gentleman who will adore you as much I have in the brief time we have had together.

Holly sighed again, blinking back her tears. Surely William had known that she could not find any gentleman in London, or anywhere else, who could favorably compare with him! Giving her heart to another, only two years after his death, would be disloyal to his memory.

I know what you are thinking, my dear Holly, and I assure you that you will be doing me no favor by remaining my widow. I wish, instead, that you actively search for a new love. Of course you must be cautious not to give your heart lightly, but I fear that you will err on the side of being so cautious as to not give your heart at all. Your first unfortunate love was a rake and a bounder, but there are other gentlemen who will not play fast and loose with your affections. Put aside your fears and use your good judgment to find one who is worthy of you. And when you find him, give your heart freely so that you may find true contentment.

"No. I cannot marry again!" Holly whispered the words, experiencing a most inappropriate surge of anger at her dear dead husband. "Surely you knew that, William!"

Holly turned back to the letter and her eyes widened as she read the next line. *No doubt you are angry with me for suggesting such a thing. This is all to the good, as I have managed to jolt you out of your complacency. Search for a husband, my darling, and do it wisely. You will please both yourself and me in the bargain. And if you disregard my final wishes, I vow that if it is within my power to do so, I shall return to haunt you most unmercifully.*

Holly smiled as she read William's final line. He had always possessed a fine sense of humor and a flair for the dramatic. But he seemed very serious about urging her to take part in his daughters' Seasons.

With a thoughtful sigh, Holly put aside the letter and blew out the candle by her bed. She snuggled down under the covers and felt a tingle of warmth invade her tired body. William had truly loved her or he would not have set aside these funds for her use. Did she not owe it to him to do as he wished?

She longed for sleep, but it did not come. Instead, Holly's thoughts turned to balls and routs and Venetian breakfasts, and a delicious shiver of anticipation swept through her. Did she dare to take part in the Season? Or would the tabbies of the *ton* cast her out for her indecorous conduct? She would not mind censure for herself, but she was anxious that Beth and Marcie might be cut as well, for such an unseemly action on the part of their father's widow.

Holly stared up at the ceiling, barely noticing the lacy pattern the moonlight created as it shone through the branches of the tree outside her window. If the tabbies of the *ton* knew that William had arranged this Season for her and had insisted on it in his final communication to her, they could not criticize her for respecting his wishes. Indeed, if the information were presented to them *before* the actual start of the Season, several of them might come to admire her obedience and intercede with the others on her behalf. It would require great tact on her part in approaching these denizens, but Holly had never possessed a faint heart. She would send off a letter to her aunt's dearest friend, Lady Pinchton, and ask for her assistance with this delicate matter.

The sky had begun to lighten and the morning birds had commenced their songs before Holly sank into an exhausted slumber. Even then her rest was not complete, for she dreamed that she was an angel, dancing in the arms of a handsome pirate, who was set on winning her heart for the second time, only to break it once again.

Five

"Oh, Mama! Are you certain this is the right house?"

Holly smiled at Marcie's astonished expression and nodded. "Yes, Marcie. This is the house your father's solicitor rented for us."

"It's very large." Beth's eyes were as wide as her sister's. "And exceedingly grand!"

Holly laughed. "It is not so grand as all that. You must not forget that you once lived at Bentworth Manor."

"You are right, Mama." Beth nodded. "Bentworth Manor is even grander than this lovely town house."

Marcie shrugged. "I fail to see what that has to do with it since we do not live at Bentworth Manor any longer. Now it belongs to Uncle Richard and Aunt Annabelle."

"The fact that we have removed to the dower cottage does not change the circumstances of your birth or alter your status in society. You are the daughters of Viscount Bentworth and you must not forget that." Holly smiled at them both. "Come, girls. We are keeping your uncle's coachman from his duties. He must return to Bentworth Manor with all possible speed so Lady Annabelle will not be inconvenienced."

Marcie giggled. "Yes, indeed. Far be it from us to inconvenience dear Aunt Annabelle."

"Marcie!" Beth shot her younger sister a warning glance as she gathered up her reticule and pelisse. "Remember the caution that Mama has given us. As the daughters of a peer, it does not compliment us to behave in a petty or spiteful manner."

Marcie sighed. "You are right, Beth. But I did think that Aunt Annabelle was about to have an attack of apoplexy when Uncle Richard informed her that we were to be carried to London in the family coach."

"Her complexion did turn a very uncomplimentary shade of red." Beth grinned, remembering her aunt's reaction to the news. "Do hand me that box, Marcie. I wish to carry in my new bonnet myself."

As Holly climbed out of the carriage and waited for the girls to disembark, she smiled in supreme satisfaction. Though the residence on High Street was modest by *ton* standards, it put her in mind of a mansion after enduring the close confines of the dower cottage. Here both Beth and Marcie would have bed-chambers of their own and she would enjoy a suite of rooms. They hadn't experienced such luxury since William had died almost two years ago.

The past three weeks had rushed by with the speed of a whirl-wind. There had been many tasks to accomplish before their departure and Holly had not enjoyed a quiet moment to herself since she had first opened Mr. Hempton's letter. The girls had helped Holly to close up the dower house for the months that they would be gone, placing Holland covers on the large pieces of furniture and securing the pantry so that the rodents should not reap the benefit of their store of supplies. There had been rooms to be cleaned and then closed off, and clothing to be stored where the moths could not destroy it. The windows had been shuttered, the chimney blocked to prevent the squirrels and birds from accessing the interior in their absence, and a small sum given to the scullery maid from the manor house who had agreed to tend Holly's herb garden while she was away.

Another matter, not so easily accomplished, had been finding a replacement for Holly. Rather than risk the good health of his tenants, Richard had obtained, on the very last day, Lady Anna-belle's reluctant permission to allow the Poole family the use

of the dower cottage. In return for this largess, Serena Poole
had promised to treat William's tenants in addition to the tenants
on the earl's estate. This decision had necessitated the reopening
of the cottage, and the undoing of all that had been done.

Holly and the girls had worked far into the night, but at last
the cottage had been ready for occupancy again. The Poole family had arrived early that morning, and Holly had seen them
installed on the premises. She had taught Serena the eccentrici-
ties of the stove, indicated which herbs would be ready for har-
vest in her absence, and handed over the keys to the cottage.
By the time all this had been accomplished, it was nearing midday and the post-chaise had long since departed. Richard had
offered the use of his traveling coach and Holly and the girls
had set off for London, exhausted by their efforts.

The girls' exhaustion had vanished the moment the coach
had arrived at the outskirts of London. Marcie and Beth had
not been so crass as to lean out from the carriage windows, but
they had peered closely at the wondrous sights they had passed.
Even Holly, who had lived in London during her First Season,
had found their excitement contagious. There had been countless comments from Marcie on the lovely styles of the ladies'
gowns, and Beth had been struck quite speechless by the sight
of a footman, dressed in splendid livery, stepping proudly down
the street. A pie seller carrying his wares on his head had been
the next to draw Marcie's attention, and Beth had not ceased to
comment on the bustle of traffic and the constant stream of
elegant coaches, curricles, and high-perch phaetons they had
encountered.

Now it seemed that both girls had lost their gift for chatter.
They stood silently at the base of the steps that rose to the front
entrance of the town house and simply stared at their temporary
home. Holly smiled, understanding the reason for their hesi-
tance, and marched up the steps to make use of the knocker.
Both Beth and Marcie were entering into another sphere of their
lives and neither girl was confident of being accepted into the
glittering world of the *haute ton*.

"Come, girls." Holly motioned for them to join her. "We must meet the staff that Mr. Hempton has hired and assure that our baggage is properly unloaded. Once we have accomplished those tasks and taken a bit of refreshment, we will retire to our rooms for a well-deserved rest."

The elderly butler who opened the door took in Holly's travel-worn gown and favored her with a quizzical glance. "Lady Bentworth?"

Holly nodded. "Yes. And these are my daughters, Miss Elizabeth and Miss Marcella."

"Hobson, madam." The butler bowed slightly and held open the door. "If you will follow me to the drawing room, I shall inform Mrs.Merriweather of your arrival and she will see to it that a tea tray is prepared. Then I will fetch James to see to your luggage."

Holly smiled, noting the nervous quaver in Hobson's voice. He was quite elderly and she had no doubt that he was glad of the position. "Thank you, Mr. Hobson. A tea tray would be most welcome, but only after we have washed off the dust of our travels. I will ring when we are ready for refreshment. And please tell Mrs. Merriweather that we should like to make her acquaintance at that time."

"Certainly, madam." Hobson gave another creaking bow. "If you will follow me, I will show you to your chambers."

Holly accompanied the aging butler up the staircase, the girls in her wake. Once Hobson had shown her to her quarters, she instructed the girls to join her when they had tidied themselves, and sent them off in Hobson's care. Then she stepped into her chambers, removed her wraps, and washed her hands and face. Once she had tidied her hair and looked presentable once again, she gazed around at the chambers that would serve as her home for the next several months.

The large bedchamber was done entirely in shades of pink. It was not Holly's favorite color, but she had to admit that no cost had been spared in its decoration. Satin draperies of a pink floral design graced the windows, and the canopy over the bed was hung with the same material. French paper that sported large sprays of pink roses covered all four walls, and the floor was laid with a carpet that resembled a field of pink daisies.

"Oh, my!" Holly sat down on the bed covers, which also matched the design of the walls, and gave a deep sigh. She felt as if she were a honeybee, in the center of a gigantic pink flower garden. The sight of so many pink blossoms was quite dizzying and she shut her eyes to block them out for a moment.

Once she had regained her composure, Holly decided to explore the other chambers that made up her suite. The door to her dressing room was ajar, and she groaned quite loudly as she realized that it was decorated in a similar manner. The chamber beyond, which she assumed was her private sitting room, had yet to be seen.

Holly rose to her feet and walked across the pink daisy carpet to her sitting room. When she pushed open the door, half-expecting that more pink blossoms would assault her, she gave a heartfelt sigh of relief. Her sitting room walls were covered with ivory satin. White lace draperies graced the mullioned windows and the furniture was upholstered in restful shades of green. The chamber was really quite ordinary, but it pleased Holly immensely as compared to her pink floral boudoir.

An amused smile crossed Holly's face. Either the mistress of this town house had exceeded her budget before she had redecorated this sitting room, or she had decided that one of her chambers was in need of a plain touch. Holly would invite the girls to take tea in this lovely sitting room before they explored the rest of the house.

Only moments after Holly had employed the bell pull to ring for the tea tray, she heard a gentle tap on her bedchamber door. She hurried through the dressing room and her bedchamber, doing her utmost to ignore the decor, and opened the door.

"Oh, Mama!" Beth started to laugh the instant she saw the dubious splendor of Holly's quarters. "My chamber is exactly the same as yours, except that it is done in violet!"

Marcie nodded, going off into a volley of giggles. "And mine is identical in yellow! The lady who lives here must be fiercely enamored of flowers."

"We'll take our tea in my sitting room." Holly smiled as she led the way. "It is quite plain in comparison and no doubt we will find it a welcome relief."

The girls followed Holly to the sitting room, and Beth smiled as she took a seat on the green velvet sofa. "This chamber is very nice, Mama."

"Yes, indeed it is." Marcie chose a chair covered in pale green satin. "There is not a flower in sight!"

Holly smiled at the girls. "We will see what we can do to save ourselves from some of the flowers tomorrow. The house-keeper will know what is stored in the attic and we shall ask for her assistance. No doubt there are other carpets we can use and it is possible there are other bed hangings as well. The French wallpaper, however, will have to stay as it is. Since we are merely renting this residence, there is no possible way that we can change it."

"Draperies of a solid color would help." Beth nodded, warming to the idea. "Perhaps the floral wallpaper will be quite lovely if it contains the only blossoms in the room."

Holly laughed. "Perhaps, but I must admit that I have my doubts. Let us pray that the drawing room has not been refurbished in the same manner."

There was a tap on the sitting room door and Holly called out her permission to enter. A moment later, the door opened and a round-faced woman in black bombazine marched in. A young maid followed in her wake, carefully balancing the tea tray. At a nod from the housekeeper, the maid placed it carefully on the table in front of Holly, gave a quick curtsy, and left the chamber.

"I am Mrs. Merriweather, madam." The housekeeper dipped her head. "I take great pleasure in welcoming you to London."

Holly smiled. "Thank you, Mrs. Merriweather. These are my daughters, Miss Elizabeth and Miss Marcella. Mr. Hempton informed me that you are in the owner's employ?"

"Yes, madam." Mrs. Merriweather bobbed her head again, favoring both Beth and Marcie with a smile. "The baroness is traveling the continent and will not return until the end of the year."

Holly nodded, noting the housekeeper's smile. It was obvious that she'd taken a liking to the two girls. "It is a lovely house, Mrs. Merriweather. Am I correct in assuming that our chambers were refurbished quite recently?"

"Yes, madam. The bedchambers were completed less than six months ago and m'lady spared no expense in the endeavor. She confided that she wished to bring the garden inside, to warm her during the cold winter months."

Holly caught the barest hint of humor in the housekeeper's voice. It gave her reason to believe that Mrs. Merriweather might share their sensibilities at the onslaught of the flowers, but she should have to be extremely tactful when she again broached the subject. "Please join us for tea, Mrs. Merriweather. I know it is somewhat unusual, but we are not used to ceremony. Do sit down and I shall pour you a cup."

"If you're certain . . . ?" The housekeeper hesitated, but Beth patted the place next to her on the couch and she took the indicated seat.

"We desperately need your assistance, Mrs. Merriweather." Holly poured a cup and handed it to the housekeeper. "Beth and Marcie have never been to London before, and I enjoyed only one Season before I married their father. It was a very minimal Season, as my aunt was not in the best of health and could accompany me to very few events."

Mrs. Merriweather sighed. "That's a great pity, madam. But your daughters will not have such restrictions."

"No, indeed." Holly nodded. "I intend to accept every invitation that is suitable, but I shall need your assistance with that as well, for I am hard-pressed to know which are suitable and which are not."

"Mr. Hobson could advise you of that, madam. He has worked in several of the best houses."

"Excellent!" Holly beamed. "Let me tell you of our situation, Mrs. Merriweather. We have just recently discovered that the girls' father left monies in trust for their debuts and I fear that we are as green as green can be. No doubt you know what is proper and what is not, and I do not wish to make any mistakes. Can we count upon you to advise us?"

Mrs. Merriweather raised her brows. "You want *me* to advise you, madam?"

"Yes, indeed." Holly nodded quickly. "I am convinced that you know far more of society than we do."

Mrs. Merriweather smiled as she nodded. "I will be happy to assist you in any way that I can, madam."

"Thank you, Mrs. Merriweather." Holly began to grin. "You may begin by telling us your opinion of the decorations in our bedchambers. Are they similar to those in the other great London houses?"

"Not at all, madam. The baroness engaged a French decorator to choose the furnishings and she followed his advice to the letter. I do believe they are quite . . . unique."

"All those flowers." Marcie giggled. "Perhaps it is not nice of me to say so, Mrs. Merriweather, but I do declare I felt the urge to sneeze when I first entered my chamber."

Mrs. Merriweather stared at Marcie for a moment, and then she burst out laughing. "M'lady said it was all the crack, but I must admit that I agree with you, miss. Dorri, the youngest maid, insists she becomes quite light-headed whenever she enters the chambers."

"Perhaps we can do something to spare Dorri's sensibilities." Holly smiled, knowing that she had found an ally. "Did the baroness happen to save the old carpets that were removed from those chambers?"

"Yes, madam. They're up in the attic, rolled up just as nice as you please. There are two in a lovely ivory, the exact color of the walls in this sitting room, and there is a third in a pretty nut brown."

"Would it be possible for us to view them, Mrs. Merriweather?" Beth looked eager.

"Of course, miss." Mrs. Merriweather turned to Holly. "Shall I have James bring them down for you, madam?"

"No, Mrs. Merriweather. That would be a waste of his time and effort. It will be far easier for us to go up to them. You will show us the way, won't you?"

Mrs. Merriweather smiled as she nodded." Of course, madam."

"Did the baroness save the old draperies as well?" Marcie turned to their housekeeper.

"No, but I did." Mrs. Merriweather grinned proudly. "And I folded the old bed hangings and packed them away in the event the baroness ever tired of her new furnishings. Shall we go up to look at them now? Or would you prefer to wait until you've rested?"

Holly laughed. "We could only rest in our bedchambers if it were pitch dark, Mrs. Merriweather. We shall go now, if you please."

Six

"Oh, Marcie. You are too absurd for words!" Holly dissolved into gales of laughter as Marcie dipped her knee in a deep curtsy, her feathered headdress bobbing quite comically. The petite dark-haired miss with eyes the color of spring violets had draped a length of table linen over her arm to simulate a train and she was dressed in her favorite cotton wrapper. The garment had once been a lovely shade of blue, but it had been washed so many times, it had faded into a disreputable gray.

Mrs. Merriweather chuckled and held her sides as Marcie backed into a table. Holly had asked their housekeeper to join them for tea in her sitting room so that the girls could tell her about their presentation to Queen Charlotte that afternoon.

"Marcie is not exaggerating *that* much, Mama." Beth was quick to defend her sister. "Of course it wasn't as humorous as she is painting it."

"Tell us your impression, Miss Beth." Mrs. Merriweather smiled at her.

"It was all very hushed and solemn, and every young lady was on her very best behavior. The Queen's drawing room was very grand with the finest furnishings I have ever seen. But the ritual was almost exactly as Marcie performed it for you."

"Except that I was wearing my presentation gown instead of my wrapper." Marcie giggled slightly. "Rest assured, Mama, we did everything correctly."

Holly nodded, remembering her own presentation very well.

Lady Pinchton had accompanied her to St. James' Palace and acted as her chaperone. In view of this fact, Holly had called upon the dowager marchioness on their second day in London, and just as she had hoped, Lady Pinchton had offered to perform the same service for Beth and Marcie. "Then Lady Pinchton was pleased with you?"

"Yes, Mama." Beth nodded quickly. "She told both of us that we should take very well."

Marcie frowned slightly. "What exactly does that mean, Mama? From the smiles Lady Pinchton bestowed upon us, I assume it was a compliment?"

"A very high compliment, dear." Holly exchanged a smile with Mrs. Merriweather. "A debutante who *takes* is accepted by London society."

Both Beth and Marcie looked very relieved by this news. They had been anxious about their introduction to court and had practiced their deep curtsies until they were exhausted. Holly had assisted them, taking the part of Queen Charlotte, and Mrs. Merriweather and Mr. Hobson had pretended to be the lords-in-waiting who had spread out their trains.

As the girls chatted with Mrs. Merriweather, drinking their tea and indulging in several of the pastries from the tray, Holly thought about all that they had accomplished in the fortnight that had passed since their arrival. Mr. Hempton had engaged several tutors for Beth and Marcie and their lessons had commenced at once. They had spent three hours each week with a dancing master, an equal amount of time with the elderly and impoverished widow who had taught them court protocol and etiquette, and two hours a week with a drawing master. They had also improved their skills upon the pianoforte, and learned several new vocal pieces, one of which was a duet. Indeed, Beth and Marcie had scarcely had time to explore their new surroundings as they had also spent countless hours in consultation with Madame Beauchamp, who had been charged with the duty of completing their new wardrobes, and even more time shopping with Holly for the necessary accessories.

Holly looked over at the girls and smiled. Their color was high and they were both still flushed with excitement over their presentation. The moment Lady Pinchton's coachman had delivered them back to the town house on High Street, the girls had rushed up to their bedchambers, which were now quite acceptable thanks to Mrs. Merriweather's foresight in saving the baroness's old furnishings. As Holly had watched, traveling from room to room to attend both girls, Beth and Marcie had disrobed in record speed, tossing off their old-fashioned gowns, along with their hoops and their crinolines.

"It was as silent as the grave in the Queen's presentation chamber." Marcie sighed, popping the last bit of pastry into her mouth.

"Far too silent." Beth agreed quickly. "Just as I feared, my knee cracked quite audibly during my curtsy and it was so loud, all in the chamber must have heard it. Her Majesty pretended to take no notice, of course, and I could not help but think that such a thing must occur quite frequently."

Marcie nodded. "When Beth's knee cracked, I glanced at the lords-in-waiting but not one exhibited even the slightest hint of a smile. They were every one of them as impassive as the walls."

Mrs. Merriweather chuckled. "They wouldn't be lords-in-waiting for long if they lost their composure in the presence of their queen. Tell me about Her Majesty. Was she very beautiful?"

"No, quite the opposite." Marcie shook her head. "Perhaps I should not say this, but she looked very ordinary to me. Her features reminded me of the rector's wife."

"Is this true?" Mrs. Merriweather turned to Beth.

"Yes." Beth nodded. "Her Majesty is far from beautiful, but she does have a very commanding presence."

"She has a purse to her lips, as if she had just recently tasted something quite unpleasant." Marcie continued her description. "Her face is far too long to be beautiful, and her eyes are most disturbing."

"Her eyes?" Holly frowned slightly. She did not remember taking special note of Queen Charlotte's eyes.

"There is no light in them, Mama, no humor or pleasure at all. Her Majesty seemed empty of all emotion, as if she were merely performing her duty without taking the least pleasure in it. Her mind was elsewhere. I am almost certain of it."

Holly nodded. "Perhaps she was anxious about the King's health. Or perhaps she was simply weary. She is nearing seventy years of age."

"You may have the right of it." Mrs. Merriweather nodded as she turned to Holly. "There is another factor that could well have contributed to Her Majesty's weariness, but it would not be proper to mention it in front of these innocent young misses."

Holly smiled. "If you refer to the number of children she bore, it is quite acceptable to speak of such things with Beth and Marcie. They have been in attendance at several births and have assisted me when I required another set of hands. The process of childbirth is no mystery to them."

"We have always helped Mama take care of the tenants." Beth smiled at Mrs. Merriweather proudly. "But she has cautioned us never to speak of such things with others."

Mrs. Merriweather nodded her approval. "Your mama is right, Miss Beth. To mention such things in polite society should be considered quite improper. I was raised in the country myself, and I cannot help but think it a great disservice to shield young misses from that aspect of life."

"I share your sentiment, Mrs. Merriweather." Holly smiled. "Please tell us what you know of Her Majesty. We are eager to hear."

Mrs. Merriweather took a deep breath and leaned closer. "Lord knows Her Majesty has the right to be weary. She gave birth to fifteen children in the first twenty-one years of her marriage and that must have taken its toll on her stamina, though I am certain she was cosseted to within an inch of her life. But not even a queen is spared the discomforts of increasing, and I have heard she could eat nothing substantial during those times.

It is ironic, is it not? Queen Charlotte had the best chefs in her employ, and all she could take while she was increasing was weak tea and wafers."

Holly raised her brows. "It is a pity that her doctors did not see fit to provide her with a remedy. I have found that a bit of dry toast, taken immediately upon awakening, calms an unsettled stomach quite nicely. And after the lady is up and about, she should drink a cup of warm beef broth with the fat skimmed away, accompanied by another bit of toast. This simple treatment will spark her appetite for the remainder of the day and dispel any uneasiness."

"Perhaps you should have been called in for Queen Charlotte." Marcie grinned. "You know all the remedies, Mama."

Holly laughed and shook her head. "Not all, Marcie. It would take me more than one lifetime to learn them all. But tell me more about your presentation. Mrs. Merriweather and I wish to know every detail."

"Yes, indeed." Mrs. Merriweather nodded. "Was the Prince Regent in attendance?"

Beth shook her head. "No, it was only Queen Charlotte."

"Tell us all from the very beginning." Holly settled back against the customs of the couch in anticipation of a comfortable coze. "I wish to know everything that occurred from the moment you stepped out of Lady Pinchton's carriage."

Beth smiled and helped herself to a second cup of tea, removing Marcie's feathered headdress from the table and placing it carefully on the back of a chair. "We had to leave our wraps in the carriage. That is required, you know. And once we entered St. James' Palace, we were escorted directly to the long gallery to await our turn to be presented."

"It was very cold." Marcie took up the tale. "I should like to have had a shawl to cover my shoulders, but that is not allowed. My teeth began to chatter and I shivered most dreadfully."

"Because you were anxious, or because you were cold?" Holly leaned forward expectantly.

"A bit of both, I believe." Marcie smiled, giving the sort of honest answer that Holly had expected. "It reminded me of the apple house in the fall, except that it did not smell as nice. I think it is cruel to require one to bare one's neck and shoulders, even in the coldest weather."

Beth nodded. "One poor lady was so chilled, her skin had a decided blue tinge. She was almost of an age with Lady Pinchton. She confided to me that she had married quite recently and was only now eligible to be presented."

Mrs. Merriweather raised her brows. "Then she was allowed her presentation by virtue of her marriage?"

"Yes. She said that her husband was a physician."

It was Holly's turn to raise her brows. "But an exception to the protocol can be made for the elderly and those in ill health. If the lady's husband was a physician, he could have written a letter that allowed her to cover her shoulders!"

"That is perfectly true." Beth nodded. "But she told me that she did not wish to set herself apart from the other ladies who were waiting to be presented. She confided that it had always been her dream to wear the proper white presentation dress and she would not give it up, regardless of the weather, her age, or her health."

Mrs. Merriweather grinned. "Vanity?"

"No doubt." Marcie giggled.

"But perhaps not. She may have wanted that moment in her life to be perfection. Most girls dream of their presentation, whether they are peers or not." Beth stopped, realizing exactly what she had said, and she turned to Mrs. Merriweather with an anxious expression. "I apologize, Mrs. Merriweather. Are you very overset that you were not presented?"

"Not at all! I do not think I should care to be trussed up like a goose with feathers stuck in my hair, wearing a hoop and pounds of crinolines, and carrying a ridiculously long train. I am not in the least bit envious, my dear, so you must put that suspicion to rest. But I am most curious about your experience, so please do go on."

Beth looked a bit uncertain for a moment, but then she nod-ded. "As I said, it was uncommonly cold in the palace, and I was thankful that we did not have to wait for too long. It was no more than a few minutes before Marcie and I were sum-moned and instructed as to which door to enter."

"It seemed much longer than that to me!" Marcie shivered, apparently remembering the chill of the hall. "We carried our trains over our left arms, and when we entered the presentation chamber, we let them fall to the floor. Two lords-in-waiting came forward to spread them out for us, and then we moved forward."

"You were announced?" Holly recalled the reading of her own name and how unfamiliar it had sounded to her ears.

"Yes." Marcie nodded. "Beth went first because she is the oldest. Tell them, Beth."

"It is a very long room, and it seemed to take me forever to reach the Queen. I kept my eyes quite properly downcast, but I did look up at her through my lashes."

"So did I!" Marcie grinned at her sister. "Go on, Beth."

"When I reached Her Majesty, I performed my deep curtsy."

"And that was when your knee cracked?" Holly grinned, imagining the worst.

"No, not then. It happened a bit later, when I attempted to rise. No doubt you remember how low the curtsy must be."

Holly nodded, remembering the countless times that she had practiced her curtsy. She had been required to hold the uncom-fortable pose for several minutes, all the while maintaining her balance.

"I was forced to wait, almost kneeling on the floor, until Her Majesty had greeted me formally and kissed me on the fore-head. Then I arose and that is when my knee embarrassed me. It was very loud, Mama, almost the volume of a gunshot."

"What did you do?" Holly's blue eyes twinkled with amuse-ment. Perhaps Beth had been discomfited then, but now she appeared to find humor in the recollection.

"Nothing. To apologize should only have drawn more atten-

tion to what had occurred. I simply bowed my head and waited
for Marcie to approach Her Majesty."

"I thought the same would happen to me." Marcie grinned
at her sister. "But I took heart from the manner in which Beth
had maintained her dignity. It was all very grand and exceedingly proper. Once Her Majesty placed a kiss upon my brow, I
stepped back to join Beth and then both of us backed out of
the chamber."

"Did you find it difficult to walk backwards?" Mrs. Merriweather was intrigued. She knew that a young miss was required
to face Her Majesty at all times, even when taking leave of the
Queen's drawing room.

"It was not as difficult as I had imagined." Beth answered
the question. "I managed it quite gracefully, I thought, and so
did Marcie. We were not at all like the Misses Hampton, who
preceded us."

Holly leaned forward, sensing a bit of humorous *on-dit*.
"Who are the Misses Hampton and what happened to them?"

"Dorinda and Dorothea Hampton are twins and they were
presented together. As they began to back out of Her Majesty's
presence, Dorinda caught her heel on the hem of her gown and
stumbled into Dorothea. Dorothea lost her balance and reached
out to Dorinda to steady herself, and both ended in a tangle of
feathers, and hoops, and trains."

"They actually fell to the floor in front of Her Majesty?"
Mrs. Merriweather was horrified.

"No." Marcie shook her head, sending her ebony curls bouncing. "But they would have fallen if two lords-in-waiting hadn't
stepped forward to snatch them up at the last moment."

"Did you see it happen?" Though she felt sympathy for the
two misses and their narrow escape, Holly could not resist
chuckling over the picture that came to mind.

"No." Marcie shook her head. "They were presented a full
hour before we arrived. But one of the Queen's footmen told
me about it as we were preparing to leave the palace."

"He actually spoke to you?" Holly was shocked when Marcie

nodded. She was aware that her younger stepdaughter possessed a candid and friendly nature, but she was surprised that a member of Her Majesty's staff should have been so indiscreet as to tell Marcie of the incident.

"He put me in mind of James, Mama." Marcie nodded. "And you know how people always tend to confide in me. Perhaps it is because I appear so ingenuous, as if I never had a thought more serious than which gown to wear, or which pastry to choose from the tea tray."

"No doubt." Holly laughed as Marcie assumed her most guileless expression.

"I am simply famished." Beth stared at the tea tray, which was quite empty. "Shall we ring for a light nuncheon?"

Holly nodded. "If you wish."

"I dare not take a bite, once I am dressed for the ball." Marcie sighed deeply. "My gown is so snug, I shall scarcely be allowed to take a breath. I should like to make the acquaintance of the gentleman who decided that a lady's waist should number her years, as I would take the greatest of pleasure in coshing him over his head!"

"You are certain that it is a gentleman who is responsible?" Mrs. Merriweather laughed merrily, enjoying Marcie's antics.

"Of course." Marcie giggled. "No lady could be so diabolical, unless, of course, she was a lady well advanced in years."

Mrs. Merriweather grinned, rising to her feet. "I shall go down to the kitchens and request something that will not add inches to your waistlines. And that includes you, madam, for your waist must, by definition, be almost as small as that of your daughters. And I shall give thanks that I have surpassed my fiftieth birthday and can live out the rest of my days in comfort!"

Seven

"I'm finished, m'lady." Dorri stepped back with a grin on her face. "You look every bit as fetching as Miss Beth and Miss Marcie. Maybe even more so."

Holly glanced in the cheval glass and her eyes widened in shock. The girls had discovered that Dorri, the little maid who had complained of feeling dizzy every time she had stepped into one of the baroness's bedchambers, possessed an amazing skill at arranging their hair. They had touted her talents to Holly, claiming that she could copy any coiffure from the pages of *La Belle Assemblée, Ackermann's Repository,* or the *Lady's Monthy Museum.* After several days of being besieged by both Beth and Marcie, Holly had promoted Dorri to the position of abigail and she was gratified to see that the girls' trust in Dorri's abilities had not been misplaced.

"You have a great talent, Dorri." Holly smiled at the youngest member of her staff. "No one has ever dressed my hair so beautifully, not even the French abigail my aunt engaged for me during my First Season."

Dorri bobbed her head, accepting the compliment with a wide smile. "Thank you, m'lady. Me mum says I'm quite handy with the needle, too, if you was ever to need something stitched."

"I'll keep that in mind. You may go to the girls now, Dorri. When they're ready, please ask them to join us in the drawing room. Mrs. Merriweather and Mr. Hobson wish to see them in their finery before we leave for the evening."

"Yes, m'lady."

Dorri bobbed her head again and hurried from the chamber. When the door had closed behind her, Holly turned back to the glass again. There was no need for the rouge pot on this evening. Her excitement over the girls' first formal ball had heightened her natural color, making any artificial means quite unnecessary. No doubt the girls were also in a state of excited anticipation and she would be required to calm their frazzled nerves before they made their entrance at Lady Pinchton's mansion.

Holly sighed and turned thoughtful, remembering the first grand ball that she had been permitted to attend. Lady Pinchton had seen to it that she had received one of the coveted invitations to the Duke and Duchess of Elmwood's masquerade ball. Holly had worn the guise of an angel and that fateful evening had nearly been her undoing. She had been a green girl at the time, dazzled by the elevated company in the ballroom and quite innocent of the ways of rakes and scoundrels.

She shivered slightly as she recalled the waltz that she had shared with a handsome pirate. The pirate had plied her with compliments, and when their dance had concluded, he had leaned against a pillar in the ballroom, his eyes never leaving her as she had danced with several other partners. Later, after they had danced a second waltz, he had enticed her onto the balcony, where they had shared their most private thoughts. It had seemed the most natural conclusion in the world when he had kissed her and Holly had tumbled into love without a second thought.

Holly sighed, remembering the warmth of his lips and the gentle manner in which he had held her. She had believed him when he had told her that he shared her emotion, but she had been sadly mistaken. The capture of her trusting heart had been an evening's amusement for him, a mere dalliance with a young miss from the country who had been foolish enough to believe his lies. No doubt she had been just one in a long line of conquests for him, a lark that he had quickly forgotten once the sun had risen over the housetops on the next morning.

Would he remember her if he saw her again? Holly faced her image in the glass with a frown. She doubted that he had given her even a passing thought in the years that had ensued since that evening. But she would remember him and make certain that Beth and Marcie avoided his presence completely.

Should she warn her stepdaughters of the charming rake who had treated her so callously? Holly considered it for a brief moment and then she discarded the notion. It was extremely unlikely that they should encounter him at any of this Season's social events. A rake of his caliber would surely have been killed in a duel by this time, or chased out of the country by an angry brother or husband.

With a final check to her appearance, Holly gathered her shawl, reticule, and gloves and exited her chambers. As she descended the staircase, she attempted to banish all thoughts of her first love from her mind, but one nagging image remained. It was the look of utter sincerity in the depths of his warm gray eyes when he had told her that he loved her.

"Mama! You look so beautiful!"

The admiration on Beth's face made Holly smile. "So do you, my darling. That gown is perfect for you. Your sister exhibited great foresight when she urged you to choose that lovely shade of sea green."

"Thank you, Mama." A blush rose to Beth's cheeks at the compliment. "But are you certain that the bodice is not too daring? I cannot help but notice that my figure is quite . . . exposed."

Holly laughed. "No, my dear, it is perfection. You simply are not accustomed to wearing ball gowns, that is all."

"If you say so, Mama." Beth nodded quickly. "Marcie will be down in a moment. When I left, Dorri was just putting the finishing touches to her hair."

"I'm here." Marcie floated into the room, wearing a lovely formal gown of the palest yellow. The full skirt swirled when she walked and a circlet of pale yellow violets had been woven in among her ebony curls.

"You look lovely, Marcie!" Beth smiled at her younger sister. "I predict that you will be the belle of the ball."

Marcie shrugged. "Perhaps, but only if they see me before they notice you. You are a picture, Beth. Did I not tell you that the color of your gown would set off your eyes?"

"Yes." Beth gave her sister a fond smile. "You are the undisputed leader when it comes to fashion, Marcie."

Marcie laughed and turned to Holly, who was seated on the couch observing them both. "Would you please stand up, Mama. I want to see if your gown drapes in the manner I imagined."

"Certainly." Holly rose to her feet and turned around slowly, letting the full skirt swirl in her wake. "Are you satisfied, dear?"

Marcie nodded. "I think so. But I cannot tell for certain unless you remove your shawl."

"But I plan to wear my shawl, Marcie." Holly objected. "If you recall, we chose it especially to complement this gown."

"That is true, but you must remove it when you enter Lady Pinchton's ballroom. You are the one who told us that ballrooms are frequently warm and exceedingly close. You will be quite overheated if you wear it for the entire evening."

Holly winced. She had been hoping that the girls would not see just how she had altered the appearance of her gown until it was too late to be helped. The deep wine color that they had foisted on her was improper enough for a widow whose husband had been dead for less than two years, but Holly had permitted them to have their way. The depth of her neckline was another matter and she suspected a conspiracy between Madame Beauchamp and her girls, as Holly was certain that the gown had not dipped quite so low at her final fitting.

"Mama?" Marcie was insistent. "Beth and I want to see your gown without the shawl."

"Yes, Mama. Please oblige us." Beth added her voice to that of her sister's.

There was no help for it. Holly sighed and took off her shawl. The expressions of dismay on both girls' faces would have been comical in any other light, but now Holly felt an unfamiliar pang of guilt for attempting to trick them.

"Oh, Mama!" Marcie appeared truly overset. "That lace fichu does not complement your lovely gown in the slightest!"

Beth nodded her agreement. "She is right, Mama. You must remove it and leave it here at home."

"But I should not like to appear without it." Holly frowned slightly. "It would not be at all appropriate for a lady in my circumstances. And it is my very best fichu."

Marcie sighed and crossed the room to Holly's side. "It may be your very best fichu, but it is not good enough for this evening. Hold still, Mama, and I will remove it for you."

"But Marcie, I truly wish that you would not . . ." Holly's protest died in mid-sentence as Marcie reached out and deftly removed her fichu.

"The difference is truly amazing!" Beth's green eyes began to sparkle as the deep décolletage of Holly's gown was exposed. "Now you are all the crack, Mama!"

Marcie stepped back and nodded. "Yes, indeed. You must not ruin the lines of your lovely gown."

"But I am a widow!" Holly protested. "I shall be roundly criticized for dressing as if I am a young lady on the Marriage Mart!"

Beth shook her head. "No, you will not. Lady Pinchton told us that you confided in her about Papa's letter and she has disclosed it to several of her friends. They all applaud you, Mama, for observing Papa's last wishes, and Lady Pinchton is certain that you will be well received."

"Perhaps, but . . ." Holly stopped as she heard a tap on the door.

"It must be Mrs. Merriweather and Mr. Hobson." Marcie grinned as she hurried to the door and opened it. "Come in, please. We are ready for your inspection."

Mrs. Merriweather and Mr. Hobson entered the drawing

room. They had taken no more than a few steps when Mrs. Merriweather caught sight of Holly and came to a halt.

"Oh, my!" The housekeeper gazed at Holly for a moment and then a happy smile spread over her face. "You could be a princess, madam! I've never, in all my days, seen anyone look so charming!"

Mr. Hobson nodded his agreement. "You are magnificent, madam."

Holly laughed, waving away their compliments. "Fustian! The girls are far more fetching than I could ever hope to be."

"They are simply lovely." Mrs. Merriweather turned her attentions to Beth and Marcie. "Your gowns are exquisite, girls, and I have never seen you look better. I shall instruct Cook to begin her baking immediately, as I have no doubt that you will have a line of morning callers that will stretch around the block. I do believe you should tell James to prepare for a lengthy parade of horses and carriages, Mr. Hobson."

"Indeed, I shall." Mr. Hobson nodded. "And do you not think that we should move several dozen additional chairs into this chamber?"

Mrs. Merriweather nodded quickly, exchanging a wink with the butler. "That is an excellent suggestion. Of course, this chamber will not accommodate the sheer volume of chairs that will be needed. Perhaps we should serve tea and pastry in the park so that all their suitors could call at once."

"You are doing it up much too brown, Mrs. Merriweather." Marcie giggled. "And you, also, Mr. Hobson. But we are not the only ones who will have callers. I am certain that dear Mama will be even more popular than we can ever aspire to be."

All eyes turned in her direction and Holly forced a good-natured smile at the jest. The girls would have morning callers. That was to be expected. But she sincerely hoped that no misguided gentleman would have the effrontery to call upon her!

Eight

"That will be all, Easton. Please have my curricle brought round." Paul Danforth, the Earl of Roxbury, waved his valet away and shrugged into his coat by himself. One glance in the mirror told him that he looked as presentable as possible on such short notice. His clothing was impeccable, a testimony to Easton's fine care and the skill of his tailor. But his dark hair insisted on curling boyishly, even though Easton had brushed it smooth only moments before.

There was a worried frown on Paul's brow as he tucked a clean handkerchief into his pocket and added another, in the event that his sister turned into a watering pot. His elder sibling was normally quite independent and entirely capable of handling her own affairs. If she required his aid, the problem was serious indeed, and only dire circumstances would have caused her to add the word "urgent" at the end of her message.

As he exited his chamber and hurried down the staircase, Paul's brow was still furrowed with anxiety. He shuddered to think in what condition he should find his sister if tragedy had befallen her husband. Willa had married the Earl of Pelham, a widower, only two years before and theirs was truly a love match. Philip, Willa's husband, was traveling the continent in the diplomatic service of His Majesty, precisely as his father had done, and his grandfather and great-grandfather before him.

Philip's patent had been established only four generations earlier, which made him the Fourth Earl of Pelham. Paul outranked his brother-in-law, as he was the Ninth Earl of Roxbury. Paul's mother, the widow of the Eighth Earl of Roxbury, found this highly amusing, for when both families were seated at formal dinner parties, she took precedence and Willa was still required to trail along in her wake.

Though his ranking was higher, Paul had to admit that Philip's family history was far more interesting. Queen Anne had awarded Philip's great-grandfather the title and accompanying lands for his diplomatic service on behalf of the Crown during the War of Spanish Succession. Philip did not know the details of precisely what his great-grandfather had done to earn such an honor from his Queen, but several historians of the age had stated that without the First Earl of Pelham's assistance, the Crown could not have claimed Port Royal and all of Acadia.

Philip did not speak of his duties often and Paul doubted that even Willa knew the precise nature of his assignments. But he had let slip to Paul, one evening when both of them had been in their cups, that his work was occasionally dangerous.

Even though he attempted to disabuse himself of the notion that something horrible had happened to Philip, Paul could not help but be anxious as he traveled the short distance to his sister's town residence. Once he had arrived and left his horses in the care of Philip's groom, he bounded up the steps and gave the knocker a sharp, urgent rap.

"Lord Roxbury." Hawkins, Philip's butler, bowed slightly, relieving Paul of his coat and hat, and handing them to a footman. "Madam asked that I bring you directly to her sitting room."

Paul knew better than to ask Hawkins what was amiss. Philip had chosen the man for his discretion and Hawkins had orders not to divulge any household business, even to close acquaintances and other members of the family. Rather than broach the subject, Paul simply followed the staid butler to Willa's quarters and waited patiently while Hawkins rapped on her sitting room door.

"Oh, Paul!" Willa, who had been reclining on a blue velvet

sofa, jumped to her feet when she saw her brother. "I am so glad you have come!"

"*Why* have I come?" Paul regarded her closely. Willa was perfectly dressed in an afternoon gown of sky blue muslin, her dark curls were carefully arranged in the latest style, and there were no signs of recent tears in her blue-gray eyes. He came to the conclusion that his sister did not look in the least bit overset and he gratefully discarded the notion that something dreadful had happened to Philip.

"It's dear Jennifer. You do remember her, don't you, Paul? She was my bosom bow at Miss Booth's Academy."

"Of course." Paul nodded quickly. He remembered the sunny redhead who had come home with his sister for a visit. "Is there something amiss with Jenny?"

"She is married now, and has need of me. Jenny is . . . it is a somewhat delicate situation, Paul, and . . ."

"Jenny is increasing?" Paul guessed the source of Willa's embarrassment and laughed. "Come now, Willa. We have never skirted around such issues before. There is nothing in the least bit unnatural about bearing a child."

Willa laughed. "You are right, my dear. It is just that I'm so accustomed to speaking with Philip's stodgy family, I quite forgot that I needn't couch my words with you."

"Tell me." Philip sat down with a smile on his face. "Is Jenny happy in her marriage?"

"Oh, my yes! And she's delighted over her pregnancy. But she's six months along, perhaps a bit more, and there are complications. The physician has confined her to bed and the poor dear's so bored, she's becoming slightly batty with it all. I received a letter from her this morning and she practically begged me to come to her, claiming she could not bear it another moment with only her mama-in-law in attendance. If I do, that well-meaning but highly irritating lady will return to her own residence until after the birth."

Paul nodded. "Then you must go to her immediately. I will be happy to see to any matters that require your attention here."

"You should not be so quick to offer." Willa's lips curved up in a smile. "There are two very important matters that require my attention and they both have names, David and Stewart."

"Philip's sons have come to stay with you for the Season?"

Willa nodded. "Yes, indeed. They arrived only yesterday and I promised Philip that I would supervise them in his absence."

"Ah-ha!" Paul grinned at his sister. "I wondered why you needed me so urgently. I assume that you wish me to take charge of David and Stewart so that you may go to Jenny?"

Willa had the grace to blush as she nodded. "I know it will cut into your time, Paul, but Jenny truly needs me. And the boys are usually no trouble to speak of."

"How would they feel about this?"

Willa gave a slight laugh. "They will be very relieved to be rid of me. David and Stewart are of an age where my very best motherly cautions fall on deaf ears. And you know, my dear, that they have always adored you. They are forever talking about their Uncle Paul."

"Then there is no problem to speak of. Pack your things and be on your way. And do not forget to give Jenny my greetings. I shall take the boys to stay with me at Roxbury House and supervise them for you."

Willa did not look convinced. "You must not let them get into any muddles, Paul. They are both quite well behaved, but this is the very first Season that they have attended."

"You must not worry, Willa." Paul grinned at his sister. "After all, I am well acquainted with any traps into which they might tumble."

Willa laughed. "By virtue of having fallen into them yourself?"

"Of course. I am a reformed scoundrel, my dear, and they shall not be able to pull the wool over my eyes."

"Reformed? That is news to me, but I knew that I could count on you." Willa smiled and crossed the room to place a kiss on Paul's cheek. "Let us go up to their chambers and tell them the news. I have accepted several dozen invitations for them and Hawkins has made a list of their schedule."

Paul's eyes narrowed as he realized that he had been outmaneuvered by his sister. "Then you knew that I'd agree to take over their care?"

"I had *hoped* you would. And I thought it best to be fully prepared in the event that you agreed to do so." Willa deftly sidestepped the trap that he had set for her. "David and Stewart will be attending the come-out ball of two young sisters from the country this evening, distant relatives, I believe."

Paul groaned. He had made arrangements to meet several friends for supper at White's, followed by an evening at the tables in that fine gentlemen's club. Now it seemed he should have to send his regrets and attend a debutante ball instead. "Where is this event to be held?"

"At Lady Pinchton's mansion." Willa frowned slightly. "I do hope this doesn't inconvenience you, dear."

Paul sighed. Lady Pinchton was a most proper dowager and any ball she hosted would be as dry as dust. But he had given his promise to Willa and he would have to make the best of it. "It's quite all right, Willa. Attending Lady Pinchton's ball and making the acquaintance of two young misses from the country will be most entertaining, I am sure."

Paul turned to his two young charges as they joined the long line of carriages that were moving slowly forward toward the entrance to Lady Pinchton's town mansion. "You must both remember not to dance more than twice with the same young lady."

"Yes, Uncle Paul." David, Philip's older son, nodded quickly. "And we are not to ask any young lady to walk in the gardens without a proper chaperone."

Paul laughed, reaching out to straighten David's neckcloth. He had to cease thinking of David as a boy, for Philip's heir was nearing his twentieth birthday.

"We are permitted one glass of champagne, no more," Stewart chimed in, reciting the rules that Paul had given them before they had set out for Lady Pinchton's mansion. "And we are not, under any circumstances, to show undue attention to any one *particular* young lady."

"Right." Paul nodded, smiling at Stewart. Philip's second son resembled his father closely, with the same light hair and dark-blue eyes. He was almost nineteen and possessed a fine athletic build that made the addition of buckram wadding to his coat quite unnecessary.

"Lady Willa has warned us that some of the debutantes may try to set their caps for us." David grinned at his uncle, his even teeth flashing whitely in his face.

"She is quite correct in that respect." Paul laughed, giving David a closer inspection. The boy's dark good looks resembled those of his mother, a raven-haired beauty who had died several years ago of a lingering illness she had contracted while traveling with Philip. "You are a prize catch, David, as you are your father's heir and will soon assume his secondary holdings as well as his lesser title. And you, Stewart, stand to inherit a tidy sum from your mother's side of the family. You must both take care not to be tricked into any compromising situations."

Stewart laughed. "Believe me, Uncle, we have been warned. Lady Willa told us that we must constantly be on our guard as some debutantes will stop at nothing to trap us into marriage."

"My sister has prepared you well." Paul bit back a chuckle at the solemn expressions on their faces. "Am I correct in assuming that you have no plans to be leg-shackled in the near future?"

David looked quite alarmed at the suggestion. "You are entirely correct, Uncle Paul! There's time enough to fall into the parson's mousetrap when we are older and more settled."

"David is quite right." Stewart nodded quickly. "I have decided to remain a bachelor like you, Uncle Paul, for the next several years at least. I think I should like to enjoy the company of beautiful ladies without taking on the encumbrances of marriage."

Paul winced slightly. At one and thirty, he was still unwed, even though Willa and his mother had both urged him to choose a suitable wife and set up his nursery. Now, it seemed, his bachelor lifestyle had influenced his younger nephew in a way that he had not intended.

"No doubt I will marry sooner or later." Paul's smile did not reach his eyes as he faced Philip's sons. "There are family obligations to consider."

David nodded, accepting his words, but Stewart spoke up. "I do not see what family obligations have to do with it. Father says a man should not marry to please someone else."

"And your father is quite right." Paul sighed. "But I am of the age where the company of a wife would warm my old bones on cold winter nights."

Both boys stared at him for a moment, and then Stewart laughed. "You are bamming us, are you not, Uncle Paul?"

"Perhaps, just a bit." Paul grinned at his young charges. "I shall not marry until I truly wish to do so, and I would hope that you follow my example. Any lady I choose must stand the test of time."

"The test of time?" David was curious.

"Yes, indeed. I shall keep company with the lady I choose for at least a year before I offer for her. By that time, I shall know for certain whether or not we will suit."

"That is very wise of you, Uncle Paul." David nodded quickly. "We would do well to practice the same caution."

Stewart nodded. "Yes. The test of time will work nicely for us, as well."

"Then let us prepare to enjoy the evening without a single thought of matrimony entering our minds." Paul noticed that their carriage was finally approaching the head of the line and he wanted one last word with the boys before Lady Pinchton's footman approached to open the carriage door. "If you conduct yourselves impeccably tonight, I shall take you with me tomorrow when I go to Gentleman Jackson's."

David's mouth flew open with surprise. "Gentleman Jackson's? Oh, Uncle! I have been wishing to go there for well over a year!"

"Me, too." Stewart grinned. "I assure you, sir, that you will have no cause for complaint over our behavior."

Paul nodded, hiding a grin. Willa had told him that the boys had been wishing to observe a sparring match and Gentleman Jackson owned the finest establishment of pugilistic skills in the entire city. Perhaps, if his nephews were truly well behaved at this evening's entertainment, he might even coax his good friend, Gentleman Jackson, into giving them a few lessons.

"Lady Willa says you have a way with the ladies and perhaps we could learn a thing or two from you." David looked very eager. "I must admit I am not well trained at the sorts of compliments that young misses seem to expect."

"I am certain you'll do admirably." Paul bit back a chuckle. Whatever had Willa told the boys about him?

Stewart cast an admiring look at his uncle. "Father says they call you *The Elusive Earl*. He told us the title was given to you by Lady Janeway when she set her cap for you and you refused to be tangled in her web."

"Father also said that we would be wise to copy your behavior so that we will not be caught by some clever young miss." David nodded solemnly at his uncle. "He said *The Elusive Earl* was a well-known expert at avoiding matrimony."

Paul laughed long and hard and then he turned to the two boys. "Your father is right in one respect. Lady Janeway did fancy to marry me and I did foil her plans."

"How did you accomplish that?" Stewart was clearly intrigued.

"There isn't time to tell you now, but I'll divulge all over breakfast tomorrow."

"Thank you, Uncle Paul." David smiled up at him. "We would be grateful for any advice that you care to give us."

Paul coughed, hiding his chuckle. It was clear that the boys had been told that he was a womanizer. The label the *ton* had given Paul was quite undeserved, but it was beyond his power to undo the whispered *on-dits* that still circulated about him. It was true that he had passed from one charming lady to the next without a backward glance. Once he had learned that a particular lady was not the one he had sought, he had moved on to try his luck in another quarter. Perhaps this made him a rake in some eyes, but Paul did not think that he had been unkind. He had promised nothing and had always presented each lady with a token gift before he had taken his leave of her. More than one lady who frequented the best drawing rooms of the *ton* would have a small gold locket in her jewel box, a sign that *The Elusive Earl* had favored her for a time.

As his carriage wheeled up at the entrance and one of Lady Pinchton's liveried footmen opened the door, Paul imagined how the tongues would wag if the *ton* knew the truth about him. Instead of that notorious rake, *The Elusive Earl,* Paul was simply a man who had lost his heart to the blond angel he'd met at a masquerade ball five Seasons ago. Since he did not know her name and had never seen her face without the mask that had obscured it, he had no clue as to her identity. But Paul had paid close attention to every blond lady who had appeared on the social scene ever since. He was on a quest to find his fickle angel again and find out precisely why she had failed to keep her promise to him.

Nine

Holly smiled as she watched her stepdaughters take the floor. They had not lacked for partners this evening, and to Holly, who was as proud of them as a mother could be, it appeared that Beth and Marcie were the most popular young debutantes in Lady Pinchton's large ballroom.

With the girls stationed between them, Holly and Lady Pinchton had fulfilled their obligations in the reception line. After this duty had been accomplished, Holly had chosen a seat with the other chaperones. She had not left her chair for upwards of two hours and she was becoming quite weary of making polite conversation with the other chaperones, all of whom were at least double her age.

Of course there had been questions about both Beth and Marcie and Holly had answered them all with a gracious smile. Now, however, she felt restless and she longed for a moment alone, away from the scrutiny of curious eyes. Since Beth and Marcie were engaged for this set of dances, there was no reason why she could not slip away to the ladies' withdrawing room and enjoy a bit of solitude.

With that goal in mind, Holly turned to the chaperone on her left, an elderly spinster who had informed Holly that she was in charge of her youngest sibling's daughter. "Excuse me, Lady Warton, but I find I must excuse myself for a brief moment. Would it be possible for you to—"

"Say no more," the elderly spinster interrupted her with a

smile. "Run along, Lady Bentworth. You may be assured that I will watch your darling stepdaughters for you."

Holly thanked Lady Warton and quickly exited the ballroom. But just as she was navigating the staircase, her eyes were drawn to three handsome gentlemen who were just now preparing to enter the ballroom.

The two gentlemen in the lead had fresh young faces and their anxiety at entering the ballroom was apparent. Holly smiled as they straightened their shoulders, pulled their coat sleeves down so that the prescribed amount of ruffled white cuff was exposed, and reached up, almost in tandem, to smooth their hair. The taller of the two had golden hair and a powerful athletic frame. The other was darkly handsome, with a build that indicated he might excel at sports that required agility. Though he was slight, the muscles in his upper arms and calves were well defined and Holly surmised that he possessed a goodly amount of strength.

It was the older gentleman who captivated Holly, though she was in position to observe only his back. He was the tallest of the three, his hair was black and worn slightly longer than fashion dictated, and he appeared quite at ease in his formal wear. He was obviously in charge of the two younger boys, for they deferred to him, stepping aside at the ballroom door so that he might enter before them.

The older gentleman turned at the door, for a last word with his charges, and Holly gasped slightly. Even though five years had passed since she had seen her first fickle love, her memory of him had not dimmed. This gentleman resembled him most uncannily in the color of his hair, his powerful build, and his height.

Could he be the pirate she had partnered at that fateful masquerade ball five years ago, the rake who had captured her heart and then failed to keep their planned rendezvous? Holly swayed slightly, grasped the polished wooden banister to steady herself, and watched him carefully as he strode into the ballroom with the two young gentlemen in his wake. No, such a coincidence was the stuff of novels and seldom occurred in ordinary life. It was not at all likely that the charming rake who had played fast and loose with her heart was still in London, and all but impossible that he should appear here, at Lady Pinchton's mansion, for her stepdaughters' debutante ball.

Chiding herself for her foolish imaginings, Holly hurried down the hall to the ladies' withdrawing room. One glance in the mirror and she chided herself again, for her outward show of emotion. Her complexion was quite flushed, her eyes were wide and troubled, and her hands were trembling slightly. She had to regain control of her emotions before one of the other chaperones asked her what was amiss.

Once she had straightened her gown, smoothed her hair, and taken several deep breaths to erase the last trace of her distress, Holly felt much more the thing. She was even able to smile with good humor at her earlier flight. What a ninnyhammer she had been to let her fears run roughshod over her better sense! She had never seen her fickle love's features beneath his pirate's mask and knew only the color of his hair and eyes, and his height. If she allowed herself to become so unsettled over the sight of every tall, dark-haired gentleman she encountered in Lady Pinchton's ballroom, she would spend the entire evening in a heightened state of anxiety.

Once Holly had regained her composure, she exited the chamber with a smile on her face. She nodded politely to another tall, dark-haired gentleman who was entering the chamber Lady Pinchton had set aside for cards, and felt marked relief at the steadiness of her heartbeat. With a lift of her chin, she reentered the ballroom to find that the set of country dances had ended and another was about to begin.

Holly glanced round the dance floor and smiled as she saw Beth place her gloved hand on the arm of the young, dark-haired gentleman that Holly had observed entering the ballroom. Marcie had taken up a place next to her sister, and Holly noticed that she had accepted his companion as her partner. The two couples were well suited and Holly watched as they took their places on the dance floor, Beth's light brown hair and slender figure forming a pleasing contrast to her darkly handsome partner and Marcie's dark beauty complementing her blond escort.

"Such well-behaved girls." Lady Warton smiled at Holly as she returned to her chair. "When your stepdaughters discovered that you were gone, they brought their young gentlemen over for my approval."

Holly nodded. "That is precisely what I instructed them to do. And you gave them leave to dance, Lady Warton?"

"Indeed I did. They have taken the floor with the Earl of Pelham's sons, a very fine family and above reproach. The elder, David, is his father's heir and will soon assume his secondary title of viscount. And his younger brother, Stewart, will inherit his mother's lands in two years' time. They told me that they have just come down from Cambridge and I thought that you would not object if your stepdaughters danced with them."

"You were correct, Lady Warton." Holly nodded quickly. She longed to ask about the gentleman who had entered the ballroom with Lord Pelham's sons, but such a question could be misconstrued. Lady Warton had shared a good bit of gossip with her in the time that they had been seated together, and Holly did not want to add to her store of tarradiddle.

Holly's mind spun, alighting on a plan to learn the information she sought. Perhaps there was a way to ask without asking and Holly turned to the dowager with a guileless expression. "I do not recall making Lord Pelham's acquaintance. Is he not in attendance?"

Lady Warton shook her head. "No, my dear. I understand he is traveling the continent in the service of His Majesty. He is an ambassador, or some such thing."

"Then his sons are here with their mother?"

Lady Warton frowned as she shook her head. "Their mother died quite some time ago and Lord Pelham has since remarried. I heard that the new countess had intended to accompany the boys, but she was called away to a friend's sickbed."

"Surely the young gentlemen have not come here alone!"

Holly lowered her eyes, unable to face Lady Warton while knowing full well that this was not the case.

"No, indeed. Their uncle has taken charge of them in their stepmother's absence."

"I see." Holly nodded quickly, repressing the smile that threatened to turn up the corners of her lips at so easily learning the information she had sought. Perhaps it was not such a bad thing that Lady Warton was a gabble monger.

Lady Warton leaned closer, deftly unfurling her fan and placing it strategically to assure the privacy of their conversation. "They call him *The Elusive Earl,* you know."

"The boys' uncle?" Holly's eyes widened.

"Yes, indeed. It is because no lady has been able to capture his interest for longer than a week." Lady Warton's eyes twinkled merrily. "The fact that he is here at all is a feather in Lady Pinchton's cap. He does not attend debutante functions, preferring the company of older and . . . shall we say more *experienced* ladies?"

Holly laughed, enjoying the impish smile that crossed Lady Warton's face. "You make *The Elusive Earl* sound most fascinating, Lady Warton, but I shall take your words as a warning to avoid his company."

"That would be wise, of course." Lady Warton gave a surprisingly girlish giggle and leaned over to pat Holly's hand. "But I have heard that he prefers ladies who share your lovely hair color. And the largest share of them have been very close to your own age. Perhaps you are the very one to capture his heart and bring him up to scratch."

Holly shook her head. "I beg to decline that dubious honor, Lady Warton. You see, I have no desire to marry again."

"Was your first marriage so dreadful then?" Lady Warton's eyes glinted in the light from the chandeliers and Holly was forewarned that her elderly companion was on the trail of yet another *on-dit* to add to her repertoire.

"Not in the least, Lady Warton. My first marriage was far happier than any succeeding one could ever be, and it is the reason that I do not seek another husband. No other could compare with the fine gentleman who shared my life for so brief a time."

Lady Warton nodded and gave Holly a smile of approval. "That is a lovely sentiment, my dear, and I have no doubt that you are sincere. But you are far too young to sit on the shelf for the remainder of your days. Lady Pinchton has told me of your situation and I agree that you must honor your dear husband's wishes. You must enjoy the Season that he has arranged for you."

"That is true and I am determined to enjoy it, but I truly do not desire to enter the Marriage Mart." Holly frowned slightly, wondering if everyone in the ballroom knew about the letter that William had left for her. If Lady Pinchton had taken Lady Warton into her confidence, no doubt the news had spread far and wide.

"How long has your dear husband been gone, dear?" Lady Warton leaned closer.

"It will be two years in a month's time."

"A month? Why, that is perfection!" A smile spread over Lady Warton's face. "I will make certain that you and your lovely stepdaughters receive an invitation to my dear sister's masquerade ball. It is to be held in five weeks, and by that time, you will be free to dance."

"Thank you, Lady Warton. You must not think me ungrateful, for my stepdaughters and I should certainly enjoy attending the affair, but I am not certain that it would be proper for me to take the floor."

Lady Warton waved Holly's concerns away with a flutter of her fan. "Of course you should take the floor, my dear! And no one will dare to criticize you, for I will ask my brother-in-law to lead you out in the first waltz. He is the Duke of Elmwood, you know, and to criticize his choice of partner would be very bad *ton*."

Holly felt her hands begin to tremble and she did her best not to show how distressed she was. She had attended the duke and Duchess of Elmwood's costume ball five Seasons ago, and it was there that she had met the handsome pirate who had stolen her heart.

"You will attend, will you not?" Lady Warton looked a bit concerned.

"Indeed, we will and with great pleasure." Holly managed a shaky smile. This was not the time to indulge her unhappy memories. It would be a *coup* for Beth and Marcie to receive an invitation to the elegant affair.

"I do believe I'll have my sister invite Lord Pelham's sons as well." Lady Warton smiled as she spied Holly's stepdaughters dancing with David and Stewart. "You would do well to encourage your girls to think kindly of their partners, Lady Bentworth. An alliance with such a noble family would do much to elevate your stepdaughters to the level of Incomparables."

Holly nodded, keeping her expression carefully neutral. "Indeed, it would, but the girls are far too young to marry at this time. After all, this is their very first Season. Perhaps, in a year or so—"

"Too young?" Lady Warton interrupted her with a laugh. "Why, that is simply not true, my dear. I do believe you married your husband in your very first Season, did you not?"

Holly nodded, sensing that Lady Warton was laying a trap for her and unable to think of a way to extricate herself. "Yes, Lady Warton, I did."

"And you told me that your marriage was happy?" Lady Warton smiled, closing in for the kill.

"It was very happy." Holly nodded quickly.

"Then you must not be concerned." Lady Warton leaned over to pat Holly's hand. "If two such suitable young gentlemen offer for your stepdaughters, you must not be so selfish as to deny their future happiness."

Holly sighed. She was well and firmly caught. "No, Lady Warton. I would never do that. But they must be Beth and Marcie's perfect matches."

"Of course." Lady Warton nodded quickly. "And only time

will tell about that. See how they smile at each other? I do believe I catch the delightful scent of romance in the air."

Holly glanced at her stepdaughters and winced as she noted their sparkling eyes and their happy smiles. Both Beth and Marcie did appear to be quite enamored of their partners. Holly stifled the urge to contradict the aging dowager, claiming that her stepdaughters were merely enjoying their first formal ball, but she could not deny their marked preference for David and Stewart.

"Perhaps you have the right of it, Lady Warton." Holly gave a reluctant nod and reminded herself to speak to her stepdaughters about forming attachments so early in the Season. "But as you so wisely stated, only time will tell."

Ten

Paul kept a polite smile on his face as he conversed with a contemporary of his mother's, Lady Priscilla Norwich. Though he had intended to watch his nephews for a moment and then take himself off to the card room, she had waylaid him quite handily by asking of his mother's health.

All the while Paul exchanged suitable comments with her, half-listening to her words, his sharp gray eyes roamed the chamber, hoping to spot the lovely blond lady he had glimpsed earlier on the stair. Though five years had passed since he had last seen his fickle angel, something about the lady's carriage and the color of her hair had reminded him of her. Was it possible that she had come to London again, to enjoy the entertainments of the Season? If so, Paul intended to find out precisely why she had failed to meet him.

"As fond as I am of you, dear boy, I must warn you to leave Lady Pinchton's *protégés* quite alone. They are delightfully innocent girls from the country and it would not be fair to expose them to your wicked charms. Only if you promise to behave yourself will I point them out to you."

Paul nodded, smiling devilishly as that was what Lady Norwich seemed to expect of him. "Please do, my dear lady. I cannot promise to behave myself if I do not know before whom I must behave."

"Do you see the charming young miss in the sea-green gown?" Lady Norwich directed Paul's attention to the center of the ballroom. "She is Miss Elizabeth Langley. And her sister, Miss Marcella, is dancing not far from her. Her gown is a lovely shade of buttercup yellow."

Paul nodded as he spied the two young ladies. "Ah, yes. I see them, Lady Norwich, and you may rest assured that they are quite safe from my attentions. They are far too young, and as it happens, Miss Langley and Miss Marcella are dancing with my nephews."

"Lord Pelham's sons?" Lady Norwich's eyes widened as Paul nodded. "Ah, yes. I recognize them now. David and Stewart, is that not correct?"

Paul laughed. "Your memory cannot be faulted, Lady Norwich. But how do you come to know of them?"

"Your dear sister made the introductions a full year ago, when they paid a brief visit to Town. They are handsome young gentlemen and their behavior, thus far, has been faultless. I saw them both seek out their hostess and make their pretties quite admirably."

"They are fine boys." Paul nodded. "Of course they are both high-spirited, but that is to be expected as this is the first Season that they have been permitted to attend. Philip charged Willa with the duty of supervising them while he is on the continent, but she has been called away to attend an ailing friend."

"Do not tell me that *you* are in charge of them!"

"Yes, indeed." Paul stifled the urge to grin as Lady Norwich's eyes widened in shock. "Come now, Lady Norwich. It is not as bad as all that. After all, David and Stewart can learn proper behavior by *not* following my example."

Lady Norwich's lips twitched up in a smile. "If the *on-dits* I have heard concerning your actions are true, dear boy, indeed they can!"

"Perhaps you would be kind enough to advise me." Paul turned to Lady Norwich a candid smile. "I should not like to be remiss in my duties and I have never taken charge of two young gentlemen before. I feel as though I am groping in the dark."

Lady Norwich laughed. "From what I have heard of your escapades, dear boy, that should not be a novelty for you!"

"That was quite wicked of you, madam!" Paul chuckled appreciatively at her *bon mot.* "But I am most sincere about seeking your advice. I would not like to fail in my obligations to my sister and brother-in-law."

Lady Norwich nodded. "Of course you would not and I would be delighted to assist you, dear boy. Your first task is to assure that young David and Stewart behave properly and I must say that you appear to have that well in hand. Whether by your influence, or that of your dear sister, none can criticize their conduct."

"Thank you, Lady Norwich." Paul accepted the compliment even though he doubted that the credit was his.

"Your second obligation is to make certain that your nephews limit their attentions to *suitable* young ladies."

Paul nodded gravely, though he felt more like chuckling. "Suitable. Yes, indeed. And how do I discover whether or not a young lady is suitable?"

"You must examine the young lady's family, dear boy. If there is the slightest hint of scandal in her background, you must warn your nephews away."

"I see. And how would you regard Miss Elizabeth and Miss Marcella, Lady Norwich? Are they *suitable* young ladies?"

An expression of distress crossed Lady Norwich's angular face. "They are certainly suitable partners for a dance. They are Lady Pinchton's *protégées,* after all."

"But there is something that you are withholding, Lady Norwich." Paul lowered his voice and leaned a bit closer to his mother's friend. "Is there a scandal in the family?"

Lady Norwich sighed and glanced around to make certain that her words were not overheard. "Not precisely a scandal, but a slight bit of tarradiddle that I chanced to hear several years ago. Of course, it could be nothing but a hum, but one cannot be too cautious when one is in charge of such impressionable young gentlemen."

"You had best tell me, Lady Norwich." Paul glanced at his nephews. "Perhaps I am mistaken, but David and Stewart seem quite taken with these particular young ladies."

Lady Norwich gazed at the boys again, and then she nodded. "I suppose it is my duty to tell you, though I do not like to repeat gossip. It concerns the young ladies' stepmother, Lady Bentworth."

"Bentworth?" Paul repeated the name. He was certain he had heard it before, but he could not seem to recall the circumstance.

"She is seated with the other chaperones, next to Lady Warton, in a deep red gown. She was the viscount's second wife and she is now his widow."

Paul's eyes widened as he caught sight of the lady in question. She was the same lovely lady that he had seen on the stair as they had entered the ballroom. "She is very young to be a widow."

"Yes, indeed." Lady Norwich nodded. "And she is also quite fetching. Lady Pinchton confided to me that she was still quite distraught over the loss of her husband."

Paul noted the dubious tone in Lady Norwich's voice. "But you do not believe it to be true?"

"I am sure I do not know, one way or the other, as I have only just met Lady Bentworth. But there was some speculation when she married the viscount."

Paul raised his brows, waiting for Lady Norwich to arrive at the crux of her conversation. When she did not continue, he prompted her. "Yes?"

"The viscount was several decades her senior with two daughters who were very nearly grown. From all I have heard, he was a kind and gentle man, not at all well acquainted with the ways of the *ton*."

"You are saying that the viscount was *naïve?*"

"Yes, indeed." Lady Norwich laughed slightly. "From the first day he met her, he was taken in by her charms."

Paul drew the obvious conclusion. "And marrying him was a feather in her cap?"

"Oh, my yes! Her family was perfectly respectable, an aunt and uncle who lived on a small estate in the country, an entail of some sort as I recall. Rumor had it that they spent their entire savings on a Season for her."

"Then they must have hoped that she'd marry well."

"No doubt." Lady Norwich nodded. "And they were not mistaken in their aspirations, for she did. I understand that Viscount Bentworth provided for them as part of the marriage settlement, and due to his largess, they lived out the remainder of their lives in comfort."

Paul raised his brows. "But it is not unusual for a young miss to marry for the purpose of providing for her family."

"Of course it is not. But none who knew her expected her to catch the eye of such a notable gentleman, and there was a great deal of speculation when they married before the end of her First Season. Some thought her an opportunist, but that was only to be expected given the disparity in their ages and the fact that the viscount possessed both title and wealth. It was a subject that was bandied about a great deal, naturally."

"Naturally." Paul nodded, smiling wryly. No doubt Lady Norwich, herself, had been one who had speculated over the viscount's young bride.

"To make matters worse, their union was accomplished in great haste by special license, and they removed to the viscount's country estate immediately after the ceremony. It led some to wonder whether or not the girl had been compromised."

Paul raised his brows. "And had she been?"

"There is no way to tell, for certain, as the couple remained childless. Still, it is quite odd that they retired so quickly to Bentworth lands and remained there until the viscount's death."

Paul felt a surge of pity for the young miss who had been the object of such gossip. "And now this greedy social climber is back to present her husband's daughters?"

"Precisely." Lady Norwich caught the irony in his tone and looked a bit discomfited. "You must understand that what I have told you is simply gossip, dear boy. Lady Pinchton insists that the viscount's widow has been an exemplary wife and step-mother. All the same, I cannot help but wonder at the reason the viscount insisted that she share in his daughters' Season."

"But that is normal, is it not?" Paul frowned slightly. "Some-one has to watch over them, and she appears to be the logical choice."

"But she is not here as a mere chaperone. According to Lady Pinchton, the viscount left monies with his solicitor, along with a letter expressing his desire that his widow cast off her mourn-ing and take an active part in the Season. This letter, which none of us has had the privilege to see, urges her to secure a suitable *parti* and remarry."

This news left Paul dumbstruck. What kind of a husband would arrange for his widow's remarriage? He cast about for some comment to make, but he was saved the trouble for Lady Norwich continued of her own accord.

"Quite naturally, she claims that she does not wish to re-marry, that none could compare to her dear, dead husband. She gives a pretty little speech that is perfectly calculated to tug at the heartstrings and I have no doubt that some will believe her."

Paul nodded, catching Lady Norwich's meaning perfectly. "Am I to assume that you suspect the letter, supposedly written by the viscount before his death, is a forgery? And that she is using it as her justification for seeking a new husband?"

"It seems a reasonable assumption." Lady Norwich raised one perfectly shaped brow. "No doubt she developed expensive tastes during her years as a viscountess and the portion her husband left to her will not support the life she prefers. I daresay that if a gentleman of singular worth and title were to come along, he would persuade her to change her mind quite quickly. After all, it cannot be pleasant to live in a small dower cottage and rely on the generosity of one's brother-in-law."

"No, indeed." Paul nodded. It was clear that Lady Norwich believed the viscount's widow was a fortune hunter, and perhaps it was true. Lady Bentworth was dressed in a fine gown, and though she was sedately seated with the chaperones, one small foot was tapping out the beat of the music.

Without realizing that he had done so, Paul began to smile. Perhaps he ought to go over and make her acquaintance. He would have a perfect excuse, as his nephews were dancing with her stepdaughters. Then he could take her measure himself.

"I do not like that glint in your eye, dear Roxbury." Lady Norwich began to frown. "What devilment are you contemplating?"

Paul smiled guilelessly. "Why none, Lady Norwich. I merely thought it might be appropriate for me to meet Lady Bentworth, since my nephews have engaged her stepdaughters in a dance."

"No good can come of it." Lady Norwich shook her head. "I am sorry, dear boy, but I must decline to assist you."

"Tell me why, Lady Norwich. I merely wish to make the lady's acquaintance."

"Not even that." Lady Norwich was firm. "She is a taking little chit and just your type. And once she hears of your title and your wealth, she is bound to set her cap for you. No, dear boy. Your mother would never forgive me if I allowed you to become entangled in her trap."

Paul laughed, reaching out to take Lady Norwich's arm. *"The Elusive Earl?* Entangled? Heaven forfend, dear lady! Give a thought to my reputation and then I beg you to reconsider. If I am as black as they paint me by half, no harm will come of it."

"There is that." Lady Norwich began to smile. "And two such consummate gamesters in close proximity can only provide an amusing diversion."

Paul grinned. "Precisely. I knew I could count on you, Lady Norwich. You have always been my favorite among Mother's friends."

"Fustian!" Lady Norwich tapped his arm with her unfurled fan. "Still, your meeting should be the source for more than one amusing *on-dit.* Come along, dear boy, and I shall introduce you straightaway."

Eleven

Holly's hands were still trembling as she sat in the carriage, barely heeding Beth and Marcie's chatter about the ball. Her stepdaughters had enjoyed the ball immensely and Holly was grateful for that. But the appearance of Lady Norwich with *The Elusive Earl* in tow had sent Holly's evening crashing into a downward spiral that would only end when she was safely ensconced in her private quarters on High Street.

She had not liked him above half! He was a rake and a bounder, and Holly had become convinced of this fact the instant that she had raised her eyes to his. But though she had felt quite breathless in his presence, a most unwelcome response to his handsome appearance and commanding manner, she had not been able to tell if he was her fickle pirate. She should be required to spend more time with him to be certain, but that was the very thing Holly wished to avoid!

The moment Lady Norwich had introduced the Ninth Earl of Roxbury to Holly, she had turned away to begin a conversation with Lady Warton. This had left Holly alone to converse with the earl, knowing nothing of him but his title and his unsavory reputation. Of course, Holly had done her best to initiate a congenial conversation, asking him if he had just recently arrived in London. His reaction to her query had been odd, to say the least, as he had merely stared at her intently, his dark brows furrowing slightly. At first Holly had thought that he had taken more than his share of champagne and had become too befuddled to reply. Surely that was the only excuse he could have for scrutinizing her so rudely! But then, when she had been about to turn from him and give up the attempt at converse, he had smiled quite politely, his gray eyes still probing hers, and told her that he had been in residence for upwards of two months.

Holly had fought to keep the smile on her face and the color from heating her cheeks. The man had no right to stare at her so! He was not foxed. She could tell that now, as his stance was steady, his eyes were clear, and his reply to her had not been in the least slurred.

Deciding it should be uncivil not to attempt further converse, Holly had mentioned that Lady Pinchton had praised Edmund Kean as Shylock, and asked if he had viewed the performance. He had smiled his charming smile, appearing for all the world to attend her words, but again it had taken him long moments to respond to her query.

During the silence, which had seemed to stretch on for hours, he had pinned her to the spot with his eyes. Holly had trembled slightly, knowing precisely how a fox should feel, pursued by a pack of slavering hounds, but she had held her ground. Then he had chuckled slightly, raking her from head to toe with his gaze, and said that he had not yet had the opportunity to take in the play, but that he had no doubt Lady Pinchton's opinion was quite accurate.

It was at this point that Lady Norwich had broken off her conversation with Lady Warton and returned to his side. She had taken his arm, begged Holly to excuse them, and pulled him away to introduce him to another group of guests. Holly had been much relieved, staring after him with a frown. *The Elusive Earl* had stared at her so openly, she had suspected that he could see beneath her very skin to observe the frantic beating of her heart!

Holly gave an angry sigh as she recalled the manner in which he had scrutinized her. It was almost as if he had examined her thoroughly and found her wanting. Though she could find no fault with his words, Lord Roxbury's action had been insufferably rude.

"What is it, Mama?" Beth heard her sigh and turned to her in alarm.

"Nothing of any significance, dear." Holly arranged her lips in a smile. "I am simply tired, that is all."

Once Beth had returned to her conversation with Marcie, Holly's mind resumed her contemplation of *The Elusive Earl*. Though she wished for no further congress with him, she had no doubt that they should meet again. His nephews had taken an interest in her stepdaughters, and their paths were bound to cross.

Holly sat, eyes closed, half-listening to Beth and Marcie's excited chatter. She was exhausted by the events of the evening and she had not slept well the night before. Was it possible that her imagination had played a trick upon her perceptions? Lady Warton had told her of the earl's reputation and she had been alerted to his faults long before she had made his acquaintance. She had prejudged him, firmly expecting him to behave as a rake and a scoundrel and she had interpreted his actions in that light. She supposed it was possible that Lord Roxbury gazed at all ladies in this manner, and he meant nothing untoward by his scrutiny. All the same, his presence had caused her great discomfort.

"I do believe I have made a conquest!" Marcie laughed gaily, rousing Holly from her troubled thoughts. "And I daresay you have made one also, dear Beth!"

Beth smiled shyly. "Oh, I do hope that you are right. I did think that Lord Redfield was dashing."

"But not as dashing as his brother." Marcie laughed. "What do you think, Mama? Have we made a conquest at our very first ball?"

"Perhaps." Holly forced herself to listen to her stepdaughters, putting aside her contemplation of *The Elusive Earl*.

"Of course we've made conquests!" Marcie was not to be

denied. "They asked if they could call upon us tomorrow, did they not?"

Holly smiled slightly in the darkness. It would do the girls no harm to think that they had made conquests and perhaps it was true. But she had also seen Lord Pelham's sons ask several other chaperones for permission to call upon their charges as well.

"Do you think they favor us, Mama?"

Beth appeared a bit anxious and Holly nodded quickly. "Yes, dear. I believe they do, but you must not count upon it over-much. It is not wise to form attachments this early in the Season."

"Why not, Mama?" Marcie began to frown.

"Because you have not made the acquaintance of all the young gentlemen, as yet. It would be much wiser of you to reserve your opinion until you have a wider base of comparison."

"Like Marcie and the kittens?" Beth laughed as she recalled the incident.

"Precisely." Holly nodded, grinning at Marcie. "Do you remember how you thought each kitten that Mrs. Darby lifted from her basket was more charming than the last?"

Marcie groaned in protest. "But Mama, I cannot have been above twelve at the time. And in truth, I wanted them all. They were each charming in their own way."

"Precisely as each young gentleman is charming in his own way." Holly smiled as she made her point. "You would be very foolish to lose your heart to one particular gentleman before you have even made the acquaintance of the rest. And you certainly cannot have them all! Why, whatever would dear Lady Pinchton say if she discovered that my stepdaughters were such flirts?"

Marcie and Beth broke into a fit of the giggles at the thought, and Holly leaned back against the squabs once more. She hoped her little lesson had served to ward off any premature attachment to Lord Pelham's sons.

"We do not want them all, Mama." Beth spoke up the moment she had regained her composure. "We are not even certain that we want any particular gentleman at all. But you must admit that Lord Redfield and Mr. Averill are exceedingly pleasant."

Holly nodded. "Indeed, they are. And they do come from a very highly respected family. Lady Warton mentioned that Lord Pelham serves His Majesty in some important capacity."

"He is an ambassador." Marcie spoke up. "Stewart told me all about it. He hopes to accompany his father on some of his travels."

Beth nodded. "David told me the same."

"Stewart? And David?" Holly began to frown. "You must not let anyone else hear you call them by their given names."

"But why, Mama?" Beth was clearly confused. "David's mother was our cousin and they came for a visit at Bentworth Hall. David recalls that we played together."

"But you do not?"

Beth shook her head. "No, Mama, and I catch your drift. It is acceptable for him to address me informally, but I must use his title."

Holly nodded. "That is it, precisely. Any informality on your part could be misinterpreted."

"Then I shall call David *Lord Redfield* in the future."

"And I will call Stewart *Mr. Averill.*" Marcie was quick to agree.

"Perhaps that is best." Holly smiled at them both. "Have you given a thought to which gown you will wear to receive them tomorrow?"

This question prompted a discussion of every gown the girls owned and Holly leaned back against the squabs once again. It was precisely as she had intended, for it spared her from any but the most general comment for the remainder of the journey home.

"Good night, girls." Holly gave them both hugs as they headed up the staircase to their chambers. "I was very proud of both of you this evening. You may be assured that you conducted yourselves very well."

"Thank you, Mama." Beth looked pleased. "Shall we ring for chocolate and have a comfy coze in your sitting room?"

Holly sighed, hoping that they would not be too disappointed at her refusal. "Not tonight, my dears. I am so sleepy, I can scarcely hold open my eyes."

"Of course, Mama." Marcie nodded quickly. "We must remember that you are older and require more rest."

"Really, Marcie! You make Mama sound ancient!" Beth turned to glare at her sister.

Marcie frowned as she turned to face Beth. "I did not say that Mama was ancient. I merely said that she was older and required more rest than we do. After all, she has done most of the work around here while we have merely attended our lessons. To my way of thinking, Mama has a perfect right to be tired."

"Thank you, Marcie." Holly tried not to laugh at Marcie's outraged expression. It was clear that her stepdaughters' emotions were running high and that was to be expected after their exciting evening. "I do believe it would serve both of you well to retire quite soon. Do ring for chocolate, if you like, but drink it quickly and then go directly to bed. Morning will be here in just a few hours and you must be at your best for your callers."

"You're right, Mama." Marcie nodded quickly and then she turned to Beth. "I'm sorry, Beth. I should not have snapped at you like that. Let us go to our rooms and leave Mama to her rest."

Beth nodded, favoring Marcie with a forgiving smile. "You are right, Marcie. And I should not have snapped at you. Perhaps we are both every bit as tired as Mama."

Holly gave a sigh of relief as the girls went down the hall, hand in hand. Their little spat had evaporated into thin air, as most of their arguments did.

The moment she had gained the sanctuary of her bedchamber, Holly sank down on the edge of the bed. It was true that she was exhausted, but there was another element to her fatigue, one that made her desire to sleep, rather than think about her problem. But think she must, and Holly stood up to remove her gown and search out more comfortable clothing.

Once she had performed her nightly ablutions and donned her nightrail and a warm wrapper, Holly sat down to put slippers on her feet. She desired a cup of tea to calm her frazzled nerves, but she did not think it fair to wake the staff at this hour. Resigned to doing without, Holly padded into her sitting room on slippered feet.

The sight that greeted her brought a delighted smile to Holly's face. The very tea tray that she had desired reposed upon the piecrust table. Mrs. Merriweather had anticipated her wishes and brought in the teapot before she had retired for the night.

"Bless you, Mrs. Merriweather!" Holly said the words aloud as she removed the cozy and poured herself a cup. Though the tea was no longer steaming, it was still quite warm and Holly sipped gratefully. Then she noticed that there were three cups on the tray and she felt a moment's guilt. Had she done her stepdaughters a disservice by refusing the coze that they had suggested?

Deciding that she had, Holly stepped out into the hall and made her way to Beth's door. She was about to knock when she heard the sounds of conversation within.

"Did you observe Mama conversing with Lord Roxbury?"

Holly recognized Beth's voice and hesitated. Perhaps she should not interrupt their private converse.

"Yes, indeed. I thought him remarkably handsome for someone so old, but Mama did not even seem to notice how dashing he was. And she had the strangest expression on her face."

"I thought the same!" Beth sounded quite puzzled.

"Perhaps she knew him from her First Season?"

"I do not think so." Beth answered quickly. "After all, they had just been introduced. If Mama had known him, there would have been no need for Lady Norwich's introduction."

"You are right. I did not think of that. I received another

impression, but I am not sure it is accurate. Did you think that Mama took him in dislike?"

"Yes, indeed." Beth sounded very definite. "I agree with you completely on that score."

"Oh, dear! You do not think that she will forbid us from seeing Lord Redfield and Mr. Averill, do you, Beth?"

"You are such a pea goose, Marcie!" Beth laughed softly. "Mama would never be that unfair."

Holly gave a soft sigh. She was well and truly trapped by the esteem in which the girls held her. It would be most unfair of her to ask her stepdaughters to avoid the company of Lord Redfield and Mr. Averill simply because she did not care for their uncle.

"Do you think he knows that Mama holds him in dislike?" Marcie posed the question.

"No. I should be willing to wager that he is completely oblivious." Beth giggled slightly. "Mama was perfectly polite, so perfectly polite that we guessed she was making an effort. No one else noticed, I am certain of it. It is only by virtue of knowing Mama's character so well that we were able to discern her true emotions."

Holly's brows lifted in surprise. Her stepdaughters were too perceptive by half! The girls had accurately judged her reaction to *The Elusive Earl,* and it gave her cause to wonder what other of her secrets they had guessed.

"I truly do not understand." Marcie's voice was troubled. "It is not at all like Mama to take a frivolous dislike to anyone."

"Perhaps he reminded her of someone and she will reconsider her opinion once she knows more of him. In any event, we can do nothing to smooth those waters at this late date."

"Perhaps it would help to change her opinion if she were to encounter him again." Marcie's voice quavered slightly. "I really do like Mr. Averill and I had hoped that we all could be friends. You do not think that Mama dislikes Mr. Averill, do you, Beth?"

"No. She appeared to be quite charmed by both Mr. Averill and Lord Redfield. And she did not hesitate to give her permission for them to call. I do believe we are brewing a tempest in a teapot, Marcie. There is no reason to think that Mama will take them in dislike simply because she does not care for their uncle."

"You are quite right." Marcie sounded much relieved. "I am brewing a tempest in a . . . where was that, Beth?"

"A teapot. It is a quotation from Cicero. You really must learn your classics, Marcie. Most gentlemen appear to be suitably impressed if you can quote from them."

"I'll leave that to you, Sister Bluestocking." Marcie giggled, causing Holly to smile. Marcie had been a reluctant student at every subject save the natural sciences. "If I encounter any gentleman who reveres his classics, I shall simply give him over to you."

There was a pause in the conversation during which Holly heard several deep sighs and yawns. Then Marcie spoke again. "I declare, I am in the same boat as Mama. My eyes simply refuse to stay open any longer. Do come and fetch me when you wake, Beth. I still have not decided which gown to wear."

Holly recognized the need for her immediate departure. She turned on her heel and sped quickly down the hall as if demons were chasing her. She had no sooner darted inside her sitting room and closed the door behind her, than she heard the sound of Marcie's footsteps heading down the hall toward her own bedchamber.

Holly leaned against her door, breathing deeply for a moment, and then she returned to the settee to pour herself a fresh cup of tea. The conversation she had inadvertently overheard had served to resolve her dilemma. She would force herself to be perfectly pleasant to *The Elusive Earl*. To do any less would not be fair to Beth and Marcie. She could only hope and pray that the girls would tire of Lord Redfield and Mr. Averill quite quickly and settle upon another pair of young gentlemen who piqued their interest.

Twelve

Paul rubbed his jaw and grinned as he recalled the events of the morning. They had arrived at Gentleman Jackson's famous establishment at the ungodly hour of nine in the morning and both David and Stewart had watched in fascination as he had entered the ring and sparred with the celebrated proprietor. Just as Paul had suspected, the late hours he had kept and his lack of proper exercise had taken its toll on his prowess. After only a few moments in the ring, it became abundantly clear that he was not as agile and alert as he once had been. Vowing to pay more attention to his diet and his exercise, Paul had done his best to block his friend's jabs and land a few of his own.

Noticing that Paul's nephews were closely observing their sparring match, Gentleman Jackson had been kind to Paul, dropping his guard and permitting Paul to land a few well-placed punches. Paul had accepted this charity gratefully as his stamina had been waning at an alarming rate and he had known that if his old friend had wished, he could easily have felled him in short order.

Just as Paul had anticipated, both David and Stewart had been impressed with this demonstration of the manly art of pugilism. When Paul had removed himself from the ring, regrettably winded and doing his utmost to conceal it, his nephews had expressed a desire to learn the skill.

While the boys had waited, watching another sparring match in progress, Paul had spoken to his old friend privately and

Gentleman Jackson had agreed to tutor his nephews in the rudiments of boxing. Once several appointments had been made for them, Paul and the boys had returned to Roxbury House. David and Stewart had rushed immediately to their chambers to ready themselves for the morning calls they had promised to pay on several young misses they had met the previous evening, and Paul had retired to his library to nurse his aching jaw.

The brandy decanter was still sitting out on the table from the previous evening, and Paul eyed it with longing. Though a stiff glass would serve to soothe his aching jaw, he had no intention of overindulging as he had last night. Once the boys had retired, he had consumed several snifters, staring at the dying embers of the fire. He had been puzzled by his reaction to Lady Bentworth and thinking about her now did not serve to erase his concerns.

He had been certain that he would recognize his fickle angel the instant he laid eyes on her again, but perhaps he had been mistaken. Lady Bentworth did resemble her quite strongly, but she had lacked the charming innocence that his angel had exhibited on their one evening together. Of course, that charming innocence could have been a scam. After all, she had failed to meet him at the spot that he had chosen for their rendezvous.

Paul sighed, reaching out for the brandy and then withdrawing his hand before his fingers could close around the decanter. Brandy would not ease the memories that plagued him. He had already attempted to find relief in that manner and it had failed.

Lady Bentworth was an uncommonly attractive female and perhaps that had caused his astonishing reaction. Though he had been on his guard when Lady Norwich had introduced them, and had merely wished to judge for himself whether the *on-dits* about her could be true, Paul had been rendered nearly speechless by her beauty. All the while they had exchanged pleasantries, he had imagined her glorious blond hair spread out on his pillow and her shapely arms reaching up to wrap themselves around his neck. He had lost himself in the sparkling depths of her sapphire eyes and now, when he attempted to recall the subject of their conversation, he was unable to remember a single word.

Had he tumbled into love again? Paul shuddered at the thought. He had been squiring the loveliest ladies the *ton* had offered for the past five Seasons and never had he experienced this intensity of emotion with any of them.

Only once before had he felt like this. Paul clenched his fist and barely managed to restrain himself from smashing it into the surface of the table that sat beside his chair. The unwelcome passions that he harbored for Lady Bentworth were identical to those he had felt when he'd held his fickle angel in his arms. Was that proof that they were one and the same?

Paul shook his head to clear it. No, it was not a valid proof. Philip had spoken to him about his first wife, and his tone of voice, as well as his words, had convinced Paul that he had loved her to distraction. But Philip also loved Willa to distraction. There could be no argument on that score. It was possible for lightning to strike a man twice, and Paul had been thusly struck.

He must fight his affliction. Paul squared his shoulders and took a deep breath. Lady Bentworth was not for him. Though she had appeared quite demure and proper, not at all what he had expected, Paul had no doubt that she was in the market for another wealthy and titled husband. Now that she had learned of his title and his deep pockets, he could be very certain that she would use all of her wiles to attract him.

How could one so lovely be so deceitful? Paul gave a bitter smile as he recalled just a few of the great men who had fallen prey to exquisitely seductive women. Sampson had sacrificed himself so that Delilah might live, and Marc Antony had given up his life in defense of Cleopatra. No doubt Lady Bentworth's beauty could inspire a like devotion in other more susceptible gentlemen, but *The Elusive Earl* would escape her wiles unscathed.

There were the sounds of clattering feet on the stair and Paul gave a grateful sigh. His nephews would pull him out of his brown study. He glanced at the standing clock in the corner and noted that it was still well before noon. His nephews must be eager to pay their calls, as they had washed and dressed in record time.

Though Paul had promised Willa that he would keep the boys under his watchful eye, he did not feel the need to accompany them on their social rounds. He was not so old as to have forgotten his first Season and the calls he had paid to debutantes. As much as a young gentleman might wish otherwise, it was quite impossible to make love to a young miss in the twenty-five minutes that were allotted for a call, especially since it must be done under the sharp eyes of the chaperones and her other callers.

"We are ready, Uncle Paul." David hurried into the library, Stewart following at his heels. "We have arranged to make four calls."

Paul grinned as he nodded. "I assume that I would be derelict in my duties if I did not ask which particular young ladies you plan to favor?"

"We will go to Miss Imogene Dunnsbury. Her home is only a few blocks away." Stewart answered him with a smile. "And then we shall call upon Miss Viola Atkins, who resides very close to her."

Paul raised his brows. "Would Miss Viola Atkins be Lady Roche's granddaughter?"

"Yes, Uncle Paul." David nodded quickly.

Paul hesitated, uncertain of how to continue. He had made the acquaintance of Lady Roche's granddaughter no more than a few days ago, a chance meeting on Bond Street. As he recalled, the girl had been a mousy little thing with a reed thin figure and downcast eyes.

"I know what you are thinking, sir, and you are quite correct," David continued. "Miss Atkins is not a beauty. But we attended Eton with her brother and he begged us to do him the kindness of calling upon her. He says his sister does not show to advantage at social gatherings, but that she is uncommonly nice."

Stewart nodded. "Harold was very anxious about her reception. He knows full well that she is not pretty, but he thought that a call from us might gain her some notice."

"So you two are scheming to launch her properly?" Paul bit back a grin.

"If we can, sir." David nodded quickly. "We began at Lady Pinchton's ball. I danced with her twice and so did Stewart."

Paul's eyes twinkled with amusement. "And what conclusions did you draw?"

"Harold was right." Stewart smiled. "Miss Atkins is really quite sweet. I should like to count her among my friends."

David nodded. "I feel the same. She knew precisely why I had asked her to dance and she thanked me for granting her brother the favor."

"And you denied that it was only a favor to her brother and told her that you had truly wished to dance with her?"

"No, Uncle Paul." David shook his head. "It would have been an insult to her intelligence. Instead, I asked her to dance with me a second time and told her that the first had been for her brother, but that the second dance was for me, alone."

Paul's smile widened and he clapped his nephew on the back. "Excellent! I am certain your attentions added to her measure and also to her confidence. Now, as I recall, Miss Atkins is but the second call you mentioned. Which lucky young lady receives the third?"

"Our third call will be upon two young ladies." Stewart answered the question. "Miss Glenda and Miss Brenda Tomley. They are Lord and Lady Gilford's twin daughters."

Paul smiled as he nodded. "And your fourth call?"

"Miss Elizabeth and Miss Marcella." David spoke up. "Once we pay our respects to them, we shall return here."

Paul managed to keep his expression pleasant, though he felt more like frowning. "Lady Bentworth's stepdaughters?"

"Yes, sir," David nodded. "No doubt there will be quite a crush in Lady Bentworth's drawing room, as I heard several other gentlemen say that they intended to call."

Paul's urge to frown disappeared. A crowded drawing room would be much to his liking. If there were many guests, his nephews would not have the opportunity to exchange more than a word or two with Lady Bentworth's stepdaughters. "You had best be on your way then. I ordered the red curricle brought round for your use."

"Your red curricle?" Stewart began to grin. "Thank you, Uncle Paul!"

Paul nodded. There was a method in his madness, one his nephews would never fathom. The sporty curricle contained room for only two and it would make it quite impossible for them to offer a ride to any young lady they fancied.

"I will trust you to handle the reins, David." Paul turned to his older nephew, for Philip had told him that the boy was an excellent whipster. "Mind the traffic on the street and err on the side of caution. My pair is quite spirited."

David nodded quickly, his eyes gleaming with excitement. "I will, Uncle Paul. You may count upon it."

As the boys made their bows and hurried out to the waiting equipage, Paul gave way to the new worry that had occurred to him the moment that he'd heard his nephews planned to call upon Lady Bentworth's stepdaughters. Perhaps Miss Elizabeth and Miss Marcella were proper young misses. The little he had seen of them appeared to bear out this fact. But they had been in their stepmother's sole care for almost two years, and she could not have set a good example for them. According to the gossip that Lady Norwich had repeated to him, Lady Bentworth had married Lord Bentworth for his money and his title. If she had managed to infuse her stepdaughters with her own dubious values, it was not unreasonable for him to be anxious when his nephews were in their company.

Holly gave a sigh of relief as she examined the cards on the silver salver. There were only two cards, not three, and they were properly bent down at the corners to signify that Lord

Redfield and Mr. Averill had come in person to call upon her stepdaughters.

"Please bring them in, Mr. Hobson." Holly favored him with a conspiratorial smile. "And could you ask James if he will garner two more chairs from my sitting room? We appear to have more callers than we anticipated."

Hobson nodded and returned her smile with one of his own. "Certainly, madam."

As she waited for Lord Redfield and Mr. Averill to put in their appearance, Holly gazed around the crowded drawing room. Beth was holding court on the settee, surrounded by three fellow debutantes and four of the young gentlemen she had met at Lady Pinchton's ball. She was wearing a lovely deep blue gown with flounces of white lace at the hem. The same frothy white lace had been used to set off the low round neckline and fill it in a bit for modesty's sake. Dorri had dressed Beth's light brown hair quite modishly with clusters of curls pulled back with a blue satin ribbon that matched her gown.

As Holly watched, Beth became engaged in what appeared to be a serious conversation with one of the young gentlemen. She heard him speak the name "Homer," and then, *"The Iliad,"* and Holly bit back a chuckle of amusement. It was clear that this young gentleman wished to impress Beth with his erudite knowledge, and he harbored no intimation that he was conversing with a young miss who had studied both *The Iliad* and *The Odyssey* in the original Greek.

Marcie, on the other hand, was holding a court of her own. She was seated in the center of a group of chairs, with several young gentlemen dancing in attendance. As was true of Beth, Marcie was surrounded by three other debutantes. One appeared to be quite a flirt, waving her fan and batting her eyes at a fair-haired young gentleman who wore a look of stoic resignation. The second was a charming young miss with a ready smile and a delightfully contagious laugh. The third debutante was Lady Warton's niece, a shy and retiring young miss that Marcie had decided to befriend, confiding to Holly that Miss Fanny

Warton was a wit of the first water when she became relaxed enough to open her mouth.

In contrast to her sister, Marcie had chosen a gown fashioned from a lively shade of pink muslin. The cut was deceptively simple, but it served to set off Marcie's petite figure to advantage. A wide white collar with deep notches in the sides drew the eye to the deepest point of the plunging neckline, which was cleverly obscured from view by an inset of pink lace that was gathered to resemble a flower in full bloom.

As Holly watched, Miss Warton tapped Marcie's wrist lightly in an attempt to gain her attention. Marcie turned to her, smiling, and bent to listen to her comment. Then she gave a tinkling laugh and nodded, causing shy Miss Warton to take on a lovely color. Then Marcie turned to repeat the comment to another young gentleman who was leaning against the mantelpiece. He laughed appreciatively and crossed the space between them to take a chair adjoining Miss Warton's.

Several of the debutantes had brought their mothers, and a group of older ladies and chaperones had gathered on the chairs around Holly, leaving their charges to their own pursuits but within a watchful distance. Holly smiled and nodded as one of the ladies made a comment about the weather, but her mind was on other matters. She could not help but wonder what would occur when Lord Redfield and Mr. Averill made their entrance. Lady Warton had told her that they were prize catches, and for that reason alone, they should cause quite a stir.

It was at this point that Hobson brought Lord Redfield and Mr. Averill to the drawing room. Both young gentlemen proceeded to her immediately, to greet her politely as their hostess and to make their pretties. As they turned from her to exchange a few polite words with the chaperones and mothers, Holly noticed that the buzz of conversation in the drawing room was diminishing in volume, leaving in its wake a hush of anticipation.

Holly had all she could do not to laugh as, one by one, the younger occupants of the chamber turned to gaze at the newcomers. She saw several of the mothers exchange speaking glances with their daughters, causing their offspring to straighten in their chairs and pinch their cheeks to add a bit of color.

The level of conversation rose once again as Lord Redfield and Mr. Averill began to walk across the room toward the younger contingency.

Several debutantes, who had formerly been conversing in a rather desultory fashion, now became newly animated. Their laughter trilled out, their fans unfurled, and they quickly rearranged their positions to present the most attractive poses. Miss Cecilia Appleby, the flirt that Holly had noticed earlier, appeared to be judging the speed of their approach out of the corner of her eye. As Lord Redfield moved to brush past her, she rose to her feet quite suddenly and came within inches of colliding with him. This caused Lord Redfield to reach out and steady her while she gazed up at him under her lashes.

Holly watched her stepdaughters, hoping that they would not behave in so foolish a manner, and they did not disappoint her. Marcie smiled a greeting to Mr. Averill, but she made to finish her conversation with Miss Warton and her new companion before turning to him.

Mr. Averill seemed a bit confused when Marcie did not favor him with her immediate attention. He stood, quietly listening for a moment, and then an expression of admiration crossed his face. Holly raised her brows at this unusual reaction. Was it possible that Mr. Averill admired Marcie for not excusing herself from her other companions the moment he arrived at her side?

Holly glanced at Beth and realized that her elder stepdaughter was favoring Lord Redfield with the very same treatment. Beth smiled, gave a slight dip of her head to acknowledge Lord Redfield's presence, and then continued her response to the young gentleman who fancied himself a scholar.

Holly bit back an amused smile as she watched an expression of consternation flood across Lord Redfield's face. She had no doubt that both boys had been roundly toad-eaten during their previous calls upon other young ladies and were surprised by the natural, unaffected manner in which her stepdaughters had greeted them.

"I do declare, Lady Bentworth." The extremely plump lady on Holly's right succeeded in gaining her attention. "These are the most excellent chocolate tartlets that I have ever had the pleasure to taste."

Holly smiled, noticing that the plate was nearly empty. "Thank you, Lady Price. If you wish, I shall have Cook write out the receipt for you."

"Indeed, I would be most grateful." Lady Price nodded. And then she went on to describe to Holly, in detail, the contents of the tea trays in the various drawing rooms that she had visited since the beginning of the Season.

After Holly had motioned for Hobson and indicated that the plate of chocolate tartlets should be replenished, she gave full attention to Lady Price's conversation. She was proud of her stepdaughters' conduct on this day and she would be certain to tell them so the moment their guests had departed.

Thirteen

David grinned as he waited for Beth to finish her conversation with the lanky young gentleman who was spouting classical quotations for her edification. The fellow was regrettably inaccurate, but that was not the reason for his grin. No other young miss had ever placed him in this position before and he found he admired Beth immensely for concluding her discussion with the dubious scholar. Most of the young ladies he'd met this morning would simply have cut off their dialogue and turned their full attention toward him.

This was the fourth drawing room that David and Stewart had visited that day. When they had entered the others, all conversation had ceased for a breathless moment and then had begun again, reanimated. Lady Bentworth's drawing room had been no exception. The same hush had fallen, and the young ladies in the group surrounding Beth had turned to gaze up at him hopefully, putting on their most attractive smiles and leaning forward to gain his attention. Beth was the only exception. She did not seem to be unduly impressed by the honor of his presence.

Rather than taking umbrage at her lack of obsequiousness, David found it most refreshing. He had noticed this aspect of her character on the previous evening, and it was the reason he had asked permission to call upon her.

Beth was an unusual young lady. She had not batted her eyes at him during the dance they had shared on the previous eve-

ning. She had not looked up at him through her lashes, or attempted to press herself more closely against him than propriety
allowed. She had failed to compliment him extravagantly on
skills that he did not possess, and she certainly had not invited
him to escort her on a walk through the moonlit gardens without
benefit of chaperone. Beth had appeared to favor him well
enough, but David had watched her dance with several other
young gentlemen and she did not seem to treat them any dif-
ferently than she had treated him. Perhaps the Season sported
prettier, livelier, and more charming debutantes, but David
found himself intrigued by the one young miss who seemed to
have not the slightest inclination to fall at his feet.

David had grown quite accustomed to the ingratiatory behavior of other young ladies and had grown to resent it. It seemed
absurd that they should revere him merely because he was about
to inherit a title. David had decided that he should prefer to be
judged by his worth and not his wealth, but thus far, he had not
found anyone except Stewart to agree with him.

David had discussed this problem with his brother at length
while they were at Cambridge. Though it was an honor to always
be the first chosen when sides were made up for games, it
caused David great discomfort when there were others in his
form who were far better at sports. Stewart had confided that
he had experienced the same deference, receiving praise that
was not truly due him from those whom he outranked.

Together, the two brothers had attempted to convince their
classmates to treat them only with the respect that they had
earned, but their attempt had failed. The English aristocracy and
the timeworn order of precedence had been in place for far too
long to be overturned by two young boys who held different
ideals.

"I am very pleased to see you, Lord Redfield." Beth's mu-
sical voice brought David back to the present. "I do apologize
for not greeting you sooner, but it would not have been kind of
me to interrupt Mr. Baxton in mid-thought."

David grinned and stepped a bit closer, so they should not

be overheard. "I agree completely. It would have been most unkind. On the other hand, you should have been spared his comment that Homer was a Roman."

"There is that." Beth giggled. "Perhaps he has confused Homer with Cicero, though I do not see how such a misconception is possible. Their works have so little in common."

"Including the language in which they were written." David grinned at her. It was highly unusual to come across a young lady who mentioned Homer and Cicero in the same breath.

Beth sighed. "Before you think me a bluestocking, I must admit that it took me nearly a year to struggle through *The Iliad*."

"You've read *The Iliad?*" David was impressed when Beth nodded. Though he had enjoyed his study of the classics, he had never met another young lady who claimed that she had read them.

"I much preferred *The Odyssey*." Beth regarded him with sparkling eyes. "I began on it immediately after finishing *The Iliad*. Of course, it is always possible that I enjoyed it more, simply because I had become a bit more adept at the language."

David's eyes widened, not quite believing his ears. "You studied Homer in the original Greek?"

"Yes, I fear I did." Beth gave a delightful laugh. "I really could not tell you why, but I suspect that I merely wished to prove that I could best the squire's oldest son."

"You did not like him?"

"Not by half!" Beth frowned slightly. "He became most insufferable when he learned that his father had made plans for him to attend Oxford, and he twitted me constantly about it. When I ventured to say that I should also like to pursue a higher level of education, he ridiculed me most shamelessly. He even had the audacity to tell me that there was no need to educate females, for all I would be required to know is how to dance, accompany myself upon the pianoforte, and draw pretty sketches of flowers!"

"I begin to understand why you did not favor him." David grinned, finding Beth intriguing.

"That is not all. He also complained to the rector that I had no business being tutored with him, for I would only slow his progress. It was then that I vowed to best him in every subject."

David nodded, liking her spirit. "It appears that you received a fine education. Are you still overset that you could not go to Oxford?"

"Oh, no. Not in the slightest!" She favored him with another of her delightful smiles. "I changed my opinion once the squire's son returned home after his first year and told me of his studies. I decided that Cambridge must be the better school, by far."

"I went to Cambridge." David grinned at her, part of him hoping that she had not known.

"You did?" Beth gave him a radiant smile, but then she sighed. "Mama is always cautioning me about things like this. I should not have told you my preference."

"Why?"

"Because you could just as likely have attended Oxford, and then I would be caught in a muddle, attempting to extricate myself."

"You did not know which school I attended?" David stared at her intently.

"Of course not. How could I possibly have known? I only know of you what my fellow debutantes told me, and they did not mention your school."

David grinned. He was almost certain what her fellow debutantes had told her, but he could not resist asking. "What did they tell you of me?"

Beth hesitated, a blush rising to her cheeks. "I really ought not to tell you."

"But I want you to tell me." David smiled at her. "I give you my word that I will not repeat anything you say. Surely it cannot be as appalling as all that!"

Beth shook her head. "Oh, no! Everything I have heard has

been quite complimentary. But I really must tell you that you are considered the catch of the Season."

"Why must you tell me that?" David's eyes began to twinkle as he noticed Beth's high color.

Beth leaned a bit closer, lowering her voice to little above a whisper. "So that you will be forewarned, of course."

"What exactly is it that makes me such a prime catch?" David could not resist teasing her a bit. Her complexion was rosy and the color in her cheeks accentuated her lovely green eyes.

Beth sighed. "I do hope I'm not speaking out of turn, but it all appears to hinge upon your circumstances, Lord Redfield. They say you will inherit your father's lesser title in less than six months' time, and that you will become quite wealthy. That, apparently, makes you a most worthy prize for the young lady who can succeed in bringing you up to scratch."

"Do you find these facts about me attractive?" David raised his brows, wondering whether or not he should believe her answer.

Beth laughed. "Certainly they are attractive. How could they not be? All things being equal, I doubt there is a young lady in all of England who would prefer to wed a poor gentleman over a wealthy one. But any lady who agreed to wed a gentleman simply because he was titled and wealthy would be a fool of the first water."

"And you are not a fool?"

"I should hope I am not!" Beth laughed. "But perhaps I am, for allowing myself to speak of it. Would you mind terribly turning over our conversation to another subject, Lord Redfield?"

As their discussion continued along a different line, David smiled to himself. He had not encountered any other young ladies who possessed Beth's candor and he found himself fascinated by her. Before he took his leave of her stepmother, he intended to ask permission to invite her for a ride through the park. He had no doubt that Beth would like taking part in the

Promenade and it would provide him with the opportunity to continue their intriguing conversation.

Holly made a valiant attempt not to show her concern over Lord Redfield's request. She had hoped that both David and Stewart would call once or twice and then lose any but a friendly interest in her stepdaughters. She had known full well that her hope was self-serving, for if the boys paid their attentions elsewhere, she should be spared the necessity of any further converse with their uncle. Now it seemed that her wish was not to be. Lord Redfield had asked for her permission to collect Beth the following afternoon and join the Promenade in Hyde Park.

"I am certain that Beth should be delighted, Lord Redfield, but I fear I must decline for her." Holly sighed deeply, knowing how bitterly disappointed Beth would be. "Since she is so newly arrived in London, I feel it would be remiss of me to allow her to accompany you without a proper chaperone."

Lord Redfield appeared quite astonished at her answer and Holly had all she could do not to smile. No doubt any other debutante's mama should have accepted his suggested outing with delight. He thought for a moment, furrowing his brow, and then he favored her with a most charming smile. "Indeed, Lady Bentworth, you must think me a sap-skull for failing to consider that. Would it serve the purpose if I asked my brother and Miss Marcella to accompany us?"

"Why, yes." Holly nodded reluctantly. "I daresay it would. I will leave it to you to make the arrangements with my stepdaughters."

As Lord Redfield returned to speak with Beth and then Marcie, Holly frowned slightly. He had been perfectly well behaved, asking her leave before mentioning the invitation to Beth, and treating her with the utmost deference. Holly found herself impressed with his manner and the polite words he had used to phrase his request, but caution was still in order. While it was true that Beth would be properly chaperoned by her sister and

Lord Redfield's brother, Holly would not leave it to chance. She firmly intended to devise a way to observe her stepdaughters as they progressed through the park and make certain that Lord Redfield and Mr. Averill had not been influenced by their uncle's rakish ways.

Paul sat in his library, listening intently to Farley's report. He had instructed his butler to gather information on what had transpired during his nephew's calls, knowing full well that the servants' gossip should provide him with a full account. Thus far, it was precisely as Paul had expected. His nephews had stayed the proper twenty-five minutes on each of their first three calls. On the fourth, however, they had lingered much longer.

"Upwards of an hour, you say?" Paul frowned slightly as his butler nodded. "Was there any explanation, Farley?"

"Yes, m'lord. There was quite a crush and it seems that they had to wait to speak to the young misses."

Paul raised his brows. "I see. And now they are in their chambers, preparing for the evening's entertainment?"

"No, m'lord. The last I heard, they were in the stables, deciding which of your carriages would serve them best."

"Which of *my* carriages?" Paul was a bit shocked. "I gave them the loan of the red curricle."

"I know that, m'lord. And very generous of you it was. But it seems they have need of a carriage that will accommodate two young ladies on a ride through the park."

Paul frowned, fearing the worst. "I see. And do you know which *particular* two young ladies they plan to escort?"

"Yes, m'lord." Farley nodded. "Lady Bentworth's stepdaughters."

Paul sighed deeply. He might have known. It was obvious that the devious and lovely Lady Bentworth had coached her stepdaughters well. He had hoped that his nephews might escape, but it was clear that they had fallen under the young ladies' spell.

When his employer did not respond, Farley continued. "I assume they will come to ask you for the loan of the carriage directly, m'lord, as this excursion is scheduled to take place tomorrow afternoon."

"I see." Paul nodded. "In that event, please have my green phaeton brought round tomorrow afternoon, immediately after the carriage of their choice departs."

Farley's lips twitched slightly at the corners. "Yes, m'lord. You plan to follow them?"

"Of course I do, Farley." Paul gave a decisive nod. "My nephews may not be aware of it, but I shall be there to make certain that they are not taken in by any young debutantes, and *especially* by Lady Bentworth's stepdaughters."

Farley's lips twitched again and then he drew a deep breath. "May I make a suggestion, m'lord?"

"Of course, Farley." Paul nodded quickly. "You have been with me too long to stand on ceremony. What is it?"

"You know their destination, m'lord. Perhaps it would not be so apparent that you intended to follow if you departed *before* them?"

"Excellent suggestion, Farley!" Paul smiled at the man. "Do you have any others?"

Farley nodded. "Only one, m'lord. I would also think that it might throw a cloak over your true purpose if you invited a young lady to accompany you."

"Yes, indeed." Paul favored his butler with another smile. "I shall see to it straightaway. Send Parker to me. I shall write an invitation to Lady Clarington and dispatch it with him."

Farley shook his head slightly. "Lady *Clarington,* m'lord?"

"Yes, Farley. I need someone who will agree to accompany me on short notice and I am certain that she will . . ." Paul stopped speaking as he noticed his butler's frown. He thought for a moment and then he sighed. "You are quite correct, Farley. Lady Clarington will not do at all. She will simply construe my invitation as a sign that I welcome her further pursuits. Do you think that Miss Winston would better serve my purpose?"

Farley nodded his approval. "Yes, m'lord. Miss Winston shall do famously. And since you have not favored her with your attentions in the past, she should not be unduly encouraged."

"Thank you, Farley. You have been a great help to me." Paul clapped the man on the back. "You may be certain that I shall keep you apprised of any further developments, as you appear to be far better at these devious matters than even *The Elusive Earl* is rumored to be!"

Fourteen

Holly had just taken the first sip from her morning cup of chocolate when Hobson appeared in the doorway of the breakfast room. There was a disapproving frown on his face and Holly knew immediately that something was amiss. "What is it, Mr. Hobson?"

"There is a gentleman to see you, Lady Bentworth. He has no card, but he gave his name as Colonel Faraday."

Holly's eyes began to sparkle with excitement and a delighted smile spread across her face. "How marvelous! I have been wishing to meet Colonel Faraday for ever so long! Bring him to me immediately, Mr. Hobson. And have another place set. I shall invite him to join me, of course."

"If Madam is certain . . . ?"

Hobson bowed stiffly, his frown still in place. For a moment Holly was quite at a loss to know why he appeared so disapproving, but then she realized that he had no notion what relationship Colonel Faraday had to her family. And she, herself, had added to Hobson's distress by saying that she had not made the colonel's acquaintance before!

"I think I had better explain." Holly suppressed the urge to giggle in the face of Hobson's frowning demeanor. It was apparent her staid butler believed that his mistress was behaving in a most improper manner. "Colonel Faraday was a dear friend of my late husband's, and he is my stepdaughter's godfather.

Though I have never met him personally, my husband confided that they were even closer than brothers."

Hobson looked greatly relieved as he nodded. "Very good, madam. I shall bring him to you straightway."

"After you do, find Dorri and send her up to wake the girls so that they may join us. Colonel Faraday has been traveling in foreign lands and I do not believe he has laid eyes on them for at least ten years."

After Hobson had gone off to do her bidding, Holly reached up to smooth her hair. If she had known that Colonel Faraday was to pay them a visit, she should have dressed in one of her new gowns. The one she wore was quite old, a remnant from her First Season that had been altered to fit her mature figure. The pretty blue muslin, printed with a design of red roses, could no longer claim to be in the first stare of fashion, but at least it was cheerful and attractive.

The sound of approaching footsteps warned Holly that she was about to meet her husband's dearest friend. She put a welcoming smile on her face and rose from her chair in preparation.

"My dear Holly! How very good of you to receive me without prior notice!"

"I am so very pleased to meet you at last, Colonel Faraday." Holly's eyes widened as she welcomed the gentleman her husband had touted as the very best crony a gentleman could have. He was really quite handsome, a fine figure of a man with a full head of silvery hair and a moustache to match. He was a bit shorter than she had imagined, perhaps because William's description of his virtues had caused her to think he would tower over lesser men, but he cut a fine figure in his well-tailored clothing.

The colonel beamed as he took the chair she indicated. "I do declare that I would have known you anywhere from William's description. It was quite accurate except that he did not mention your exceptional beauty."

"Thank you, Colonel Faraday." Holly felt the color rise to her cheeks at his compliment.

"Sunny." Colonel Faraday corrected her with a smile. "It is the name my goddaughters gave me."

Holly raised her brows. "But why did they call you that?"

"Colonel Faraday was more of a mouthful than they could pronounce at a young age and they began to call me Uncle Sunny. At first we were equally puzzled, but then William realized that they had misinterpreted my family name."

"Faraday?" Holly smiled as the obvious explanation occurred to her. "Of course! A fair day is a sunny day, and so you became known as their Uncle Sunny."

The colonel nodded and returned her smile. "We all thought it was quite charming of them. I wonder if they will still call me that, now that they are almost grown."

"We shall soon see, for I have sent someone to wake them and tell them that you are here. Will you be remaining in London for the Season, Sunny?"

"No, my dear. I have simply come to conclude a bit of business, and to see how you fare, now that William is gone. He provided for you well then?"

"Yes, indeed he did." Holly nodded quickly. "And he left an amount in trust for his daughters' Seasons. We did not know this until quite recently. It was a most pleasant surprise."

Colonel Faraday nodded. "He wrote to me that he intended to do so. And he also wrote that marrying you had turned out to be a true blessing for him and for the girls. He claimed that you were the very best wife that he could possibly have chosen and the best stepmother for Beth and Marcie. William did not give praise lightly, and I knew that you would be a remarkable lady."

"I loved William very much." Holly blinked back a tear. "And I do love the girls. In the five years that we have been together, they have become much more than stepdaughters to me. In truth, we are as close as a mother and daughters could be."

"William also mentioned that you would be alone in the world, once his daughters married. He desired that you marry again, but he claimed that you might be so stubborn as to refuse that option."

Holly could not help the smile that hovered at the corners of her lips. "William knew me very well, indeed. Though I am following his wishes to take part in this current Season, I truly do not wish to remarry."

"Then what *do* you wish to do, once Beth and Marcie have left the excellent home that you have provided for them?"

Holly frowned slightly, hoping that confiding her wishes to the colonel would not shock him. "I intend to start a genteel business, using my knowledge of the healing arts. I wish to teach my knowledge to others, and once they are practiced, secure placement for them with those who have need of their services."

"An excellent notion!" Colonel Faraday nodded. "I have no doubt that William would have approved."

Holly drew a breath of relief. She was glad that her husband's dearest friend approved of her plans. "How long do you stay in London, Sunny?"

"I must leave in two days' time. I shall be sure to give you my direction before I go, so that you can call upon me if you have need."

Holly nodded. "Thank you, Sunny. It is good to have a friend. Perhaps you can give me the benefit of your advice while you are here. I find I am quite at a loss, at times, in deciding precisely how to supervise my delightful stepdaughters."

"I am no expert, but I shall do my best." Colonel Faraday leaned forward. "What is it you wish to know, my dear?"

It took several minutes, but Holly managed to tell her late husband's friend all about Beth and Marcie and their apparent preference for Lord Redfield and Mr. Averill. When she had finished, she sighed deeply. "I do trust them to behave properly, but this is their First Season and they have never encountered such sophisticated young gentlemen before."

"You are wise to be concerned." The colonel nodded quickly.

"Especially since the two young gentlemen they appear to prefer above all others are the nephews of *The Elusive Earl.*"

"Then you have heard mention of him?"

"Indeed, I have." Colonel Faraday nodded again. "I have excellent connections in Town, my dear, and I shall take it upon myself to investigate the backgrounds of these two young pups. The girls are young and could be quite easily impressed by the trappings of Town Bronze."

Holly breathed another sigh of relief. Just having the colonel's advice for a day or two had relieved some of her anxiety.

"Even if the young gentlemen are not of an unsavory bent, they are still in the initial high-spirited stages of manhood. And they are bound to be influenced by their uncle's reputation, as they are currently residing with him. You say that you gave your permission for them to join the Promenade through the park this afternoon?"

"Yes." Holly dipped her head. "Perhaps I should not have done so, but—"

The colonel interrupted her by holding up his hand. "No, my dear. To refuse the young gentlemen should have been over-playing your hand. If Beth and Marcie believe that you trust them, they will do their utmost to earn that trust and not become a cause of disappointment to you."

"That was my thinking on the matter." Holly nodded quickly. "Still, I would prefer to keep them under a watchful eye."

Colonel Farady grinned. "Then we shall. My sister's equipage is at my disposal while I am in London. I will come to collect you and we shall take a turn through the park, this very afternoon."

"Oh, thank you, Sunny!" Holly drew a deep sigh of relief. "That will serve the purpose very well, indeed."

"And I will regale you with all the latest tarradiddle about the luminaries that we will meet. My sister has been bending my ear for the past several hours about all that has happened since I've been away."

"Perhaps she would like to join us?" Holly made the suggestion quickly.

"No, my dear. I love my sister dearly, but I must tell you that she is the source of most of the *on-dits* she told to me. What if we were to observe one of our young charges tottering on the edge of propriety? We should not be able to speak of it candidly in her presence for fear it would spark her tongue. And even if that should not happen, there is another factor to consider. I should not like our every word memorized by my sister for its further repetition."

Holly nodded. "You are quite right, of course. It is best that we limit this excursion to the two of us."

It was at that moment that Beth and Marcie rushed in and greeted their Uncle Sunny with affectionate hugs. The colonel appeared inordinately pleased that they still called him by their childhood name, and Holly sat back to enjoy the flow of conversation and the excellent breakfast that was served to them.

Paul had to admit that Miss Winston looked delectable in a frilly green gown with a parasol to match and a delightfully silly confection of straw, green ribbons, trailing leaves, and a most realistic rendition of a canary perched atop her shining black tresses.

"La, Lord Roxbury! It is so delightful to see you once again!" Miss Winston lifted her skirts enough to provide a glimpse of one well-turned ankle as she was assisted into his phaeton. "And such a lovely equipage! I do declare, sir! I shall be the envy of every young lady in London!"

Paul grinned as he attained his own seat and took the ribbons from his waiting tiger. It seemed that Miss Winston had fluff for brains, but perhaps she was merely a bit nervous in his presence. "Shall we proceed, my dear?"

"Indeed, let us hasten on our journey!" Miss Winston's voice was breathless. "The Promenade should be delightful, as it is such a fine day! Such lovely weather for this time of year, do you not think?"

"Yes, very fine." As Paul sprang his horses, he wondered how it would be possible to endure a ride through the park with such an animated young lady. Hoping to temper her bubbling enthusiasm, he decided to engage her in more thoughtful converse. "Do you ever wonder, Miss Winston, why we feel compelled to dress in our finest and take a turn through the park every afternoon at this time?"

Miss Winston gave him a curious glance and then her laughter trilled out. "La, no, sir! It is quite clear why we do so!"

"And what reason would that be?"

"Why, to see and be seen, of course! My dear mama says that is the purpose of life, and I do believe I agree with her completely!"

Paul decided that she had fluff for brains, just as he'd thought, but he could not resist asking another question. "But why do we choose Hyde Park? And why precisely at three in the afternoon?"

"Because that is when everyone else is there!" Miss Winston's laughter trilled once again. "If we went to another place, or arrived at a different hour, there should be no one there to see us!"

"You have answered my questions completely." Paul bit back a chuckle of laughter. He really should not have teased her. It was clear that Miss Winston had been raised to be an emptyheaded young miss who parroted everything she had been told.

"I have heard that Prinny has come to Town!" Miss Winston smiled as if she were divulging a delicious secret. "Do you suspect that he might favor us with his presence at the Promenade?"

"I do hope most sincerely that he will not!"

"But why ever not?" Miss Winston appeared quite astonished by his answer.

"The Promenade is such a crush as it is, without adding

Prinny to the mix. I daresay that if he is rumored to appear, we shall be stuck in line for hours."

"Oh." As Paul watched, two glistening tears appeared in the corner of Miss Winston's eyes. "And you should not care to be stuck for so long in my company?"

Paul winced. Miss Winston was not as hen-witted as he had at first assumed, for she had immediately caught his meaning. "No, my dear. I am certain the interlude should pass most delightfully with you at my side. My only concern was for my pair. They have a regrettable tendency to become restless when they are not in motion."

"Of course! I have heard Papa complain of the very same thing!" Miss Winston favored him with a happy smile. "Then I, also, shall hope that Prinny will not be there."

Several moments of blessed silence ensued while Paul maneuvered around a cart with a broken axle and a slow-moving landau. All the while he could feel Miss Winston's eyes upon him. Finally, she spoke again.

"I am given to understand that the question of Catholic emancipation is to be discussed once again in Parliament. Do you have an opinion on the issue, Lord Roxbury? I should be eager to hear it."

Paul sighed, not inclined to enter a discussion on this sensitive subject with a young miss who could not possibly be interested, one way or the other. "Since I have not yet had the opportunity to listen to debates on the subject, I am not certain whether I favor the opinion of William Pitt and his followers, or that of Sir Robert Peel. I do know that it is much too weighty an issue to be taken lightly."

"How insightful of you, Lord Roxbury!" Miss Winston nodded, smiling at him. When no further response from him was forthcoming, she looked slightly taken aback for a moment and then quickly regained her composure. "I have heard that the exhibition of watercolors is excellent. Are you also of this opinion, Lord Roxbury?"

Paul sighed. No doubt she had been told to discuss politics

and then to move on to the arts. "I have not had the pleasure of attending, as yet. I must reserve my opinion until that time."

Miss Winston nodded quickly, causing Paul to wonder which subject she would attempt to broach next. No doubt it would be the Season and its entertainments.

"I thought the decorations at Lady Pinchton's ball were delightfully lavish." Miss Winston favored him with yet another smile. "You were in attendance, were you not?"

Paul nodded. It was time to put his poor companion out of her misery by giving her a subject to discuss. "Indeed, I was. And I believe your judgment quite accurate on that score. Would you permit me to ask you a personal question, Miss Winston? If I overstep my bounds, you need not give me an answer."

"Of course, Lord Roxbury." Miss Winston appeared a bit apprehensive, but she nodded.

"It is your bonnet. I find it particularly fetching. Would you mind telling me how you came to select that particular one?"

"Why certainly, Lord Roxbury!" Miss Winston's smile reached a shade of brilliance that quite superseded her previous attempts. "But are you certain that you are truly interested in such things?"

Paul could not help but smile back at her, as she appeared so pathetically eager. "I assure you that I am most fascinated. My sister's birthday will occur quite soon, and I should like to purchase the perfect gift for her. I thought perhaps a new bonnet might be the thing, but it must be exquisite, as yours is."

"Oh, I shall be delighted to assist you with that!" Miss Winston's eyes began to sparkle. "First we must decide upon the color. Then we shall move on to the style, and from there, we must make a decision on which particular milliner would serve you the best."

Paul was spared the necessity of a reply as Miss Winston went on to explain the types of bonnets that were available and the reputations enjoyed by several London milliners. Her chatter was pleasant and he listened with half an ear as he guided his team into the park and took his place behind the other equipages. In truth, he did not roust himself from his meditations until he spotted another equipage, several places ahead of him in line. It was an old-fashioned landau and it had two occupants, a silver-haired gentleman and a much younger lady. It was not until the lady turned to glance behind her that he gave an involuntary gasp of surprise.

"What is it, Lord Roxbury?" Miss Winston turned to him in alarm.

"Nothing, my dear." Paul reached out to pat her hand. "Please continue. I find your comments most enlightening."

Under his encouragement, Miss Winston resumed her prattle, extolling the virtues of cut straw over other materials. As soon as it was possible to do so without appearing rude, Paul turned his eyes to the landau once more and confirmed his earlier suspicions. The female who had given him such a start was indeed Lady Bentworth, and every one of his suspicions about her were realized. As Paul watched, she smiled most radiantly at her companion, an expensively dressed gentleman who was old enough to be her grandfather!

Fifteen

Beth exchanged smiles with Marcie as Lord Redfield's driver reined in the horses and wheeled them into place behind the line of other equipages. They were seated quite properly in the open carriage, the girls facing forward and Lord Redfield and Mr. Averill occupying the opposite bench.

Beth knew she looked her best in the gown Marcie had urged her to wear, a delightfully ruffled, dark peach muslin that was printed with a motif of tiny white daisies. Her bonnet matched the color of her gown and was trimmed with larger white daisies.

"Why do the ladies always face forward?" Marcie raised her brows as she asked the question.

Mr. Averill shrugged and turned to his older brother. "I've never given a thought to that before. Do you know?"

"Not for certain." Lord Redfield shook his head. "But I do know that it is customary and that it has been done in this fashion for years."

"I have always suspected that it is because ladies are believed to be more delicate than gentlemen and most think it more comfortable to ride facing forward than back," Beth offered.

"No doubt you are right." Mr. Averill nodded. "Perhaps if ladies are seated facing forward, they are less apt to develop carriage sickness."

Marcie giggled. "Then I have no doubt that the grooms had

their say in developing the custom. Just think of the disagreeable task they should be required—"

"Marcie!" Beth interrupted her quickly. "Let us speak of something more pleasant."

Marcie sighed. "Yes, of course. I should not have been so descriptive. But Beth and I were discussing the very same question a week or so ago, and I gave the matter a great deal of thought. I have come up with another theory on why the custom may have developed."

"Tell us, please." Mr. Averill leaned forward to smile at Marcie.

"Perhaps it is a basic difference in the sexes. Gentlemen do not mind facing the rear because they take pleasure in seeing where they have been. Ladies prefer seeing where they are to go."

"Oh, Marcie!" Beth could not help the giggle that escaped her throat. "Do you really believe that gentlemen prefer to recall past accomplishments while ladies prefer to contemplate the future?"

Marcie shrugged. "Perhaps."

"Miss Marcella has a point." Lord Redfield grinned at Beth. "If you had your choice, Miss Elizabeth, would you not prefer contemplating the future?"

Beth spoke without thinking. "Not my particular future, Lord Redfield!"

"And why is that?" Lord Redfield stared at her intently.

Beth winced. She had not meant to utter such a telling remark. Now she was at a loss, attempting to think of a way to explain it. While she remained silent, not certain precisely what to say, Marcie provided the answer.

"Because Beth's future holds even more boring calls from Mr. Baxton. And that prospect does not please my dear sister by half!"

"Marcie! That is not kind of you at all." Beth gave her sister a warning glance.

"You are quite right, as always," Marcie continued, un-

daunted. "But what I said was perfectly true. Perhaps I am sadly
lacking in tact, but you must admit that I am unfailingly honest."

Mr. Averill chuckled, clearly appreciating Marcie's answer,
but Lord Redfield looked thoughtful as he turned to Beth. "Is
Mr. Baxton the young fop who misquoted the classics to you?"

"One and the same." Beth gave a little sigh.

"It's apparent that he's quite taken with Beth." Marcie ig-
nored the rather sharp jab from Beth's elbow. "Lady Baxton
desires him to marry and I do believe that he has settled his
sights upon Beth."

Beth winced, attempting to crush the urge to reply, but quite
unable to resist. "I am not the only member of my family who
is being pursued. Mr. Baxton's cousin, Mr. Montley, seems
equally taken with Marcie. He has already sent several bou-
quets."

"Motley Montley?" Mr. Averill gave a derisive chuckle.
"Surely you do not fancy him, do you, Miss Marcella?"

"Not even if he were the very last young gentleman in all of
England!" Marcie replied promptly.

Beth sighed, the color high on her cheeks. "I beg your in-
dulgence, Lord Redfield. It is not proper for us to discuss this
at all, but since we have already fallen into this bramble, perhaps
you could grant me a favor."

"Of course." Lord Redfield nodded. "What is it?"

Beth exchanged a speaking glance with her sister and then
she continued. "We are so recently come to London, we find
ourselves at a distinct disadvantage, not knowing the ways of
the *ton*. Would it be terribly forward of us to ask you and your
brother for a bit of advice?"

"I shall be glad to oblige you." Mr. Averill nodded.

Lord Redfield nodded also. "I am not certain what value our
advice should have, but we shall be delighted to proffer it to
you."

"Is there a way to discourage Mr. Baxton and Mr. Montley
without causing them undue distress?" Beth knew her color was

still high as she spoke, but that could not be helped. She had discussed this very problem with Marcie this morning and neither one of them had known precisely how to go on.

"You could send back Mr. Montley's posies." Mr. Averill suggested.

"No, that should be considered impolite," Lord Redfield corrected him quickly. "But perhaps you could arrange to be otherwise occupied when either of the two gentlemen come to call. After two or three such instances, I should think that they would be discouraged from pursuing you further."

Beth sighed as she shook her head. "I attempted that very thing, but it had quite the opposite effect. Mr. Baxton sent round a note, early this morning, requesting that I accompany him to his mother's musicale this afternoon. When I responded by pleading a prior engagement, he sent a second note, accompanied by an indecently large floral display, with an invitation to take tea with his mother and younger sister on Tuesday of next week."

"And how did you respond to his second invitation?" Lord Redfield seemed highly amused.

"I penned a note, thanking him for the flowers, but I declined his invitation by again pleading a prior engagement. I assure you that it was not a falsehood, Lord Redfield. Both Marcie and I had already accepted an invitation to tour the National Gallery with Lady Pinchton at that exact time."

"And this did not discourage Baxton?" Mr. Averill was intrigued.

"Not in the least. Did you not see the basket of yellow roses that was delivered as we took our leave?"

Lord Redfield nodded. "Now that you mention it, I did."

"They were from Mr. Baxton. I fear that the more invitations I decline, the more interested in me he becomes. It is the very reason I asked for your advice, Lord Redfield. I am hard-pressed to know what to do. I thought that perhaps you could tell me whether you have been discouraged by a young lady in the past and precisely how it was accomplished."

Lord Redfield threw back his head and laughed, and when he turned back to her, his eyes were twinkling. "I am the wrong gentleman to ask. I have not courted any young ladies in the past, and for that reason, I have not had the opportunity to be politely refused."

"And he would not have been refused, in any case." Mr. Averill frowned slightly. "We appear to share your dilemma, Miss Elizabeth, as my brother and I also find ourselves pursued."

Beth's color rose even higher and she favored Lord Redfield an apologetic glance. "Forgive me, Lord Redfield. It was henwitted of me to forget that you are the catch of the Season. Of course you should not be refused."

"And you would not be refused, either, Mr. Averill." Marcie turned to him with a smile. "I have been told that you are also considered a prize catch. Why, I wager to say that if I were in the market for a husband, I should throw myself at you most shamelessly!"

Paul pulled himself out of his reverie as Miss Winston placed her gloved hand on his arm. "Yes, Miss Winston?"

"I asked if you had noted the direction to Madame DeVolette's Millinery."

"Yes, indeed." Paul tore his eyes from the sight of Lady Bentworth, who was leaning close to her companion, and turned his attentions to Miss Winston. "You said her shop was on Bond Street?"

"No, Lord Roxbury. It is just *off* Bond Street. I shall write out her direction for you when you return me to my home. May I ask if you are acquainted with the lady in pink, several carriages forward from us?"

Paul attempted to gather his wits once again. It was clear that Miss Winston had noted the cause of his distraction. "I am almost certain I made her acquaintance, but I do not believe I recall her name."

"It is Lady Bentworth." Miss Winston sighed deeply. "And

I do not blame you in the slightest for staring. She is making rather a spectacle of herself with Colonel Faraday. Perhaps he will be her next husband. I have heard it said that she is searching for an appropriate match and she seems to prefer the elderly. I understand her first husband was thirty years her senior."

"You say her companion is Colonel Faraday?" Paul seized on the name, wishing to know more about the gentleman.

"Yes. He is an acquaintance of Papa's and has just recently returned to our shores. Papa told me that he had been away for many years in India or the East Indies. They are so similar, I am forever confusing them."

Paul nodded, suppressing the urge to inform Miss Winston that India and the East Indies were not at all similar and continents apart. "The colonel is unmarried?"

"Yes. And he would be quite a prize for Lady Bentworth. Papa says his holdings are extensive and he is quite wealthy in his own right. I do believe poor Papa was attempting to give me a push in the colonel's direction, but I am not like Lady Bentworth and I should not like to marry a gentleman just to nurse him through his last illness."

"No, I shouldn't think you would." Paul did his best to keep the sarcasm from his voice. "Did your father say that Colonel Faraday was in the Petticoat Line?"

"Not precisely. He merely thought that the colonel might be lonely when he returned to his huge estate. I believe it is somewhere near the Lake District and Papa claims the winters there are quite long. I should hate to be forced to endure winter in a place with no amusements, shouldn't you?"

"Perhaps." Paul nodded, visualizing a lovely house, nestled in a grove of pine trees, with fields of white snow stretching as far as the eye could see. "I should think that would depend entirely on whether one was blessed with a suitable companion."

"But there would be no parties, or formal dinners, or dances." Miss Winston shivered slightly. "However would a lady in such a situation contrive to amuse herself"

"With her children, and her husband, and an extensive library, I would assume. There are winter amusements, you know. I should think it would be quite enjoyable to ride through the snow in a sleigh."

Miss Winston shivered. "Perhaps, but it all sounds quite dreadful to me. I much prefer London. There is such excitement here."

"Which amusements do you prefer in Town?" Paul asked a question that was certain to garner a lengthy response. Then, while Miss Winston waxed eloquent about balls, routs, and the theatre, he resumed his observations of the fascinating Lady Bentworth.

"I do believe that they are behaving quite properly, my dear." Colonel Faraday turned to smile at Holly.

"You are right, Sunny." Holly returned his smile. "Perhaps I was foolish to be so concerned. I must apologize for involving you in this horrible crush, but I had no notion the Promenade should be so crowded."

"Nonsense! I find I am quite enjoying myself."

"Truly?" Holly turned to him with anxious eyes.

"Yes, indeed. You forget, my dear Holly, that it has been many years since I've taken part in the Promenade. And even then, I was not so lucky as to have the prettiest lady in all of London seated in my carriage."

"Fustian!" Holly laughed merrily. "But all the same, it is generous of you to say so."

The colonel laughed, too, and then he gestured toward the equipage they were about to meet. "I do believe that is Lady Erbinger and her newest *cicisbeo*, Lord Pearsol. I cannot vouch for the truth of my sister's *on-dit*, but she did tell me that Lord Erbinger offered for his wife five times before she came to accept his proposal. And then, it was with the condition that she could continue to enjoy her association with Lord Pearsol."

"Oh, my!" Holly stared at the lady in question with high

curiosity. She did not appear that attractive and her manner was loud and boisterous, not befitting a lady of her stature at all. "Was Lord Erbinger truly smitten with her?"

"Not in the slightest. He was more smitten with her father's wealth, which she has just recently inherited. Her family was in trade."

Holly nodded, knowing that such marriages were known to occur. It was not at all unusual for a penniless but titled gentleman to marry a rich heiress for the sole purpose of relieving his debts. "Perhaps it would be wise not to mention the generous dowries that dear William set aside for the girls?"

"I could not agree with you more." The colonel reached out to pat her hand. "Though it is not certain to assure them happiness, let us encourage Beth and Marcie's suitors to marry them for love."

They all laughed long and hard at Marcie's comment about throwing herself at Stewart. Once David had collected himself, he turned to Miss Elizabeth. "Your sister claims that she is not in the market for a husband. Are you of the same mind, Miss Elizabeth?"

"Most certainly!" Beth appeared quite sincere. "Perhaps I may be of a different opinion next Season, but I have no desire to seek a husband at this time."

Marcie nodded. "Beth and I are having too much fun to spoil it all by becoming engaged. We have made it a point to inform everyone we meet that we are not in the Marriage Mart, but it seems to make certain young gentlemen even more determined to change our minds."

"So you truly do not wish to marry this Season?" David could not help feeling slightly suspicious. Miss Elizabeth and Miss Marcella certainly appeared to be sincere, but perhaps it was only a clever ploy on their parts.

"No, Lord Redfield. We do not wish to marry this Season." Beth faced him squarely. "Even if we happened to meet our perfect matches and tumbled into love quite thoroughly, we still would refuse to marry."

"But why?" Stewart raised his brows.

"Because we could not leave our dear stepmama alone." Marcie answered his question. "Beth and I have decided that it would be cruel for us to leave her until she is happily settled with a new husband."

David nodded, beginning to believe that he had met the only young ladies in all of London who had no desire to marry either Stewart or him. "Will Lady Bentworth marry in the near future?"

"I do hope she will, but I have my doubts." Beth sighed deeply. "To be quite honest about the subject, our stepmama has shown no interest in marrying again. All the same, we must try to find a suitable match for her."

"It was Papa's dying wish that we play matchmaker." Marcie spoke up quite candidly.

"Marcie! You should not have told!" Beth favored her sister with a frown.

"Why ever not?" Marcie appeared completely guileless, causing David to smile. "We will need assistance if we are to be successful, and we have already asked their advice about Motley Montley and Mr. Baxton. Why must there be further secrets between us? Lord Redfield and Mr. Averill appear to be regular fellows and perhaps they will agree to become our accomplices."

"I will agree." Stewart spoke up quickly, a wide smile spreading across his face. Then he turned to David. "Will you also agree?"

David grinned at his younger brother, reminded of the larks they had shared in the past. "Of course I will. You may count upon me, Miss Elizabeth."

"I suppose this is really most improper." Beth appeared a bit concerned. "But there is no doubt that you will be of great assistance to us. We must learn more about the gentlemen of the *ton,* so that we will not choose an inappropriate suitor for our stepmama."

"I am certain we can ferret out any information you may require." Stewart nodded quickly.

"Thank you." Beth smiled at both of them. "But cooperating in such a venture should require that we spend a great deal of time together. It is not fair of us to ask you to dance attendance on us when you would prefer to be elsewhere."

Stewart laughed. "But we would *not* prefer to be elsewhere. Tell them, brother."

"Stew is right." David smiled at Beth. "As you said earlier, we are the prize catches of the Season. With the exception of you and your sister, all the other young ladies we have met have done nothing but court our favor, hoping to engage our interest and bring us up to scratch. It is quite flattering, I admit to that, but neither of us desires to marry at this time and we find it difficult to discourage these young ladies without causing them distress."

"It is not so much the young ladies as it is their mothers." Stewart began to frown. "They seem determined that their daughters marry well and will go to any lengths to see to it that they do so."

Beth nodded. "Their mamas urge them in your direction and become angry with them when they do not succeed. I have seen it with my own eyes."

"Did Miss Appleby's mama urge her to deliberately topple into me?" David raised his brows, knowing the answer but waiting for Beth to respond.

"Yes, I fear she did. Cecilia exchanged a speaking glance with her mama, and then she jumped up, for no apparent reason, the precise moment that you passed by her chair."

"I thought it was all an accident!" Marcie's eyes widened. "I guess Mama is right and I am really quite *naïve.*"

"You are." Beth smiled at her sister fondly before she turned back to David. "I must admit that I do not envy you your position, Lord Redfield. I suspect that these ploys will grow more blatant before the Season is over."

David began to smile as a thought occurred to him. "Perhaps I have a solution to our common problem, if you will hear me out. You, Elizabeth, and you, Miss Marcella, are both plagued by unwelcome suitors. And you do not wish to marry at this time. Is that not correct?"

Beth nodded. "You are quite correct, Lord Redfield."

"And Stew and I are plagued by young ladies who desire to trap us into marriage against our wishes." David turned to Stewart. "Is that not correct?"

"It is." Stewart nodded.

"Then why do we not combine forces?" David smiled at the two young ladies. "That should serve all four of us well."

Beth caught his meaning immediately and an impish grin spread across her face. "You are brilliant, Lord Redfield! If we are seen often enough in each other's company, all will assume that we are courting and leave us well enough alone!"

"Oh, what a hum!" Marcie began to giggle. "But do you think anyone will believe us?"

Stewart shrugged. "There is no reason why they should not. You will be saving us, and we will be saving you. I should think it will all work out to our mutual advantage."

"And it will give us enough time together to find a suitable husband for your stepmother." David smiled at Beth. "Shall we swear a pact on it?"

Beth held out her gloved hands. "Let us all hold hands and swear that we shall protect each other from unwelcome suitors and refuse to be trapped into marriage this Season."

"And that we will all endeavor to find a suitable match for Lady Bentworth," David added, finding the touch of Beth's hand very pleasant indeed.

When the oath had been taken, Stewart leaned back against the squabs, a broad smile on his face. "Tell us about your stepmother. If you describe her interests and her character, it will assist us in finding her perfect match."

David listened as Beth and Marcie told them about their step-mother. He frowned as they described her first fickle love and how he had left her, and he smiled as they told of the enjoyable times they had shared in the manor house and then in the small dower cottage. When they were finished, he raised his brows. "Perhaps we should consider Uncle Paul as a match for Lady Bentworth. He is handsome and well situated, and he told us that it was past time he set up his nursery."

"Uncle Paul and Lady Bentworth?" Stewart considered it for a moment and then he nodded. "You may have hit upon a so-lution, David. There is no reason why they should not like each other."

Beth began to frown slightly. "I do believe there is. They met at our debutante ball, but they did not seem to rub along well together."

"Describe their meeting." David leaned forward. "Tell me everything that transpired."

"I did not hear their conversation, but Mama appeared quite uncomfortable in your uncle's presence. She was unfailingly polite, of course. Mama would never be uncivil. But her color was high and she looked to be quite anxious."

"Do you concur with your sister's assessment?" Stewart quizzed Marcie.

"Yes, indeed. I was a bit closer to them than Beth was, and I noticed that her hands trembled and she appeared to have great difficulty in meeting his eyes with her own. That is quite un-usual, for Mama is always the picture of composure."

David exchanged a speaking glance with Stewart and then he turned to Beth with a grin. "Do you suppose it is possible that your stepmother's discomfort was due to the fact that she found my uncle attractive?"

"Oh!" Beth began to blush quite prettily. "I had not thought of that!"

"We must place them in a situation where they can become better acquainted. Perhaps we could . . ." Marcie stopped in mid-sentence as the carriage lurched and a heavy missile came sailing into their midst. "What was that?"

"A rock." David retrieved it from the floor of the carriage. We're extremely fortunate that it missed . . . Stew! Are you all right?"

Stewart attempted a nod, but he crumpled forward instead, brushing the skirts of Marcie's gown as he slumped to the boards and leaving an alarmingly large smear of blood in his wake.

Sixteen

"What are you doing?" David stared at Beth in utter amazement as she lifted her skirts and ripped a strip from her petticoat.

"We must staunch the blood." Beth slid down on the boards next to Stewart and pressed the swatch of white cloth against the wound, which was slightly above Stewart's left brow. "Do not attempt to move him, Lord Redfield. I am not certain as to the extent of his injuries. Oh, how I wish Mama were here!"

"Lady Bentworth?" David felt his head spinning. "But why?"

Marcie spoke up. "Mama is a healer. But do not be anxious, Lord Redfield. We have assisted her in dealing with injuries of this type in the past."

Just then an old-fashioned landau pulled up beside them and Lady Bentworth jumped out, not bothering to wait for assistance. She took in the scene at a glance and motioned for David to open the door.

"Keep the cloth pressed tightly to the wound, Beth, until I am able to relieve you of the duty. Marcie? You must hop out, dear, so that I may take your place."

Marcie nodded and immediately climbed down from the carriage, standing aside so that her stepmother could enter. Lady Bentworth did not stand on ceremony or even give David the time to assist her. She lifted her skirts and climbed in, moving nimbly across the seat until she had taken up a position immediately above and slightly to the right of her older stepdaughter.

"Listen carefully, Beth." Lady Bentworth's voice was firm. "When I give the word, remove your hand and climb up on the opposite bench. I will slide to the floor and take your place."

"What shall I do to help, Lady Bentworth?" David's voice was trembling slightly. His brother's face was very pale and he appeared to have lost consciousness.

"Nothing right now, dear. Beth and I will switch positions and then we shall see."

David watched while Beth and Lady Bentworth exchanged positions. A fresh spurt of blood appeared on the cloth at the instant the pressure was relieved, and he began to frown. "There is so much blood. Shall I fetch a surgeon, Lady Bentworth?"

"No, dear. A surgeon is not necessary, as I have the situation well in hand. Wounds to the head tend to bleed profusely, but I am convinced it is not so serious as it appears."

David took heart from Lady Bentworth's answer. Her tone was encouraging, as she did not sound unduly anxious. "But do you not have something that I might do to help?"

"Yes, indeed I do." Lady Bentworth motioned for Beth to tear a fresh strip of cloth from her petticoat, and once it was done, she eased it in place over the old. "Take Marcie to the landau and ask Colonel Faraday to carry her home. Then speak to your driver and tell him to use all caution in conveying us as smoothly as he's able to our town home."

"Yes, Lady Bentworth." David nodded quickly, taking Miss Marcella's arm and leading her away to the landau. He glanced back once more, to see his brother's eyelids fluttering slightly, and breathed a deep sigh of relief.

Just as David was helping Miss Marcella into the landau, another equipage pulled up. A familiar voice hailed him, and David turned to see his uncle, driving a high-perch phaeton with a lovely lady seated beside him.

"What happened here, David?"

His uncle's tone was anxious and David hastened to reassure him. "Stewart has been injured. One of the horses kicked up a rock and it hit him on the head."

"Then we must get him to a surgeon immediately!"

His uncle made to leave the phaeton, but David stopped him. "No, Uncle Paul. Lady Bentworth said that a surgeon was not necessary. She has the situation well in hand."

"Lady Bentworth?" His uncle's eyes snapped and he began to frown fiercely. "What does *she* know of such matters?"

David struggled to find exactly the right words to explain the situation to his uncle. Though he did not understand the reason, his uncle had become quite angry the moment he had mentioned Lady Bentworth's name.

"Lady Bentworth appears quite capable, sir." David gave him a tentative smile. Perhaps he was just anxious about Stewart and this was his way of showing that emotion. "She told me that she has treated such injuries in the past and she says she does not believe Stewart's wound is serious. I really must hurry back to her, sir. We are to carry Stewart to her home for treatment."

"Not without my permission, you're not!"

David stared at his uncle in utter confusion, but he did not have much time to consider what had caused this outburst. Before he could utter another syllable, his uncle had leaped from the perch, grabbed him by the arm, and was propelling him toward the carriage that contained Stewart, Beth, and Lady Bentworth.

"What is the meaning of this, madam!" Paul glared at the occupants of the carriage.

"The meaning of what, Lord Roxbury?" Lady Bentworth turned to stare up at him. "Your nephew has been injured and I am seeing to his care. There is really no need for alarm. The wound is shallow and should present no problem once I cleanse it thoroughly and apply a bandage."

Paul felt his heart thud quite alarmingly as he noted the amount of blood on the floorboard of the carriage. Stewart was stretched out, as pale as death, and Lady Bentworth was pressing a cloth to his head. He could not help but notice that there was a goodly amount of blood on her skirts, as well as those of her stepdaughter, and he feared the worst for his nephew.

"Please stand aside, Lord Roxbury." Lady Bentworth's voice held a note of command that served to set Paul's teeth on edge. "We must be off immediately. The longer the wound is exposed to these unsanitary conditions, the greater the possibility of infection."

Paul stared at her in utter amazement, not quite believing his ears. When he spoke again, he could not control the irony that crept into his speech. "You are fobbing yourself off as a medical expert, Lady Bentworth?"

"I *am* a medical expert, sir." Lady Bentworth's voice was firm but soft, serving to draw attention to his lack of control. "I have been well trained in the healing arts and I assure you that I shall take all precautions with your nephew. Perhaps you should like to follow us in your equipage? The town home I have rented is only a few blocks from here."

Paul glared at her, despising her high-handed manner. He would not be taken in by her as easily as his nephews had been. "You will not move my nephew until I fetch a surgeon!"

"A surgeon will be quite unnecessary, Lord Roxbury." As he watched, she brushed back a lock of golden hair and settled herself more comfortably beside Stewart. "In fact, it should be a capital waste of your coin. I am quite capable as you shall see when you observe my treatment of the boy."

Paul's eyes glittered with rage. How dare this chit of a woman tell him how to spend his money! "I shall fetch a surgeon, nonetheless. I order you to wait here for me to return."

"That should not be in your nephew's best interest. I beg you, sir, to stay calm and think rationally." She faced down his ire with a smile and that served to make Paul even more enraged. "While I am certain that your intentions are admirable, the only purpose you serve is to delay treatment of your nephew's injury."

"Please let her treat Stewart, Uncle Paul." David turned to

him and Paul noted that the boy met his eyes unflinchingly. "If you wish, carry the surgeon to Lady Bentworth's home so that he can offer his opinion. But it cannot serve Stewart well to leave him here, on the floor of the carriage, without any treatment at all."

Paul stared at his elder nephew for a moment and then he nodded. As much as it rankled him, the boy was correct. "You may proceed. I shall join you with the surgeon as soon as I am able."

"Thank you, Lord Roxbury." Lady Bentworth favored him with a smile. "Colonel Faraday awaits us at the entrance to the park and I shall tell him to give you our direction."

Paul was still frowning as his injured nephew was borne off with David, Miss Elizabeth, and Lady Bentworth in attendance. He had intended to fetch the best surgeon in Town with great dispatch, but when he turned back to his own equipage, he realized that Miss Winston was sitting in the only passenger seat. He could not take her with him to fetch the surgeon and he had not the time to carry her home. He must think of an alternate plan, and quickly.

"What is it, Lord Roxbury?" Miss Winston noted his frown and raised one perfect brow with the question.

"An accident. My younger nephew is injured and I must fetch the surgeon immediately." Paul glanced around and saw salvation in the carriage that approached his. "There is Lord Beresford. I will ask him to carry you home."

Miss Winston's eyes widened with alarm. "Lord Beresford? But I cannot ride with him, sir. He has the reputation of being a rake!"

"As do I, but that did not keep you from accepting my invitation." Paul was aware that he was speaking out of turn, but he had no time to spend on soothing Miss Winston's sensibilities. "I see he has Miss Ewell with him, and I am certain that you shall be quite safe. Please step down, Miss Winston. The situation is grave and I must not delay any further."

The deed was accomplished in short order, and Paul sighed

as he wheeled his horses out of the park. Miss Winston had been regrettably overset at the summary treatment she had received at his hands. He would order a large floral tribute delivered to her home, and it should serve to ease her wounded pride.

Paul turned down an avenue that he knew to have little traffic this time of day and headed toward Belgrave Square. Mr. Lawrence Browne, a well-known surgeon with an impeccable reputation, had recently inherited a home from his maiden aunt and set up his offices there. As he traveled over the nearly deserted streets, Paul sighed as he thought of his innocent nephew under Lady Bentworth's care. It was clear that the lady had convinced David that she was capable of caring for his brother, but he was not so easily taken in. He should be regrettably remiss in his duty if he entrusted poor Stewart to the dubious ministrations of the scheming, wealth-seeking, social-climbing widow for any longer than was absolutely necessary.

"How is he, Lady Bentworth?" David jumped up as she entered the drawing room, where Holly had sent him to wait with Marcie and Beth.

"Quite well, David." Holly smiled as she faced the earnest young man. "You do not mind if I call you *David,* do you?"

"Not at all, Lady Bentworth. I would consider it an honor after the kindness that you have done for us. I am convinced that Stewart could not have received better treatment in all of London."

"You are far too kind." Holly brushed his compliment away. "I'm happy to report that Stewart is awake and complaining that he is sharp-set. A good appetite bodes well for his condition, but I fear he is not happy to be denied the supper he craves."

Beth began to frown. "Mr. Averill cannot eat?"

"He can, certainly, but he should not." Holly smiled at her elder stepdaughter and then she turned to David to explain. "Concussion may sometimes occur after a head injury, and it is best to give only liquid nourishment for the first full day. When I left your brother, our housekeeper, Mrs. Merriweather, was feeding him broth by the spoonful."

David raised his brows. "That must be a blow to his pride. No doubt he feels like a child again, being fed by his nurse."

"Perhaps, but he does not appear to mind. He took an immediate liking to Mrs. Merriweather and even asked her if she would sit with him through the night."

"He cannot return home?" David looked concerned.

"It is best not to move him any more than is necessary. Your brother has been jounced around quite enough. He will recover much faster if he is allowed to rest quietly until morning."

Marcie began to frown. "But he will recover by tomorrow, won't he?"

"Yes, dear." Holly smiled at her younger stepdaughter. "By tomorrow, I daresay all Stewart will have left of his unfortunate encounter is a good-sized bruise on his head."

They all turned toward the window as the sound of an approaching carriage was heard and David frowned as he recognized his uncle's phaeton. "It is Uncle Paul. There is another gentleman on the perch beside him and I suspect it is the surgeon. I do hope he does not insist on carrying Stewart home in spite of your cautions, Lady Bentworth."

"I am certain he will not." Holly shook her head, hoping that her words would be prophetic. From what she had seen of the earl, thus far, she doubted that he would bow to anyone's wishes if they conflicted with his own.

"I am sorry Uncle Paul was so ill-tempered with you earlier." David looked very apologetic.

"It does not matter," Holly hastened to reassure him. "It was obvious to me that your uncle was concerned for your brother's well-being."

David sighed. "That is still no excuse for being rude. When he realizes that he treated you badly, I am sure that he will apologize."

"Of course." Holly dropped her eyes. She was almost certain

that there would be no apology tendered by *The Elusive Earl,* but it would not be polite of her to say so.

"What is taking the blasted surgeon so long? He has had ample time to examine Stewart!"

David stared at his uncle, who was in a rare taking, and decided that it should not be wise for him to answer. Instead, he gestured toward the decanter that Lady Bentworth's aged butler had left on the side table. "Would you care for a brandy, Uncle Paul?"

"No! Brandy is the last thing I need at a time like this! But perhaps . . . yes, I do believe you're right. It may serve to settle my nerves. Pour me a glass, will you, David? Half full, no more."

David crossed to the table and poured the amount his uncle had requested. He had never seen Uncle Paul so agitated. David had attempted to reassure him earlier, by repeating everything that Lady Bentworth had divulged about Stewart's condition, but it had served only to agitate him further. Perhaps it was best that Beth and Marcie had gone to their chambers to change their gowns, leaving him as the sole witness to his uncle's ill humor.

David had no sooner handed the snifter of brandy to his uncle than they heard the sound of approaching footsteps. A moment later, the door slid open and Mr. Browne entered the drawing room.

"You need have no further worries, Lord Roxbury." The surgeon smiled widely. "Lady Bentworth has done all that was needed and more."

David noticed that his uncle's dark brows shot up and hovered at their highest point. "And more? Kindly explain what you mean, Mr. Browne!"

"She has cleansed the wound to perfection and applied a most unusual and effective bandage. It is really quite ingenious."

The earl's brows hovered dangerously at their highest apex. "A bandage? Ingenious?"

"Yes, indeed. It is cleverly fashioned to hold the edges of the wound together, eliminating the need for sutures. I daresay your nephew will escape without a scar."

The earl's brows lowered slightly, but David noted that he still did not appear content. "Then you can find no fault with her treatment of my nephew?"

"None at all, sir. I would say that you were extremely fortunate that Lady Bentworth happened upon the scene when she did. She is an excellent practitioner and you need have no fear of leaving young Stewart in her care."

"Leaving Stewart?" The earl's brows lifted again. "I shall not leave him! I plan to carry him home."

Mr. Browne shook his head. "I would strongly advise against it, Lord Roxbury. It is best that young Stewart rest quietly for the next twenty-four hours. There is always the possibility of concussion in head injuries of this type and moving him may have disastrous results. Surely you would not care to gamble your nephew's health over so trivial a matter?"

David found he was holding his breath, waiting for the answer. Would his uncle bow to the surgeon's wishes?

"Of course you are right, Mr. Browne." The earl nodded. "Stewart shall stay if you think it advisable. But I insist that you stay with him until he is recovered. I will pay your fee, never fear."

"It is not a question of money, Lord Roxbury, but rather, of time. Other patients have need of my services and there is nothing I can do for your nephew that Lady Bentworth has not already done. He will be in good hands here, and you may carry him home at this time tomorrow."

David turned to his uncle. "I can stay with Stewart, sir. I am certain that Lady Bentworth would not mind."

"I forbid it, David. I will give you my reasons when we are in private, but for the meantime, you will simply have to accede

to my wishes. Perhaps you will catch my meaning if you remember our converse on the way to Lady Pinchton's ball."

"Yes, sir." David nodded, still puzzled as to what his uncle
had meant. They had discussed many subjects on their drive to
the ball.

"Come along, Mr. Browne. If you have finished your examination, I will carry you back to your offices." The earl turned
to David again. "When I have concluded my business with Mr.
Browne, I shall fetch Easton. Once I have seen him settled here,
you and I will return to Roxbury House."

David stared after his uncle in some confusion as he strode
out of the drawing room with the surgeon following closely
behind. He could not think of a single reason why his uncle
would refuse to let him stay with Stewart, unless . . .

David's eyes widened as he hit upon a possible explanation.
They had discussed the tricks young ladies and their mothers
played to trap young gentlemen into marriage. Surely his uncle
could not believe that Lady Bentworth was attempting to set
some sort of a trap by keeping Stewart under her roof!

Seventeen

"Join me for a brandy, David?" Paul turned to his nephew the moment they gained the library at Roxbury House.

"A brandy? Well . . . certainly, sir."

Paul stifled a chuckle at his nephew's surprise. No doubt the boy had been expecting a severe dressing-down for speaking out of turn in the carriage. On their return to Roxbury House, David had informed his uncle, in no uncertain terms, that he was completely wrong about Lady Bentworth's motives and owed her a sincere apology.

"Thank you, Uncle Paul." David accepted the snifter of brandy and took a small sip. He did not cough or sputter, as one who had never before tasted strong spirits was apt to do, and Paul raised his brows. Perhaps his nephew was not as green as he had thought.

"I was wrong about Lady Bentworth, David." Paul had decided that the best way to glean information from the boy was to appear to be entirely candid. "What do you think I ought to do in the way of an apology?"

David grinned, meeting his uncle's eyes. "I should think a bouquet of flowers would be appropriate, Uncle Paul."

"Flowers." Paul nodded. "Yes, indeed. I will order them sent round immediately. But you do see how I could have arrived at my conclusion, do you not? I had heard that Lady Bentworth was in the market for a wealthy husband and I assumed she was using your brother's unfortunate accident as an excuse to ingratiate herself with me."

David frowned. "I have heard the gossip, Uncle, and it is quite false. Both Miss Elizabeth and Miss Marcella have assured us that their stepmother does not wish to marry again."

"Balderdash!" Paul began to smile. "Perhaps that is what she says, but I am certain that her intentions are quite the opposite. After all, it would be extremely unwise of her to admit that she is on the Marriage Mart so soon after her husband's death."

David took a moment to think about what his uncle had said, and then he nodded. "A valid point, sir. Lady Bentworth could not admit it if she *were* seeking a husband. But I am convinced that she is not. Miss Elizabeth and Miss Marcella have told us that she has refused several invitations from extremely suitable gentlemen. Indeed, both Beth and Miss Marcella are most overset that their stepmother will not agree to entertain a suitable *parti.*"

"Then they would prefer that she marry again?"

"Of course." David nodded quickly. "They told us that they would desire it above all else."

Paul's eyes narrowed as he thought about what David had said. Did the two little minxes have their sights set on him as a possible suitor for their stepmother? "No doubt Miss Elizabeth and Miss Marcella regard me as a suitable *parti.*"

"You?" David began to chortle. "Oh, no, Uncle! Certainly not *you!*"

Paul felt an unaccustomed flash of anger. How dare this halfling tell him that he was not a suitable match for Lady Bentworth! "And what is wrong with me? I'll have you know that I am considered a prize catch!"

"I am certain you are." David sobered quickly in the face of his uncle's retort. "But everyone knows that *The Elusive Earl* will not be trapped into marriage."

Paul favored his nephew with a stern look. "But I already

told you that I must marry, sooner or later. Perhaps Lady Bentworth is the perfect match for me."

"Never, Uncle!" David shook his head. "Just consider the angry words that you exchanged this very afternoon. Why, the two of you should be continually at loggerheads, neither willing to give way to the other. What kind of marriage would that be?"

Paul laughed, highly amused. "An interesting one. At least Lady Bentworth would never toad-eat me, and you may be certain she would tell me when she thought I was wrong."

"Indeed, she would!" David chuckled. "But you could not win Lady Bentworth, Uncle, even if you should decide to make the attempt."

Paul's eyes began to gleam with amusement. His scamp of a nephew had no conception of his power to win a lady's heart. "I could not?"

"No. Lady Bentworth knows of your reputation, Uncle, and I believe that she has taken you in dislike. I daresay she would reject your overtures out of hand."

"We shall see about that!" Paul gave a decisive nod. "Lady Bentworth may have hoodwinked you, and perhaps she has hoodwinked her stepdaughters as well, but I still say that she is seeking a wealthy husband who is capable of supporting her in the style she desires. Even if she regards me as a rake and a scoundrel, she will be attracted to my money and my title. I would wager to say that the moment I favor her with my attentions, she will fall into my arms like a ripe plum!"

David looked doubtful. "Perhaps it is foolish of me to disagree with a gentleman who knows the workings of a lady's mind so much better than I do, but I am certain that you are mistaken. Lady Bentworth will never allow you to pay court to her."

"Never?" Paul raised his brows. There was nothing he liked so much as a challenge.

"No, sir. She will be polite. Of that, I have no doubt. But I do not believe that you can succeed in winning her good favor."

Paul began to grin. He had intended to make a pretty apology and then leave the irritating widow to her own devices, but his nephew's assertions had put a different spin to his plans. The urge to prove David wrong was much too strong to resist, and he was determined to succeed in changing Lady Bentworth's mind about him before the Season was over.

Beth's mouth dropped open almost as far as her sister's as Lord Redfield repeated the conversation he'd had with his uncle. "But why did you tell him that Mama had taken him in dislike?"

"To bring them together." Lord Redfield grinned. "Now that he is determined to force your stepmother to change her mind about him, he will dance attendance on her."

"But only to prove his point to you!" Marcie gave an exasperated sigh. "What good will that do?"

"He will *begin* paying his attentions to your stepmother with a less than admirable motive, but I am convinced that she will soon captivate him."

Beth began to smile as she caught his meaning. "I do believe I understand your ploy, Lord Redfield. Once your uncle realizes that Mama will not be swayed by his charms, he will become intrigued."

"Precisely!" Lord Redfield favored her with a conspiratorial grin. "He will wonder why she is so different from all the other ladies he has met."

Marcie nodded. "And while your uncle is busily attempting to solve the puzzle of why dear Mama is not swooning at his feet, he will be tumbling into love with her!"

Mr. Averill grinned, looking rather rakish with a bandage over his brow. "Well done, Brother! But you have overlooked one slight matter. How will we convince Lady Bentworth to accept our uncle's attentions?"

There was silence in the small pleasure garden, where the four had gathered to await the earl's arrival with the carriage that would carry Stewart back to Roxbury House. They exchanged several anxious glances and then Beth clapped her hands.

"I have it!" Beth motioned them closer. "We shall use guilt to gain our objective. Marcie and I shall speak to Mama and offer to cut you, Lord Redfield, and you, Mr. Averill, out of our circle of acquaintances for her sake. We shall say we know that she does not regard your uncle with favor and we do not wish to force her to have any further congress with him."

Marcie grinned. "Perfection! And then we shall pull long faces and blink back tears until she says that we are being silly and that she will gladly endure your uncle's attentions for our sakes."

"Risky, but brilliant." Mr. Averill favored her with an admiring grin. "Have you thought of what you will do if Lady Bentworth accepts your offer to end our acquaintance?"

Beth shook her head. "She will not accept it. Mama would never deprive us of pleasure for her sake and she genuinely likes both of you. Our plan will work. I am certain of it."

"When will you make this attempt?" Lord Redfield looked a bit anxious.

"The moment you've left." Marcie made the decision. "Will you be attending Lady Whittington's dinner party this evening?"

Mr. Averill nodded. "Yes. I know her youngest son quite well and I will ask him to influence the seating so that we will be partnered with you at dinner."

"Excellent!" Beth nodded quickly, hoping that Lord Redfield also desired to influence the seating so that he should be near her. "Marcie and I shall meet you there and tell you precisely what Mama says."

Lord Redfield chuckled slightly. "But we will be hard-pressed to wait until then. Will you send round a note telling us whether or not you have been successful?"

"Of course," Beth agreed, but then she frowned slightly. It was on the edge of propriety, as it was, for her to send a personal note to Lord Redfield. "I do believe it should be in code, in the event that it is read by any other than you. If we are successful, I will pen a passage from Homer. If not, it will be Cicero."

Mr. Averill groaned. "If someone had but told me that it would serve such a useful purpose, I would have paid closer attention when we read the classics at Cambridge. I fear my brother shall have to interpret your note for me."

Marcie giggled at his dismayed expression. "Perhaps I should pen a note, as well, in my area of expertise."

"What would that be?" Mr. Averill turned to her expectantly.

"Horses, of course. I have always been enamored of them. Did you know that the Thoroughbred can trace its ancestry through the male line directly back to three Eastern stallions?"

Mr. Averill grinned as he nodded. "Indeed, I did. They are the Byerly Turk, the Darley Arabian, and the Godolphin Barb. Do you know when they were imported to our shores?"

"Of course I do. It was well over seventy years ago. Up until that time, we had mostly cold-blooded horses, which were perfectly fine for size and strength."

"But not so fine for pleasure riding or racing. Perhaps it's just as well that we began cross-breeding hot-blooded and cold-blooded horses, for I cannot imagine you seated on the back of a draft horse."

"But I have ridden a draft horse and enjoyed it immensely." Marcie giggled. "I was raised in the country, you know. Why, I daresay I could outride you, Mr. Averill, with one hand tied behind my back."

Mr. Averill laughed. "Never! But if you like, we'll put it to the test. Would you care to join me for a ride through the park early tomorrow morning?"

"I should enjoy it above all else!" Marcie replied enthusiastically. But then she frowned and shook her head. "But I fear I cannot. We did not bring our mounts with us."

Lord Redfield turned to Beth. "If you agree to join their excursion, Miss Elizabeth, I will see that both you and Miss

Marcella have suitable mounts. My uncle keeps a full stable here in Town and there are my father's horses as well."

"I accept with pleasure." Beth smiled happily. "A morning ride will be much to my liking. When we were in the country, we rode every day and I have sorely missed those times."

Mr. Averill nodded, pleased at the entertainment he had suggested for them, and then his eyes began to sparkle. "My uncle is a bruising rider and I am certain he would agree to accompany us. Tell me, Miss Marcella . . . does your stepmother ride?"

"Indeed, she does." Marcie nodded and answered the twinkle in his eye with a giggle. "If we ask her to join our party as our chaperone, I am almost certain that she will accept, so long as we do not mention that your uncle will also be joining us."

Lord Redfield laughed. "We are nothing if not devious, but it should serve to throw the two of them together in a pleasant setting. And I suspect that it will be difficult for my uncle and your stepmother to brangle on horseback."

"Perhaps." Beth smiled sweetly, rising to her feet at the sound of an approaching carriage. "But you do not know Mama nearly as well as we do."

"No, my dears. I cannot let you make such a sacrifice for me." Holly sighed deeply. "Lord Redfield and Mr. Averill are suitable escorts for you and I know that you favor them."

Beth's lower lip trembled slightly. "But we should be willing to give them up for your sake, Mama. We do not like to see you so distressed."

"Beth is right." Marcie nodded quickly. "It would be cruel of us to force you to be polite to someone you hold in such dislike."

Holly sighed deeply. "It is not that I dislike him so much, personally. It is his reputation as a rake and a scoundrel that disturbs me."

"But why, Mama?" Marcie frowned slightly. "Surely you do

not think that Lord Roxbury would attempt to compromise you?"

Holly stared at her younger stepdaughter in some amazement. Marcie had always spoken her mind, but she had never been quite this candid before. But the question had been asked and she must answer. "Certainly not! If what I have heard about him is accurate, *The Elusive Earl* would not waste his energy on a lady he could not conquer."

"It is settled then. Since neither you nor the earl is interested in any sort of"—Beth stopped, attempting to find the proper word—"of romantic entanglement, you can base your association on another front."

Holly could not help but laugh at Beth's earnest expression. "Perhaps, though I cannot fathom what front that would be. We have very little in the way of a common interest."

"But you do, Mama!" Marcie spoke up. "The earl cares about his nephews and you care about us. That is a lot in common, if you ask me! And since the earl has no experience with young gentlemen, he does not truly know how to supervise Lord Redfield and Mr. Averill. No doubt he would be extremely grateful if you would offer to assist him with that duty."

Holly shook her head. "I doubt the earl needs any assistance from me."

"Oh, but he does." Beth sighed deeply. "He has admitted as much to Lord Redfield and Mr. Averill. You see, the earl is dreadfully anxious that some mamas and their daughters will attempt to trap his nephews into marriage. They are prize catches, you know."

Holly nodded. "Indeed, they are. Lady Warton made certain to tell me that."

"But Lord Redfield and Mr. Averill know they are perfectly safe with us." Marcie took up the argument. "You are far from a scheming mama and not the least bit devious."

Holly raised her brows. "I am gratified to hear that they do not think so."

"How could they?" Marcie gave a little laugh. "You never

let us out of each other's sight. And most of the time you are in close proximity to us."

Beth nodded. "And you have never encouraged us to make sheep's eyes at them or to make a blatant show of courting their favor. Lord Redfield and Mr. Averill have told us that it is the very reason they prefer to spend their time with us. They know that we would never attempt to trap them into an alliance."

Holly nodded. "Then they are not in the Petticoat Line?"

"Most certainly not, Mama!" Marcie giggled. "They merely wish to enjoy the Season, as we do. We have all, the four of us, become good friends and we wish to protect each other from the dangers of a hasty and ill-suited match."

Holly nodded again. "That all sounds quite reasonable. Am I to assume, then, that neither of you desires a match with Lord Redfield or Mr. Averill?"

"Yes, Mama." Beth smiled happily. "Lord Redfield does not wish to marry for at least two years. We have discussed it."

"You discussed *marriage* with him?"

Beth nodded. "Of course. He took me into his confidence and he was delighted to find that I was of the same mind."

"And Mr. Averill told me the same, except that he wishes to wait a bit longer." Marcie smiled happily. "And when I confided that I had no intention of marrying during my debutante Season, the four of us made a pact to keep each other safe from schemes that would force us to marry before we wished to do so."

Holly blinked and took a deep breath. She had no doubt that her stepdaughters were being truthful with her, and she suspected that Lord Redfield and Mr. Averill had been equally honest with them. It was a most unusual agreement for two debutantes and two young gentlemen to make, but she could truly find no fault with it. "But what if you meet your perfect match, Beth? Or you, Marcie?"

"Then he shall have to stand the test of Lord Redfield and Mr. Averill's scrutiny." Marcie laughed merrily. "And if he passes muster with them, perhaps he *is* a perfect match."

"And if Lord Redfield or Mr. Averill meet their perfect matches?"

"Then she must pass muster with us," Beth answered. "And in the meantime, we shall all be able to enjoy the Season without fear of unwanted entanglements."

Holly began to smile. "It does sound most reasonable, almost as if you have found two brothers to protect you from harm."

"That is precisely what Mr. Averill said!" Marcie nodded quickly. "And then Lord Redfield said they felt as if they had found two sisters to guard their interests."

Holly gave each of the girls a smile. "I daresay you have found the perfect way to go on through the Season. I am very proud of you for thinking of it. But you will still have the need of chaperones for propriety's sake, and I shall do my best to be friendly toward Lord Roxbury."

"Thank you, Mama."

Beth jumped up to hug Holly, and then it was Marcie's turn. Holly felt much relieved at having had this discussion, but even as she smoothed back a lock of Marcie's hair, she wondered how it would be possible to be friendly toward *The Elusive Earl* without giving him a clue as to how very discomfited she was in his presence.

Eighteen

When Holly caught sight of the massive bouquet that had just been delivered, she was astounded. It was fully three feet in circumference and took up most of the surface of the piecrust table where Hobson had placed it. The blooms were exquisite, a sampling of every blossom that could possibly be grown in a country garden, and all were in a state of perfection. It was truly the most glorious floral display she had ever seen.

As she walked closer, Holly spied several varieties of lilies among the other flowers and her smile changed to a frown. What a pity that lilies should be included in this truly lovely bouquet. She despised lilies and had never permitted them to be planted in the gardens at Bentworth Manor. There was nothing wrong with the flower itself. It simply served to remind her of her anguish, five Seasons ago, when she had waited for her first love in the lily garden at the park. Just the barest hint of their scent brought back all the despair that she had felt upon that day when her handsome pirate had failed to keep their rendezvous.

"Mama?" Beth entered the room with Marcie behind her. "Dorri is ready to dress your hair."

Holly sighed. She was not anticipating this evening's dinner party with any degree of enthusiasm. Though the cuisine at Lady Whittington's table was rumored to be quite excellent, her hostess had confided that she intended to pair Holly with her elderly uncle, a nice enough gentleman, but one who was afflicted with an unfortunate hearing loss. "Yes, dear. I shall go up directly."

"Oh, dear!" Beth gave a gasp of dismay as she noticed the huge floral tribute. "Please tell me these flowers are not from Mr. Baxton, Mama!"

"And please tell me that they are not from Mr. Montley!" Marcie looked equally horrified.

Holly laughed, shaking off the dreary thoughts the sight of the lilies and the contemplation of her evening's dinner partner had prompted. With deliberate cheer, she linked arms with her stepdaughters and walked to the table where Hobson had placed the floral offering. "I cannot tell you anything, my dears, for I have not examined them as yet. But I have no doubt they are intended for one or the other of you."

"No, they are not." Beth drew out the card that was tucked into the massive display. "These flowers are for *you,* Mama!"

Holly blinked as she saw that her name was, indeed, written on the card. "But who would send me such a splendid bouquet? Unless . . . did your Uncle Sunny send these flowers?"

"No, Mama. They are from Lord Roxbury." Marcie grinned as she flipped over the card and read the sentiment on the other side. "He apologizes most profusely for doubting your ability to care for Mr. Averill and begs that you forgive him for his rude behavior."

"Naturally, he assumes that I will! No doubt he has not yet encountered a lady who will not be soothed by such an lavish display." Holly regarded the flowers, which had pleased her only moments before, with a baleful look.

"Mama?" Beth reached out to touch her sleeve. "You promised us that you would put your differences behind you and treat Lord Roxbury with the utmost of courtesy."

Holly sighed. "And I will. But you cannot deny that he was insufferably rude to me."

"No one is denying that, Mama." Marcie spoke in a soothing tone. "But I am certain that he will be most polite when you encounter him again. After all, he was most anxious about his nephew and he had only just met you. If one of us were injured, would you leave us in the care of a casual acquaintance whose qualifications you did not know?"

Holly thought about it for a moment and then she shook her head. "No, of course I would not. You are right, girls. It is unfair to judge Lord Roxbury by his behavior in this one instance. It is clear that his concern for Stewart overrode his civility."

"That is very kind of you, Mama, to excuse him in that manner." Beth gave her a smile of approval. "When you meet him next, will you thank him for his lovely bouquet and tell him that you accept his apology?"

Holly stared from Beth to Marcie. Both girls seemed to be anxiously awaiting her decision. "Of course I will. You need have no worry on that score. I only wish that he hadn't sent so many lilies!"

"You do not care for lilies, Mama?" Marcie raised her brows.

"No, I cannot abide them! Their scent is so . . . so cloying. I should really prefer to toss them out."

"Yes, they have a heavy perfume." Beth nodded. "But it would be a pity to toss out the whole bouquet merely because it contains a few lilies."

Marcie began to smile. "I have an idea. Let's pick out the lilies and make a second bouquet for Mrs. Merriweather. I'm certain she'd like them."

"An excellent suggestion." Holly smiled at them. "Perhaps you could accomplish that task while I dress. I should be grateful not to be forced to see them again."

When they agreed, Holly thanked them and turned to leave the room, but not before she had caught the speaking glance that passed between Beth and Marcie. There was no possible way they could know, but as she climbed the stairs to her chambers, Holly wondered if her very perceptive stepdaughters had guessed the true reason she could not abide the sight and the scent of lilies.

* * *

Paul's eyes found her the instant he entered Lady Whittington's drawing room. She was dressed in a deep blue gown only a shade darker than her eyes. Her lovely golden hair was drawn up in loose curls that framed her face and she wore no jewelry save a small string of pearls clasped about her slender neck. There was no doubt that she was the loveliest lady in the room, despite her simple gown and hairstyle. Even their hostess, who always dressed in the latest stare of fashion, did not possess Lady Bentworth's quiet elegance.

He managed to catch her eye and she moved quickly in his direction, surprising him mightily as he thought she might attempt to avoid his company. When she arrived at his side, she smiled up at him sweetly, but he could not help but notice that her smile did not reach her eyes.

"I wish to thank you for the lovely bouquet, Lord Roxbury. It was quite unnecessary for you to make such a grand gesture, but the girls and I appreciate your generosity. And I do accept your apology, though it was also unnecessary."

He swallowed with difficulty, fighting the urge to be drawn into the lovely blue depths of her eyes. "My treatment of you was boorish, madam, and it is kind of you to forgive me."

"Nonsense." Her smile became a bit less strained. "I daresay I should have done the same thing in your place. You did not know me and there was no reason for you to believe that I was a competent healer. If Beth or Marcie had been injured, I should certainly not have left them in your care on your word alone."

Paul grinned. "And you would have been wise not to do so. I know very little about caring for injuries."

"Be that as it may, Lord Roxbury, but do let us put the unfortunate incident behind us" She took a deep breath and faced him squarely. "I should like our acquaintance to be amiable. If it is not, I fear our charges shall be quite disturbed. I am quite willing to be the soul of civility toward you, if you will agree to be equally civil toward me."

Paul's grin widened as he nodded. "Of course, Lady

Bentworth. May I say that you look particularly charming this evening? Your gown is lovely."

"Thank you, Lord Roxbury." The color rose to her cheeks as she dipped her head in acknowledgment of his compliment. "I am gratified that you like it, for I fear it is the only one in my wardrobe and you will be seeing it at every dinner party this Season."

Paul raised his brows in surprise. What an odd thing for her to say! "I beg to differ, madam. You wore a lovely gown to your stepdaughters' debutante ball. It was fashioned of wine-colored velvet, as I recall."

"Your recall is excellent, Lord Roxbury." She laughed slightly. "The wine velvet is my ball gown. The blue silk I am wearing this evening is the gown that I shall wear for dinner parties. Of course, I have several others which have been altered for me from my First Season, but they are only for morning and afternoon wear."

"Why do you have only two evening gowns?" Paul asked the question that was uppermost in his mind. "Most ladies of my acquaintance have dozens."

She gave a charming laugh. "I thought it more important to clothe Marcie and Beth well. I am only a chaperone, after all, and I need not be dressed in the height of fashion to supervise their Seasons."

Paul remembered the gown she had worn at the park and he began to frown. He should be a regrettable slowtop if he did not surmise where her converse was heading. "My youngest nephew managed to ruin the gown you were wearing in the park. You must allow me to replace it, Lady Bentworth. I should be delighted to stand the cost of a new gown as a way of thanking you for treating Stewart."

"Certainly not, Lord Roxbury!" She appeared genuinely shocked. "It was a very old gown and its loss does not matter in the slightest. I do not expect repayment and I could not accept such a personal gift. It was my pleasure to assist Stewart and I am delighted that he has recovered so rapidly. And I must say he looks rather dashing in his bandage."

"He does." Paul accepted her change of subject, but he was puzzled. He had been wrong in his suspicion that she was hoping for a new gown, for she had declined his offer. Could it be that his initial assessment of her was in error? A lady in pursuit of wealth should have jumped at the chance for a new, expensive gown. But there was the question of Colonel Faraday, the wealthy bachelor who was old enough to be her grandfather. She had appeared to enjoy his company immensely, and he had assumed that the elderly gentleman was her targeted husband.

"I noticed that you accompanied Colonel Faraday in the Promenade, madam." Paul scrutinized her carefully. "Have you known him long?"

"No, I made his acquaintance only two days ago. He was a dear friend of my husband's, you see, and he has just recently returned to England. Both Beth and Marcie were delighted to see him after such a long absence."

Paul was confused. "Your stepdaughters knew him, but you did not?"

"No doubt that is a source of confusion." She laughed lightly. "Colonel Faraday spent much time with my husband and his first wife, and he is Beth and Marcie's godfather. The girls grew up calling him Uncle Sunny."

"Uncle Sunny? Of course!" Paul laughed, catching her meaning immediately. "For Faraday or *Fair Day,* no doubt."

She beamed at him as she nodded. "That is precisely right! Colonel Faraday is a wonderful gentleman and I do hope we have the opportunity to see him again."

"Then he is not here this evening?" Paul raised his brows with the question.

"No. He concluded his business and has already left Town to return to his estate in the Lake District. I suspect he will retire there as he is weary of traveling and he did mention that he was eager to see his neighbor again."

She grinned impishly and Paul caught her meaning. "The colonel's neighbor is a lady?"

"Yes, and she is only a few years younger than he is. From the affection in his voice when he described her to me, I suspect that they shall remove the fence that separates their properties at some time in the near future."

Paul gazed at her intently, but she did not seem in the least disappointed that the colonel's heart was engaged by another. "Will you and your stepdaughters visit them there?"

"Perhaps." She smiled. "I should like to make this lady's acquaintance. His eyes fairly sparkled when he spoke of her and she must be a true paragon to have waited for him all these years."

Paul was saved the necessity of a reply by the arrival of their hostess. Lady Whittington was dressed in dazzling purple silk and the bodice of her gown dripped with diamonds. He made a slight bow and took her hand, bringing it close to his lips. "Lady Whittington. May I say that you look lovely this evening, as always?"

"You may say it, dear Roxbury, but I shall be the one to decide whether it is true or not." Lady Whittington gave a tinkling laugh as she turned to Lady Bentworth. "You put us all to shame with that exquisitely simple gown, Lady Bentworth. Only a classic beauty could wear it and you do so to perfection. The rest of us must make due with flounces and furbelows to hide our faults."

Lady Bentworth laughed merrily. "You put me to the blush, Lady Whittington. But I must admit that your lavish compliment does lead me to suspect that you wish some favor from me."

"She is very clever, is she not?" Lady Whittington exchanged a wink with Paul and then she turned back to Holly. "Yes, my dear, I do. I hope you will not be too disappointed, but Uncle Kingsley has sent his regrets."

Lady Bentworth frowned slightly. "I do hope that he is not ill."

"Not at all, my dear. He simply desired to rest this evening and requested that we excuse him from attending the festivities. And now for my favor. Would it distress you to accept Lord Roxbury as your dinner partner?"

Paul came dangerously close to chortling at the shocked expression that flickered over Lady Bentworth's face. He had made the arrangements with his hostess the moment he had arrived, and she was playing her part to perfection.

Lady Bentworth quickly recovered her aplomb and dipped her head in assent. "I am sorry your uncle cannot join us this evening, Lady Whittington, but I am most pleased to be paired with Lord Roxbury."

"Excellent." Lady Whittington smiled. "And now I must be off. Do hurry to the orangery, my dears. Dinner will be served quite soon."

The moment Lady Whittington had taken her leave, Paul turned to Lady Roxbury with a grin. "I commend you for your civility, madam. Not only did you claim that you were sorry not to be saddled with an elderly, half-deaf dinner partner, you accepted your change of dinner partners with remarkable aplomb. And now, shall we adjourn to the orangery as Lady Whittington wishes?"

"Of course, Lord Roxbury." Holly found her hand was trembling slightly as she took his proffered arm and let him escort her to Lady Whittington's orangery, where small tables had been set up amid the greenery. She was relieved that she was not to be paired with Lady Whittington's elderly uncle, but she was not at all certain how she could endure a whole meal at Lord Roxbury's side. The place cards at the small four-person table indicated that their dining companions were to be Lord and Lady Timberly, a newly married couple who had not yet arrived.

Holly took her place as gracefully as possible, and turned to watch Lord Roxbury slide into his chair. He was seated in the worst of all possible locations, for even though he was slouching slightly in his chair, the fruit-laden branch of an apricot tree was brushing against the top of his head.

"Let us switch places, Lord Roxbury." Holly favored him with an amused smile. "I am not so tall as you are, and that branch will not bother me."

Lord Roxbury nodded, sending the green balls of unripe apricots bouncing. "Thank you, Lady Bentworth. I accept your kind offer, as it has come in the nick of time. I was just considering the possibility of plucking this perky fruit and hurtling it at our hostess."

"We can't have that, though I must say she deserves it for seating you so close to the tree!" Holly giggled as she quickly switched places with Lord Roxbury and reached out to rearrange the place cards.

"There is no need to change the cards, madam." Lord Roxbury reached out to stay her hand. "I happen to know that Lord and Lady Timberly will be delayed. I am certain they will arrive eventually, and when they do, we will sort out the seating."

Holly could not control her reaction to the heated sensation of his hand on hers. She pulled back, as if she had been burned, and regarded him with what she hoped was a polite but curious expression. "Then it will be just the two of us at table for the present?"

"Yes, indeed." Lord Roxbury gave her a rakish grin. "Lord and Lady Timberly have a reputation for arriving late at ton functions. They have been married for less than three months and I suspect that they would rather spend their time together in other pursuits."

"I . . . I see." Holly searched her mind for some topic of conversation, other than the habits of newlyweds. It should be inane to discuss the weather and equally silly to comment on the placement of the tables. All who knew her claimed that she was a gifted conversationalist who could draw even the most reluctant partner into a lively discourse, but she found herself quite suddenly at a complete loss for words.

Lord Roxbury reached out to cover her hand with his again.

"I beg of you, Lady Bentworth, do remain precisely where you are."

"But why, Lord Roxbury?" Holly's brows lifted as she noticed the intent expression on his face.

"If you move so much as an inch, those apricots will entangle themselves in your hair and entrap you."

Holly laughed, but she held perfectly still. "They are that close to me, sir?"

"One is insinuating itself into your coiffure as we speak." Lord Roxbury nodded solemnly. "Reach up with your hand and see if I am not correct."

Holly raised her hand and encountered one of the hard green balls of fruit, precisely where he had said it would be. "Oh, dear. You are entirely correct, Lord Roxbury."

"This will not do at all." Lord Roxbury shook his head in dismay, but Holly noticed that the corners of his mouth were twitching with amusement. "I cannot stand by idly and see you accosted by that tree. If I had an ax, I would gladly chop it down to free you."

Holly giggled at his fierce expression. The situation was embarrassing, but it was also quite humorous. "I doubt that an ax would be appropriate, sir. But perhaps, if you are very circumspect, you might attempt to pluck off some of the fruit."

"Yes, I do believe I could manage the feat." Lord Roxbury nodded. "Will you explain your tactics before I make the attempt?"

"It is very simple, sir. If the branch were not so heavy with fruit, it would rise of its own accord, freeing my hair in the process."

"A capital idea and one worth pursuing." Lord Roxbury's eyes twinkled with humor. "Please maintain your current position, Lady Bentworth, and I will capture the fruit."

Holly did her best to stifle her mirth as Lord Roxbury reached behind her to pull off the lowest piece of fruit. He passed it to her and moved his chair a bit closer so that he could grasp another piece.

"You are quite correct, Lady Bentworth." Lord Roxbury plucked off several more green apricots and presented them to her with the gravity of a soldier, performing a service for his general. "The branch is rising slightly."

Holly glanced down at the pile of green apricots she held in her lap and a giggle rose to her lips. They had not given a thought what to do with the collection of apricots she held.

"What has you so amused, Lady Bentworth?" Lord Roxbury added three more green apricots to the growing pile.

"The apricots." Holly's voice shook with mirth. "Am I to sit here and hold them all evening? Or am I to slip them into my soup bowl when Lady Whittington's footman is otherwise occupied?"

Lord Roxbury chuckled. "I must admit that I failed to consider the disposal of the dastardly fruit. What do you say we toss them on the floor?"

"We should not, sir. Someone might trip on them and fall." Holly gazed about the room, searching for another solution. "Do you see that basket next to the largest lemon tree? Perhaps we could manage to toss them in there."

Lord Roxbury raised his brows. *"We,* madam? It would be most unladylike for you to make the attempt."

"Indeed, it would." Holly nodded, her hair free of the branch at last. "But I daresay you do not think that I could hit the basket, and that is the true crux of your objection."

Lord Roxbury spread his hand against his chest and assumed an injured expression. "Never, madam! You wound me by suggesting that I harbor an ulterior motive. I am merely protecting your reputation as a lady."

"Bother my reputation as a lady!" Holly giggled, feeling suddenly young and carefree. "This is a crisis, sir, and we must take extreme measures. Let us divide these green projectiles among us and see which of us is the better shot."

Lord Roxbury's eyes began to gleam and he nodded quickly. "Done! And what spoils will go to the winner, madam?"

"Spoils?" Holly thought for moment. "I am not certain. What would you like, sir?"

Lord Roxbury seemed about to speak, and then he shook his head. "I am not certain, either, but it must be a worthy prize. Ah! I have it! David and Stewart have praised your cook's strawberry tarts. If I win, I should like a dozen of them."

"You shall have your wish, sir, *if* you win." Holly could not help but wonder at the prize he had chosen. She had expected him to ask for a kiss, or perhaps even more, and she had been fully prepared to refuse him. Perhaps he was not such a rake as the gossipmongers painted him.

"And what will you choose if you win, madam?"

"Do you have a kitchen garden at Roxbury House?" Holly began to smile when he nodded. "In that case, I should like to have some chamomile leaves, as none grows in mine."

"Chamomile leaves?"

"Yes, Lord Roxbury." Holly smiled at the stunned expression on his face. No doubt he had expected her to ask for an expensive trinket of some sort. "The supply I brought with me is running quite low and chamomile is very useful for treating several common ailments."

Lord Roxbury recovered himself and smiled at her. "You shall have your chamomile leaves, whether you prevail or not. Will you take the first shot, madam?"

"Thank you, yes." Holly selected a hard green ball from the collection on her lap and hefted it in her hand. She knew she could hit the basket, as she had played similar games as a child. The only problem she could foresee was the shallow bottom of the basket. If she tossed the green apricot with too much force, it would simply bounce out. She must hit the far rim of the basket to cause it to bounce inside.

"I shall keep watch and tell you when to lob your first piece of fruit." Lord Roxbury gazed around the orangery with a grin. "We are quite safe at the present, madam. No one is paying us the least bit attention."

Holly nodded and immediately let her apricot fly. As she had planned, it hit the far rim of the basket and bounced in.

"Very impressive, my dear!" Lord Roxbury appeared amazed at her expertise. "Have you been practicing this art for long?"

Holly giggled. "Indeed I have not, sir. I can quite honestly state that this is the very first green apricot that I have ever thrown."

"Then it is merely beginner's luck. Choose one for me, madam, and I shall have my try at it."

Holly deliberately chose an apricot that was not quite round. It also felt a bit bottom-heavy and she handed it to him with a challenging grin.

"You have chosen well, Lady Bentworth." Lord Roxbury scowled down at the fruit. "An egg-shaped apricot is the most difficult to throw."

Holly felt a teasing grin slide across her lips. "Would you care for another? I have no need to put you at a disadvantage, for my superior skill shall earn me the win."

"Never!" Lord Roxbury laughed. "The difference in the sexes shall prevail, my dear. Everyone knows that gentlemen throw green apricots much more skillfully than ladies."

Holly's laugh pealed out before she could stop it and she felt a blush rise to her cheeks. "Oh, dear! Several guests have turned to observe us. You must hold your fire for a moment, Lord Roxbury."

"Let us pretend to be discussing something terribly boring and they will turn away. It is fine weather we are having, is it not, Lady Bentworth."

"Exceedingly fine, Lord Roxbury. Of course, it could change at any time. Perhaps we will have rain before the end of the week, or even several days of fog. There is also the possibility that the weather will hold until . . ." Holly stopped speaking of her own accord, and nodded to him. "You were right, sir. They have turned back to their earlier pursuits. You may toss your apricot with impunity."

Lord Roxbury hefted his apricot, tossing it expertly into the basket. "We are tied, madam. Take your next shot."

The contest went on until there was only one apricot left, neither of them missing a single shot. Holly shrugged and turned to Lord Roxbury with a smile on her face. "There is only one left, sir. We must declare the contest undecided unless you wish to climb up the tree for another."

"No, thank you, madam. Let us end in a tie and we shall each claim victory and our prize."

"An excellent suggestion." Holly smiled at him. "But what shall we do with this last piece of ammunition?"

"Ammunition? That is an amusing choice of words, madam. If you will please pass it to me?"

Holly shrugged and passed him the last apricot, a lovely rounded and quite heavy projectile. "What will you do with it, sir?"

"You shall see. Tell me, Lady Bentworth, what do you think of Lady Whittington's butler?"

"A stuffed shirt of the first water!" Holly spoke without thinking and then she clamped one hand over her mouth. "I should not have said that."

"Perhaps not, but I find I agree completely with your opinion. There he is, standing near the door, with a disapproving expression on his face. Do you see him?"

Holly nodded, spotting the butler near the doorway. "Yes, indeed. He appears to be sneering at Lady Whittington's guests."

"The man is forever looking down his nose at me. Several times, when I arrived to call upon Lady Whittington, I suspected that he should like to check the bottom of my boots to make certain that I did not sully her carpets."

"I received that very same impression, sir." Holly nodded. "It is almost as if we are the servants and he is Lord of the Manor."

"Precisely correct, Lady Bentworth. Since we are in complete agreement in assessing the man's character, let us see how he deals with this."

Holly watched, in utter amazement, as Lord Roxbury hefted their very last apricot. "Surely, Lord Roxbury, you would not dare to—"

"I certainly would, madam." Lord Roxbury interrupted her with a chuckle and let the missile fly.

"Oh, dear!" Holly gasped as the ball of green fruit found its target and landed forcefully against the butler's backside. He gave a most undignified yelp and turned quickly to survey the room, searching for the culprit who had caused his discomfort.

"Quickly, Lady Bentworth. Let us discuss the weather again." Lord Roxbury's eyes twinkled merrily.

"I . . . I cannot!" Holly brought her napkin to her mouth and did her best to stifle her laughter.

"Oh, but you must. It would not do to appear amused, for then he will know." Lord Roxbury reached out to take her hands and leaned very close to her. "I do believe this calls for drastic measures. Stare into my eyes as if you loved me, and perhaps his gaze will not linger on us."

Holly did her best to comply, hoping that Lady Whittington's butler would not notice the smile that tugged at the corners of her lips. And then Lord Roxbury reached up to touch her face and she gasped. "What . . . what are you doing, Sir?"

"Hiding your face behind my hand. You look altogether too amused, Lady Bentworth. Think of something very solemn for his gaze is almost upon us."

Holly did her best, but her mind was a blank. Then she remembered the tray of cakes that Cook had burned that morning, and sighed deeply.

"We are safe now. He is no longer gazing at us." Lord Roxbury dropped his hand and leaned back. "Whatever did you think of? You achieved a most convincing doleful expression."

Holly laughed. "The tray of cakes that Cook burned this morning. They were my very favorite."

"I see." Lord Roxbury nodded. "I compliment you on your

cleverness, Lady Bentworth. And now we must be exceedingly circumspect, for Lady Whittington's footman is about to serve our first course."

Holly nodded, smiling slightly, as the liveried footman arrived. But she could not help wishing that Lord Roxbury had not leaned back to a more proper position and removed his hand from her cheek. She could still feel the warmth of his fingers against her skin, and to her stunned surprise, she found that she had enjoyed his touch very much indeed!

Could he have been so thoroughly mistaken about Lady Bentworth's motives? Paul sighed as he played another card. He had retired to the card room soon after dinner, but his mind was not upon the game. She had refused his offer of a new gown and seemed genuinely delighted that Colonel Faraday had left her side to court his neighbor in the North. And when he had given her carte blanche to choose any prize she wished, she had chosen chamomile leaves from his kitchen garden! Her actions were simply not consistent with those of a scheming social-climbing lady who sought a wealthy and titled husband.

Paul's lips turned up in a smile as he remembered the game they had played. Though she had been shocked by his fruited assault on Lady Whittington's stodgy butler, once he had accomplished the impish deed, she had giggled like a schoolgirl and joined forces with him to hide his guilt. She had a sense of humor, that was certain, and she was not above enjoying a good prank. On the whole, he found her quite admirable, and preferred her company to that of any lady in the room.

"Woolgathering again, Roxbury?"

Paul shook himself out of his reverie and turned to face his partner, the husband of their hostess. "Sorry, Whittington. I fear I have done you a disservice by agreeing to partner you this evening."

"Your mind is not on the cards." Lord Whittington chuckled.

"Perhaps you should remove to the ballroom and ask the lady for a dance."

Paul's brows lifted. "What lady?"

"I have no idea, but we are losing quite handily and you are usually a superb player. Whoever she is, your mind is on her and not the game."

Paul sighed, nodding at Lord Whittington and rising from the table. "You are quite right, sir. Perhaps young Olmsby could take my place?"

The substitution was accomplished without delay and Paul walked down the hall toward the ballroom. When he entered, his eyes were drawn toward a group of chaperones, sitting on chairs at the rear of the chamber. Lady Bentworth was among them, and he made his way around the crowded dance floor to approach her.

"Lord Roxbury!" She looked startled at his appearance and blushed prettily. "Do not tell me that you have pockets to let this early in the evening."

Paul laughed. "No, madam. I took my leave before that dire event could transpire. Would you care to join me in a dance?"

"I should adore it!" Her blue eyes sparkled at his suggestion. "But I fear I must refuse you, Lord Roxbury."

"But why?" He was confused by her answer, as it was apparent that she desired to join him on the floor.

"I cannot dance for several more weeks. I am still in mourning."

Paul frowned slightly. "But you are not wearing black?"

"No, and I understand your confusion. My husband left me a letter, requesting that I cast off my widow's weeds for his daughters' Seasons, but I cannot bring myself to take the floor before the two-year period has ended. Perhaps it is silly of me, but it does not seem right."

Paul nodded, admiring her resolve. "When will that period end, Lady Benworth?"

"On the night before the Duke and Duchess of Elmwood's

masquerade ball. And dear Lady Warton has threatened dire consequences if I do not dance at that time."

Paul turned to nod at the dowager seated next to Lady Bentworth. He knew Lady Warton only slightly, but she enjoyed the reputation of being the *ton's* most notorious gabble monger.

"Lady Warton." Paul dipped his head and reached out to raise the dowager's hand near his lips. "Am I wrong in sensing that I recognize an ally in you?"

Lady Warton laughed. "You are quite right, sir. It is past time for Lady Bentworth to reenter society, and I have convinced her to attend my dear sister's ball. Perhaps, if you ask her in advance, she will agree to dance with you then."

"Madam?" Paul raised his brows as he turned to Lady Bentworth. "Since the duke's ball will not have the diversions of Lady Whittington's orangery, will you give me your promise to dance with you?"

Lady Bentworth nodded, her lips quivering with suppressed laughter at his mention of the game they had played. "Indeed, I should be delighted, sir. But it is a costume ball and you must find me among the guests."

"Of course." Paul nodded. "Have you given a thought to your costume?"

"Indeed, I have. But I shall not tell you, Lord Roxbury. You must recognize me to claim your dance."

Paul grinned as he bowed to her. "I shall recognize you, madam, never fear. And I ask that my dance be a waltz."

"Certainly, sir." She smiled back at him. "I am promised to the duke for the first waltz, but I shall save the second for you."

Paul made his goodbyes and walked away. He felt absurdly happy and he had not the slightest notion why. He had waltzed with countless ladies before, but he found that just the thought of holding Lady Bentworth in his arms pleased him above all else.

Nineteen

Though she was careful not to show her pleasure, Holly was delighted when Lord Roxbury appeared at her door the next morning, accompanied by David and Stewart. Beth and Marcie had not told her that the earl should be joining them for their morning ride, but perhaps they had not known. For some unfathomable reason, Holly found she no longer thought of him as *The Elusive Earl,* that dangerous rake who had courted so many young ladies and then left them for the next who had piqued his interest.

When he had left her the previous evening, after eliciting her promise to dance with him at the masquerade ball, Holly had asked Lady Warton whether he had ever been actually accused of compromising a young lady. That good lady had begun to nod, but then a strange expression had spread over her countenance.

Now that I contemplate the matter, I do not believe that he has. He has been perfectly shameless about gaining a young lady's affection and then tossing her aside, but none he has courted has accused him of improper behavior, or even of uttering false promises. And I do believe that every one of them still claims him as a friend.

After returning home and gaining the sanctuary of her bedchamber, Holly had pondered this new bit of information. Could it be that Lord Roxbury had done nothing disgraceful to earn his reputation? That instead of a being rake, he was simply searching for a lady that he could love? The question was so disturbing, Holly had contemplated it long into the night, but she was still unsure whether Lord Roxbury was truly a rake, or whether he had been unjustly accused by the mamas of the young ladies who had fancied their daughters as his countess.

And now he was here, before her, waiting for her to acknowledge him. Holly had decided that it should be unfair of her not to give him the benefit of the doubt and she was prepared to treat him as a friend.

"Lord Roxbury." Holly dipped her head in a nod.

"Lady Bentworth." He returned her polite greeting. "I hope I am not intruding, but it occurred to me that supervising four lively young people on horseback might be too large a task for you to accomplish alone."

Holly noticed the smile that hovered about the corners of his lips and she smiled back at him. "You are quite correct, sir. You will be joining us then?"

Lord Roxbury nodded. "Yes, with your kind permission. Will you instruct your footman to remove the box from my carriage? My gardener has cuttings and some small seedlings for you."

"Chamomile?" Holly's eyes began to sparkle as he nodded, but she made a small gesture toward Beth and Marcie, who were listening to their every word. "How kind of you to remember, Lord Roxbury, when I merely mentioned it in passing."

Marcie turned her with a puzzled expression. "Lord Roxbury brought you chamomile, Mama?"

"Yes, indeed. I mentioned that none grew in our kitchen garden and I had need of it. In return, I have agreed to supply him with a tray of Cook's best strawberry tarts."

Lord Roxbury grinned. "Not apricot, madam? I understand they grow in profusion this year."

"No, sir." Holly bit back a giggle. "I fear they are not yet ripe. I do believe they are still firm green balls upon the branches and quite unsuitable for any other purpose than tossing away."

* * *

Beth managed to ride ahead with Marcie, motioning furtively for the young gentlemen to join them. After a rousing gallop, they outdistanced Lord Roxbury and their stepmother, and pulled up their horses by a stand of trees.

"Did you hear what Mama said about apricots?" Beth turned to Lord Redfield with a puzzled expression on her face.

"I did. And did you notice how they were smiling at one another, almost as if they shared a secret?"

Marcie looked very thoughtful. "They were seated at a table beneath one of Lady Whittington's apricot trees in the orangery. Perhaps that has something to do with their secret."

"You do not suppose . . ." Mr. Averill stopped and shook his head. "No, I am almost certain that neither of them could possibly be the culprit."

Beth's eyes widened as she asked the question. "You refer to Lady Whittington's butler and his unfortunate accident?"

"Yes, and I do believe you've hit on it, Stew!" Lord Redfield began to chuckle. "I would not put it past our uncle to have lobbed that green apricot at his . . . er . . ."

"Backside." Marcie giggled as she supplied the word.

"But Mama would never join in such a prank." Beth seemed very certain at first, but then she turned to Marcie. "Would she, Marcie?"

Marcie laughed. "Perhaps she would. She does possess a wickedly impish sense of humor on occasion. I doubt that she would be the one to throw it, but I am certain that she would not give Lord Roxbury away if she knew that he was the culprit."

"Partners in crime." Mr. Averill chortled. "Now that I think on it, I have no doubt that we have hit on precisely what occurred. Uncle Paul has always despised Lady Whittington's butler. He claims that the man looks down his nose at him and is far too impressed with himself. I would not put it past him to have seized the opportunity for revenge."

Beth giggled, remembering the snobbish butler's yelp as the apricot had found its mark. "We simply must find out if we are correct. Let us mention apricots at every opportunity and watch Mama carefully to see if she is put to the blush."

"A fine plan." Lord Redfield nodded. "We'll assist you by watching Uncle Paul to see if he exchanges any speaking glances with your stepmother."

Marcie giggled, glancing down the path. "Here they come. Look at Mama, Beth. Her color is so high, we shall never be able to tell if she is blushing or not."

"She looks to be enjoying herself immensely." Beth raised her brows in surprise. "I had thought that they would brangle mercilessly, but they are smiling at each other as if they are the best of friends."

An hour later, ensconced in Lady Bentworth's drawing room with a full plate of strawberry tarts before him, Paul found himself quite content. He turned to his lovely companion with a smile and indicated the two couples who were engaged in spirited converse at the other end of the room. "Tell me, Lady Bentworth. Do you think they have tumbled on to our secret? Miss Marcella mentioned apricots several times during our ride."

"I fear they are quite suspicious, but they are not yet convinced." Lady Bentworth sighed, but there was a merry twinkle in her eye. "Perhaps, if we are very cautious, we shall be able to keep the Bow Street Runners at bay."

Paul laughed. "At least we are safe for the present. They seem much more interested in each other than in our suspected crime. Does that worry you, Lady Bentworth?"

"No, not as yet." Lady Bentworth smiled back. "Though both Beth and Marcie have told me that they prefer your nephews' company to any other, they claim it is because none of the four are seeking a romantic entanglement."

Paul nodded, but he was not completely relieved. "Do you

honestly believe that it can be as simple as that? That they can remain friends without becoming . . . entangled?"

"I do, for the present." Lady Bentworth nodded quickly. "But we shall have to keep them under close scrutiny to make certain that they do not change their minds."

Paul smiled. There was nothing he should like more than assisting Lady Bentworth in supervising their charges. She was an amusing companion and he had nearly forgotten that once he had regarded her as a schemer. "I am perfectly willing to assist you, madam."

"Thank you." Lady Bentworth smiled. "But do not feel that you are obliged to pay all of your attentions to us. I am certain that you have other . . . interests."

"I have no prior claims on my time, Lady Bentworth." Paul was pleased to see that the color was rising to her cheeks.

"But . . . the Season." She cast her remarkable blue eyes downward and blushed even more fiercely. "I have no doubt you will soon grow weary of supervising your nephews and my stepdaughters. Would you not prefer to enjoy some of the entertainments with a . . . a young lady of your own choosing on your arm?"

Paul chuckled. She was easily embarrassed. It could be a ploy, of course, but he was very nearly convinced that it was not. "I am not in the Petticoat Line, madam. I have no desire to escort any young lady other than you to *ton* functions."

"Oh. I see." The color in her cheeks heightened, causing Paul to wonder whether he ought to ring for her vinaigrette or a supply of burnt feathers, but she continued to speak. "I think it only fair to tell you that, contrary to what you may have heard, I am most certainly not on the Marriage Mart. I know of your reputation, sir, and though I do not believe it is entirely accurate, I wish our relationship to be perfectly . . . circumspect."

Paul nodded, fighting back a burst of laughter. She was utterly charming in her innocence. "As do I, madam. May I have your permission to be blunt?"

"You may." She nodded quickly. "I should prefer it."

"Good. Do you enjoy my company, Lady Bentworth?"

The color rose to her cheeks again as she nodded. "Yes, Lord Roxbury. To my great surprise, I find that I do."

"And I enjoy yours. I see nothing amiss with escorting you to various entertainments. I doubt that the tongues will wag, so long as my nephews and your stepdaughters are with us. Do you agree?"

"Yes." Her voice was breathless. "I should be pleased by your escort. But you are wrong about the tongues, sir. They will wag quite fiercely."

He frowned slightly and then he sighed, acknowledging the wisdom of her words. "Perhaps you are right, but I intend to ignore them. Is it possible for you to do the same?"

"Of course." She gave a sad little smile that tugged at his heart. "I have fallen victim to mean-spirited *on-dits* before, and it truly does not matter so long as it does not affect Beth or Marcie adversely. If I am cut by some of the denizens of the *ton,* it will not be new to me."

Paul was surprised. Did she truly not care if her good offices suffered? "Then you will not mind?"

"Of course I will mind!" She gazed at him, perplexed. "It is never comfortable to be cut, even if it is done by someone you have taken in dislike. But the gossip will last only until the next scandal surfaces and then it will be forgotten. And tongues will be stilled quite effectively at the conclusion of the Season when it is revealed that you have not offered for me."

"Yes. Of course they will be stilled." Paul nodded, experiencing a most inexplicable twinge of loss. It made no sense, as he had only desired her company for the remainder of the Season and she had agreed to his wishes. Certainly the future could not be so bleak without her as he suddenly imagined it should be!

Twenty

Holly wore a smile as she sipped her morning cup of chocolate. The past two weeks had been filled with a hectic round of parties, balls, and excursions. Lord Roxbury had taken them all to Vauxhall Pleasure Gardens, where they had enjoyed the entertainments under the lights of a thousand lamps. Along with Beth and Marcie, Holly had enjoyed the jugglers, the amazing acrobats, the magician who had pulled a coin from Marcie's ear, and the parade of humanity that had passed by on the walkway in front of the box that Lord Roxbury had procured for them. They had listened to the concert, munched on the highly touted wafer-thin slices of ham, and watched their charges enjoy several dances. When Lord Roxbury had suggested that they stay to view the fireworks display at the conclusion of the evening, Holly had agreed and gasped in awe with the rest of the throng as the colorful bursts of flowerlike pyrotechnics had blossomed against the darkened sky.

Ever since Holly had agreed to join forces with Lord Roxbury, their entertainments had been both varied and pleasurable. They had attended Astley's circus, where both Marcie and Mr. Averill had been most favorably impressed with the equestrian exhibition, and attended the theatre, where they had seen Mr. Kean as Shylock. Both Holly and Lord Roxbury had been highly amused as Beth and Lord Redfield had mouthed Mr. Shakespeare's words right along with the players, and the evening had been most enjoyable. They had also taken a tour of

Carlton House, where Holly had at last viewed the fabled chandelier in the Crimson drawing room, and they had walked along Bond Street to peer in the windows of the fashionable shops. On another day, they had taken tea at Gunther's and sampled an abundance of their touted ices. After they had eaten their fill, they had concluded their afternoon excursion by exploring the volumes at Hatchard's Bookshop, nearly losing both Beth and Lord Redfield in the section that had housed the classics.

Holly's favorite entertainment had been their foray to the Pantheon Bazaar. Never had she seen such an array of goods in one place. Lord Roxbury had offered to buy them each a trinket to put them in mind of their enjoyable day, but Holly had refused, quite properly, claiming that they should remember the afternoon quite well without depleting his pockets.

And then, only yesterday, there had been a picnic in Kensington Gardens. Holly had not known their destination or she should have asked that they choose another place. She had voiced her objection when Lord Roxbury had suggested a tour of the lily garden, averting her eyes as they had passed it by, and suggested that the rose garden should please her more. But Lord Roxbury had stated that he did not care for roses, and they had settled upon a walk through the grove of lilacs instead.

Proof that Holly's stepdaughters had been accepted into the glittering world of the *ton* had come when they had received an invitation to Almack's. Though the famous assembly rooms were actually quite dreary and the refreshments left much to be desired, Lord Roxbury had duly accompanied Holly to that establishment. He had stayed by her side the entire time, the only exception being the courtesy dance that he had requested from their hostess of the evening, Lady Jersey.

Of course there had been whispers about them. Holly had expected no less. But since his nephews and her stepdaughters were also in attendance, the conjectures about them were thankfully mild. Holly did note that more than one mama of a debutante in attendance had cast glances of disapproval in her direction, but Lord Roxbury had appeared to take no notice as he had been deep in a discussion with her about their plans for a projected outing upon the Serpentine.

Even during the evenings that they had attended ton functions, Lord Roxbury had been the perfect escort. He had never failed to compliment her on her appearance and he had been prompt in offering his arm whenever the occasion had warranted. He had suffered the prattle of the other, much older chaperones with remarkable forbearance, and he had been unfailingly considerate and polite.

Holly chuckled lightly as she remembered the incident in Lady Whittington's orangery, when she had realized that Lord Roxbury's sense of humor precisely mirrored her own. She could not count the number of times his eyes had sought hers from across a room, and they had exchanged speaking glances at some humorous comment or bit of outrageous behavior. With every day that passed, Holly's esteem for the earl had grown until now she found that she enjoyed his company to the exclusion of all others. Indeed, she was anticipating the arrival of the Duke and Duchess of Elmwood's masquerade ball with mounting excitement, hoping that he would recognize her in her costume, and take her in his arms for the waltz that she had promised.

As she stared down at her cup of chocolate, Holly sighed deeply. She wished that Lord Roxbury were here with her now, for she felt quite incomplete without him. She could picture him sitting across the table, reading his paper and glancing up to tell her the items of interest. It would be cozy, talking together in the early morning, before the girls had risen from their beds. They would discuss the coming day and she would ask him which invitations he should like to accept. Perhaps he would say that he should prefer to spend a quiet evening with her at home, so that they could retire early and . . .

"Good morning, Mama. I see that you are woolgathering again."

Holly looked up in surprise to see that Beth had joined her in the breakfast room and was already sipping her own cup of chocolate. She blushed slightly at being caught out with her mind in the clouds, and smiled at her elder stepdaughter. "Good morning, Beth."

"What were you contemplating, Mama?" Beth reached for the jam pot. "You had such a contented expression on your face."

"I . . . I do not recall, dear." Holly dropped her gaze. It would never do if Beth guessed that she had been dreaming of Lord Roxbury!

Beth laughed, taking a generous measure of Cook's excellent jam. "It must have been wonderful, whatever it was, for I do not believe I have ever seen you look quite so happy."

Paul put down the letter he had received in the post and sighed. It was a quarterly report from Hugh McPherson, his agent at Midvale Park, and the news was not to his liking. Despite the amount of money Paul had spent to improve his aunt's estate, the lands were showing even less of a profit than they had when he had first inherited them. McPherson was full of ideas for further improvements, but Paul doubted that throwing more blunt at the problem would solve it. Unfortunately, he could not accurately assess the situation unless he traveled to Midvale Park, and even then, he would be at a decided disadvantage. Roxbury holdings had always been devoted to the care and breeding of fine cattle. Paul knew little of agriculture and his aunt's estate consisted entirely of farmland.

There was a light tap at the library door. Paul relegated McPherson's report to the stack of unfinished business on his desk and called out for his visitor to enter.

"Uncle Paul?" David opened the door and looked a bit anxious as he saw that his uncle was at his desk. "I can return at another time, if this is not convenient."

Paul shook his head. "No, I have finished my work for the morning. Come in, David."

David stepped in, shut the door behind him, and crossed the room to take a chair near the desk. The anxious expression did not leave his face and Paul could see that something had the boy worried. "What is it, David?"

"It is Beth, Uncle. When I told you that I wished only friendship with her, I was not untruthful."

"I did not suspect that you were." Paul was hard-pressed to curb a grin. He had wondered how long it would take his nephew to form a *tendre* for Beth.

"It is like this, sir." David sighed deeply. "I find that I prefer her company to the exclusion of all others. Perhaps it is because our interests are so similar, but in the past sennight, I have found myself contemplating . . ."

Paul nodded as his nephew's voice trailed off, and heated color rose to stain his cheeks. "You have been contemplating how Beth would react if you were to kiss her?"

"Yes! But I would not, of course! You must not think that I would take liberties with someone I so admire. It is just that I find myself thinking of her, day and night, and wishing that I could . . . could *court* her!"

This time, Paul could not hide his grin. "And Beth is not averse to this courtship?"

"She is not, sir. She has told me that she would welcome my attentions most . . . most favorably."

Paul nodded. "Then you must speak to Lady Bentworth and ask for her permission to court Beth."

"That is the problem, sir." David sighed deeply. "Beth will not allow me to speak to her stepmother."

"But why?" Paul was puzzled.

"She says we must wait until Lady Bentworth's future is assured."

Paul began to frown. "But you told me that Lady Bentworth did not wish to remarry."

"She does not. Both Beth and Marcie have urged her to reconsider, but she will not hear of it. You know full well how stubborn she can be, Uncle. She did not fall into your arms like a ripe plum, and certainly that is proof that she does not intend to remarry."

"Perhaps it is." Paul began to smile as the perfect solution occurred to him. "Would it satisfy Beth if her stepmother did not remarry, but accepted a genteel position, instead?"

David pondered it for a moment and then he nodded. "I should think that it would suffice, sir, so long as it suited her status as a widow of a peer. But Lady Bentworth has not been offered such a position, has she?"

"Not as yet." Paul smiled at his earnest young nephew. "But I do have such a position in mind, and I will broach the subject with her. I have no doubt that before this evening is over, Lady Bentworth will agree to accept my offer of employment."

David eyes widened. "But, Uncle! Surely you would not . . ."

"No, David." Paul chuckled as he imagined the path his nephew's thoughts had traveled. "I have in mind a respectable position which comes with a residence where Beth and Miss Marcella can reside in comfort until they are wed."

David nodded. "What you describe seems ideal, Uncle. But what is the nature of this position?"

"I need someone to take charge of a country property for me, to judge which further improvements should be made, and to make certain that they are accomplished. Lady Bentworth and her stepdaughters will be welcome to live at the manor house and call it their home, and I shall pay a generous salary for the benefit of Lady Bentworth's expertise."

David began to grin as he nodded. "Lady Bentworth would be perfect for the position, Uncle. When Beth's father became ill, she saw to the running of the estate."

"I know." Paul rose to his feet and walked around the desk to put his hand on David's shoulder. "Not a word to Beth about this, David. Lady Bentworth is quite independent and she would refuse my offer of employment out of hand if she suspected that we were conspiring over her welfare."

Twenty-one

Lord Roxbury had asked for a word in private, and they had slipped out onto Lady Sutherland's balcony, where they were still in sight of the crowd in the ballroom and no one could accuse them of impropriety. Holly smiled up at him in the darkness, enjoying the chill of the night air after the stuffy atmosphere in the ballroom. "Why so mysterious, Lord Roxbury? I swear you practically spirited me away from my chair in dowager's row."

"Are you not grateful that I did?"

Holly nodded quickly. "Indeed, I am! And you were not one moment too soon. If Lady Warton had repeated her story about her brother's stallion one more time, I should have screamed in a most unladylike manner."

"Her brother's stallion? I do not believe I have heard that one."

Holly giggled. "You are baiting me, sir, and it will do you no good, for I will not repeat it. It is dreadfully boring and did not bear telling in the first place. But you did not bring me out here to speak of Lady Warton's conversational skills."

"No, I did not. I must ask you a question, and since it is a rather a delicate matter, I did not wish to mention it with others nearby."

Holly nodded. "Of course. What is it, Lord Roxbury?"

"Several years ago, I inherited a small country property with a manor house. Just this morning, I went over the household accounts and I suspect that the amount spent for food is excessive."

Holly's eyes widened as Lord Roxbury named a sum. "You are right to be concerned, Lord Roxbury, as it is a very large expense. How many persons are fed there?"

"Only eight. There are the housekeeper, four maids, the cook, and two grooms."

Holly began to frown. "It is far too high, Lord Roxbury, unless . . . are there frequent guests?"

"There are no guests. My agent has his own cottage, though he may occasionally take a meal at the manor house."

"Then you are being cheated, sir." Holly nodded emphatically. "The sum you named is enough to feed a staff of eight for a half-dozen years, even if your cook is indulgent."

"Then I was correct in suspecting that all is not right with the accounts?"

"You were. It is possible, I suppose, that this waste could be laid at the feet of an inexperienced housekeeper, but I do not see how she could spend such a large sum. What of your agent? Does he see nothing amiss with the household accounts?"

Lord Roxbury shook his head. "They are not his concern. The housekeeper sends them directly to me."

"You must look into the matter straightaway, Lord Roxbury." Holly turned to face him earnestly. "I would strongly suspect that your housekeeper is lining her pockets with your coin."

Lord Roxbury nodded. "Now you have arrived at the crux of my problem, madam. I know nothing of running a household and could not judge which expenses were valid and which were not. I do know that the property has become a drain on my finances over the past few years. It was turning a small profit when I took it over, but that has long since disappeared and the expenses keep mounting. My agent is constantly haranguing me to send money for repairs and I fail to see how so many repairs can be needed."

"Are the lands used for farming?"

"Unfortunately, they are. And that is another problem. I know very little of agriculture and cannot assess the crop yield in any intelligent manner. All I know is that the estate is not turning the profit I had come to expect from the previous owner's records."

Holly smiled. "But I am able to assess crop yield. I ran my husband's estate while he was ill and I learned much of the business of farming. If you have the figures, I should be happy to tutor you in the essentials."

"Thank you, Lady Bentworth, but I fear I'll need more than a tutor." Lord Roxbury chuckled. "I am woefully ignorant and I doubt I could learn the essentials in time to be of any use. I would rather find someone to live on the property and spend several years assessing the situation for me. How would I go about hiring such a person?"

Holly sighed. "It could well be difficult. You must locate someone in whom you can place your trust. That is of paramount importance. And this person must be married, for his wife would be required to quiz the housekeeper on her expenditures and judge the worth of her staff. Ideally, this couple should have experience in running a similar estate so that they will be fair in their judgment."

"Well said, Lady Bentworth, and I shall keep all of your comments in mind. I will offer a generous salary, of course, but I know of no one who has those particular qualifications, unless . . ."

Holly raised her brows as the earl's voice trailed off. "You have thought of someone, sir?"

"Indeed, I have!" Lord Roxbury laughed. "The very person I need is you, Lady Bentworth! Now that I think on it, you meet every one of my qualifications."

Holly joined in his laughter. "You are quite correct, sir, but I am not searching for employment."

"I know." Lord Roxbury sobered and then he gave a deep sigh. "It is a great pity, Lady Bentwoth. You could solve all of my problems for me if you would see fit to move into the manor house with your stepdaughters and live there for a year or so.

Beth and Marcie could entertain their friends there and I would gladly give you leave to do what you wish with the dwelling, so long as you send me quarterly reports on the status of the estate. You cannot fathom how relieved I should be to put this wretched situation behind me."

"But I cannot become your employee, Lord Roxbury." Holly laughed at the thought. "The prospect is ridiculous!"

"Is it ridiculous, Lady Bentworth?"

Holly opened her mouth, prepared to tell him that it was, when another thought occurred to her. Lord Roxbury had proposed a business arrangement, and without realizing that he had done so, he had offered a tidy solution to her dilemma. If she took the girls and moved into his manor house, she could leave the confines of the dower cottage behind. And since he had promised that she could use the dwelling in any manner she chose, she could start her school of the healing arts and house her students in the extra chambers of his manor house!

"You are so quiet, Lady Bentworth." Lord Roxbury moved a step closer. "Tell me, are you considering my offer?"

Holly came to a sudden decision. "Yes, Lord Roxbury, I am. But this must be a business arrangement."

"Of course. Then you will move onto my property at the conclusion of the Season?"

Holly took a deep breath and nodded again. "You said that I could do as I wished with the manor house, sir. Are you certain?"

"Short of burning it down, I am. What did you have in mind, Lady Benworth?"

Holly took a deep breath and told him her plans for the school. When she had finished, she looked up with shining eyes. "Well, sir? What do you think of my plan?"

"It's a fine plan, Lady Bentworth." Lord Roxbury smiled gently. "And I say that you should forge ahead."

Holly was so excited, she did not stop to consider her actions. She reached up, placed her arms around his shoulders, and brushed her lips against his cheek. "Thank you, Lord Roxbury.

You have made all of my dreams come true. But you have not told me. Where is this estate?"

"It is a journey of only a little over three hours from here. It was my maiden aunt's estate and it is called Midvale Park."

"Midvale Park?" Holly's eyes widened in shock and she stared at him in mounting horror. *"You* are the owner of Midvale Park?"

"Yes. I have owned it for the past three years. It passed to me when my aunt died."

Holly swayed slightly on her feet and she grasped the rail of the balcony to steady herself. All her dreams of a rosy future had turned to ashes, for she would never accept a position from the man who had callously refused to fix the Pooles' roof. He was the enemy, the absentee earl who was more concerned about profits than his tenants' welfare!

Lord Roxbury smiled and offered his arm. "Let us go in and tell your stepdaughters our news. I am certain that they will enjoy living in such lovely country."

"I am certain they will, but it will be in the dower cottage on Bentworth land and not at Midvale Park!" Holly glared at him, her eyes snapping. "You are a . . . a scoundrel, sir! And I find you utterly despicable! If I am very fortunate, I shall never have to encounter your likes again!"

Paul paced across the floor in his library, a worried frown upon his face. He had been utterly confounded when Lady Bentworth had turned on her heel and marched back into the ballroom. It had been quite obvious that she had been offended, but though he had reviewed their entire conversation in his mind, Paul had been able to remember nothing he had said to cause such a reaction.

Once he had taken a few moments to regain his composure, Paul had returned to the ballroom. He had intended to ask Lady Bentworth how he had offended her so deeply, but she had disappeared. The chair she had occupied beside Lady Warton's had been empty and that good lady had clucked in sympathy when he had inquired after her. It seemed that Lady Bentworth had complained of a megrim, asked Lady Warton for the favor of supervising her stepdaughters for the remainder of the evening and the loan of her driver to carry her home.

Upon hearing that news, Paul had seen to it that the evening came to an end quite quickly, informing Beth and Marcie that their stepmother had taken ill and carrying them home to attend her. He had remained in the coach while David and Stewart had seen the girls safely inside, fully prepared to fetch a doctor if one was needed. But when his nephews had joined him, a full fifteen minutes later, they had assured him that a doctor was not at all necessary.

During their return journey to Roxbury House, Paul had listened to David's report with a sinking heart. It seemed that Lady Bentworth was his country neighbor and that was the reason her name had sounded so familiar when they had first met. She had often ridden over Midvale lands to tend his tenants' ailments and had found the conditions deplorable. One of his employees, a schoolmaster named Poole, had gone so far as to move his family into Lady Bentworth's dower cottage in her absence, as the Pooles' roof resembled nothing so much as a sieve. Lady Bentworth had even spoken to McPherson about it, and he had informed her that since the property was not showing a profit, the owner had refused to make any repairs at this time.

Paul could not fault Lady Bentworth for her reaction to the news that he owned Midvale Park. According to both Beth and Marcie, his tenants were living in squalor, his manor house was in a sad state of decay, and his fields were lying fallow as no seed had been provided for the planting. It was no wonder that Midvale Park was failing to show a profit if the accusations that Lady Bentworth and her stepdaughters had made were true.

"There is no mention of the Pooles' roof, Uncle Paul." David looked up from the stack of reports that Paul had given him.

Stewart frowned, turning the last page of the reports that he had studied. "If your agent can be believed, he has repaired the fences, reroofed every one of your tenant cottages, and put a fresh coat of paint on every structure."

"I have one report that claims McPherson has cleared all the brush from the sides of the roadway." David held the paper aloft. "But Beth said that she had traveled the road no less than three months ago and it was near to impassable."

Stewart pulled a sheet of paper from his stack. "And here is a letter from the workmen, demanding payment for clearing the road. You have written a note at the bottom, Uncle Paul, giving the date that you sent the funds, and it is a full four months ago."

"You must go to Lady Bentworth and tell her that you have paid for work that was never accomplished." David offered his opinion. "Once she knows that you authorized the repairs and sent the funds, she will no longer think you a negligent landlord."

Paul sighed. "Yes, she will. And she will be right. I have not paid a visit to Midvale Park for three long years, trusting solely in the reports that McPherson and the housekeeper sent to me. The moment the estate ceased to turn a profit, I should have gone there to assess the situation for myself."

"But you know nothing of farming." Stewart looked puzzled.

"That is no excuse. I should have hired an agricultural expert to accompany me. And I should have made certain that the funds I sent were being used for the correct purpose."

The boys were silent as Paul paced the floor, pondering the problem. After a few moments he stopped, turned toward them, and posed a question. "Do you boys know anything of farming?"

David nodded quickly, his face breaking into a smile. "I am no expert, of course, but I have read several books on the subject, and I have toured Father's lands."

"And I know precisely how a working stable should be run." Stewart grinned at his uncle.

"Then pack your bags immediately, for we leave at first light." Paul answered their smiles with one of his own. "Perhaps

we will not know all that we should, but I am certain that between us we will discover precisely who has been lining his
pockets at my unfortunate tenants' expense."

Twenty-two

As she hurried down the stairs, Marcie on her heels, Beth found herself counting the days that Lord Redfield had been gone. Nearly two weeks had passed without a word and she missed him more every day.

"The post has arrived early today." Marcie picked up the pile of envelopes from the tray in the hallway and looked through the sheaf of letters. "Here is one for you, Beth, and it is written in a hand I do not recognize."

Beth took the letter and opened it with trembling fingers. She glanced at the signature and gave a relieved sigh.

"Is it from him?" Marcie's eyes widened as Beth nodded. "Quickly, Beth. Let us hurry back to your chambers to read it!"

Once they were safely ensconced in Beth's chamber, sitting side by side on the bed, Beth perused the letter. When she had finished, she turned to Marcie with a smile. "Lord Roxbury has charged Mr. McPherson and he is awaiting trial. He has also dismissed the housekeeper, who was McPherson's accomplice in the scheme."

"That is good news." Marcie smiled.

"He has also seen to the repairs on the tenant cottages and hired Mr. Poole's brother as his new agent."

Marcie nodded, remembering Mr. Poole's brother with affection. "He will do well at the job and it will be wonderful for Mother Poole to have both of her sons with her."

"The entire Poole family will live in the agent's house, which is far larger than their cottage. And Serena is to receive a salary for her work with the tenants."

"That is very good news, indeed!" Marcie smiled. "But you have not told me the most important part. Lord Redfield and Mr. Averill have been gone for nearly a fortnight and I confess I sorely miss their company. When will they return to London?"

Beth's eyes sparkled as she gave the answer. "They are expected to arrive this very day! Lord Redfield writes that they leave at first light and should reach London by midday. And since it is already well past that time, I have no doubt that as we speak, they are back in residence at Roxbury House."

"I am so glad that they have returned!" Marcie laughed in delight. "Will we see them this evening at Lady Amesworth's musicale?"

"No." Beth shook her head. "Lord Redfield writes that there are several more tasks that they must accomplish here in Town, not the least of which is obtaining their costumes. We are to meet them at the masquerade ball tomorrow evening. Lord Redfield writes that he shall be wearing the costume of a Spanish bullfighter and Mr. Averill has chosen to dress as a centaur."

Marcie giggled, imagining Mr. Averill as one of the mythical Greek race that bore the upper body of a man and the lower body of a horse. "I might have guessed that Mr. Averill would make use of the horse in his costume. What has Lord Roxbury decided to wear?"

"Lord Redfield does not say, though he does mention that his uncle plans to attend."

Marcie sighed deeply. "I wish that we could tell Mama that they have set Midvale Park to rights."

"No, Marcie. I promised Lord Redfield that we would keep their secret. He told me that Lord Roxbury wishes to present Mama with a *fait accompli.*"

Marcie looked very troubled. "Do you think that Mama will forgive him?"

"I do not know." Beth's worried expression matched that of

her sister's. "Mama is usually most forgiving, but she is acting quite peculiar when it comes to Lord Roxbury. I do not see how she could possibly blame him when he knew nothing of the deplorable conditions at Midvale Park, but she appears to hold him to a higher standard."

"That is true. I wonder why she . . ."

Beth gazed at her sister in astonishment as Marcie stopped speaking, and a knowing smile spread across her face. "What is it, Marcie? You have the look of the cat who has got into the cream pot."

"Mama loves him!"

"What?" Beth stared at her sister in disbelief.

"Mama has tumbled into love with Lord Roxbury, but she will not admit that she has, because she is so frightened of love. Do you not remember the phrase Mama used when the squire's youngest son fell off his horse and refused to go near the stable again?"

"Of course I do." Beth nodded. "She said, *A once-burned child fears the fire.* But how does that concern Mama and Lord Roxbury?"

"She tumbled into love with her fickle pirate and suffered heartbreak because of it. And now she refuses to give her heart to any other gentleman."

Beth frowned. "But you proposed that she was in love with Lord Roxbury."

"She is. But Mama is so busy searching for reasons why she should *not* love him, that she has failed to realize that her heart is already engaged."

Beth considered it for a moment and then she nodded. "I do believe that you have the right of it, Marcie. No doubt Mama compares Lord Roxbury with her first fickle love."

"But Lord Roxbury is not at all like the rake who broke Mama's heart!" Marcie's eyes flashed with anger. "He is kind and good, and I do believe that he loves Mama very much."

Beth nodded quickly. "I believe that also. But Mama will not give Lord Roxbury the opportunity to prove his worth to her."

"Is there nothing we can do to change her mind?"

"Perhaps there is." Beth looked thoughtful. "What if we could recreate the events that led to Mama's broken heart, and prove to her that Lord Roxbury is not at all the same as her first fickle love."

"But how are we to accomplish that when we know so very little about it?"

"We know enough." Beth's smile grew as she refined her idea. "He made Mama's acquaintance at a costume ball and he was dressed as a pirate."

Marcie raised her brows. "I begin to understand your plan, dear sister, and it is admirably devious. You plan to make use of the costume ball that we are to attend tomorrow evening?"

"Yes, indeed." Beth nodded. "We must be certain that Lord Roxbury dresses as a pirate. And I do believe we must divulge Mama's secret to him so that he will understand why it is necessary."

Marcie nodded. "I agree. Will you send him a message?"

"No, Marcie. It is far too sensitive a matter to commit to paper." Beth's eyes sparkled, anticipating her sister's reaction to what she was about to propose. "We must go to Roxbury House and request an audience with the earl."

Marcie gasped. "But, Beth . . . we cannot! You know that Mama would never permit us to call upon a gentleman alone!"

"That is very true, but we will not ask for her permission. We shall simply say that we are to visit one of the other debutantes and go!"

Holly roused herself enough to give her permission when Beth and Marcie expressed a desire to meet Miss Teasdale and her mother for an afternoon stroll through Kensington Gardens. She had not been as attentive to them in the past fortnight, excusing herself from this duty by reason of Lord Redfield and Mr. Averill's absence. As the young gentlemen had gone from the city to visit country relatives, Holly had decided that her constant vigilance was not required.

"Mama?"

"Yes, dear?" Holly looked up from the slim volume of poetry that she was not reading to find Beth staring at her intently.

"Would you care to join us? I am certain that Miss Teasdale and her Mama should welcome your company."

"No, Beth." Holly sighed, not relishing the thought of a walk through the very gardens where she had so recently enjoyed an outing with Lord Roxbury. "I shall remain here and read. But you must return by five at the latest, as Madame Beauchamp has promised to deliver your costumes for their final fitting."

After the girls had left, Holly closed her book and returned it to the shelf. Lord Byron's romantical verses served only to deepen her despair. They caused her to long for what might have been, and there was no purpose in that.

As she climbed the stairs to her sitting room, Holly wondered if there was any excuse she could offer for not attending the costume ball. She should dearly like to beg off, but she had promised Lady Warton that she would take the floor for the first waltz with the duke. It was no little honor to be singled out in this manner, and to send her regrets should be an insult. Barring death or disaster, she would be forced to attend and enter into the festivities with a smile upon her face. And that smile would have to serve her well to disguise the fact that her heart had been broken not once, but twice.

"You do know that we shall be ruined if anyone catches wind of this. It is highly improper for a debutante to call upon an unmarried gentleman alone." Marcie averted her face from a passing carriage and hurried to keep up with Beth's long strides.

"We are not alone, we are together." Beth turned the corner and walked swiftly up the street that led to the earl's residence. She had deliberately chosen to say that they were to visit Miss

Teasdale, as her residence was only a short distance from Roxbury House.

Marcie giggled. "That will not fadge, sister. It would not matter whether we were two, or twenty. Our action would still be considered quite beyond a small breach of etiquette. If we are caught out, we will be thoroughly censured by the *ton.*"

"Does that matter more to you than Mama's happiness?" Beth turned to her sister with a frown.

"Of course not. You are the one who is concerned about what others think of you. I merely wished to make certain that you knew precisely what you risked."

"I do know." Beth climbed the steps that led to Lord Roxbury's door and took a deep, calming breath. What she was about to do would contradict all she had been taught of genteel behavior, but there was no help for it. With a hand that trembled only slightly, she employed the knocker and stood back, waiting for admittance.

"What will we do if Lord Roxbury is not at home?" Marcie looked worried.

"We will wait until he returns. I am determined to see him and we shall not leave until we do."

"Beth and Miss Marcella?" Paul began to frown as Farley handed him their cards. "And you say that they are *alone?*"

A smile of amusement hovered round Farley's lips. "Yes, m'lord. Naturally, I whisked them in before any passersby could see them standing at your door. I can only hope that they were unobserved."

"Quite right, Farley." Paul nodded. "Their reputations should be thoroughly ruined if word got out that they were calling upon *The Elusive Earl* without a suitable escort. I wonder what brought them here?"

"I do not know, m'lord. They appeared quite anxious, and most relieved when I told them that you were at home. I did ask them if they would divulge the nature of their visit."

"And they would not tell you?"

"No, m'lord. The younger of the two seemed about to speak, but the elder stilled her with a glance. And then she informed me, rather abruptly, that their business with you was private and of no concern to me."

"She did, did she?" Paul laughed. "I would never have thought Beth capable of such cheek. But you did deserve it, Farley."

Farley joined in his employer's laughter. "I suppose I did, m'lord."

"It is not at all like either Beth or Marcie to disregard the proprieties in this manner." Paul turned thoughtful. "Is it possible that they have run away from home?"

Farley shook his head. "I am almost certain they have not. As I left to order a tray of refreshments, I heard the younger miss say that she hoped you would not keep them long, for they should be in a terrible muddle if they were not home in time to have their costumes fitted."

"That is something, at least." Paul chuckled as he rose to his feet. "Ask David and Stewart to join us immediately, and we will discover the reason that Miss Elizabeth and Miss Marcella have defied convention to arrive on my doorstep."

Paul watched as Beth poured their tea. Her hands were trembling slightly and the color was high on her cheeks. Marcie appeared similarly anxious, but thus far, neither young lady had seen fit to discuss the reason for their unconventional visit. Instead, they had passed several minutes discussing the improvements that had been made at Midvale Park. Fearing that they should never divulge their true reason for seeking him out if he did not introduce the subject, Paul turned to Beth with a smile.

"I am certain you did not come to discuss Midvale Park with me, Beth. Precisely why are you here?"

As Paul watched, her color grew even higher. She took a deep breath, as if girding her loins for a battle that was about to occur, and met his eyes squarely. "Do you love our mama?"

"Yes." Paul spoke without thinking, but his answer was no less than the truth. He had mulled over the question for the past fortnight and he had decided that there was no other explanation for the terrible sense of loss that he had experienced when Lady Bentworth had turned on her heel and left him standing on Lady Sutherland's balcony.

"She loves you, too." Marcie spoke up. "But she will not admit that she does. That is why we have risked all to come to you. Mama's happiness is at stake."

Paul turned to David and Stewart, who were grinning widely. "You were quite correct to prefer these two young ladies over all the others. They have bottom."

"Like a horse has bottom?" Marcie giggled as he nodded. "I have never heard that before, and I am not sure whether we should be gratified, or offended."

Paul smiled. "Perhaps you should be a bit of both, but rest assured it was intended as a compliment. Now tell me exactly why you have come, and what you require of me."

"You must go to the costume ball dressed as a pirate." Beth answered the question. "And you must dance the waltz with Mama."

Marcie nodded. "We are attempting to recreate the past, to prove to Mama that you are not like her first fickle love. Mama met a pirate at the duke's costume ball five Seasons ago. She does not know that we know, but she tumbled into love with him that very night and he broke her heart."

"You say this gentleman was dressed as a pirate?" They nodded and Paul's eyes widened at the incredible coincidence. "But I attended a costume ball five Seasons ago. And I was dressed as a pirate. I partnered a lovely young lady dressed as an angel and we agreed to meet in the park the next day. I waited for hours, but she did not appear."

Beth gasped in shock. "That was Mama! Papa left us a letter telling us about it. Mama also waited for hours, but her pirate did not appear. She searched for him at every dance and party, but she never saw him again."

"It was the reason she agreed to marry Papa." Marcie nodded quickly. "He comforted her when her heart was broken. When he told her that he was dying and he needed a wife to take care of us, she agreed to marry him for our sake. Papa said she despaired of ever making a love match after the man she'd loved had left her sitting there waiting, alone at the garden."

Paul shook his head. "But I was there! It was your mama who failed to keep our rendezvous. I sat on the stone bench, next to the rose garden, for upwards of three hours."

"The rose garden?" Beth's mouth dropped open. "But Mama waited at the lily garden!"

There was a shocked silence in the sitting room as all of them digested this fact. Then David spoke. "This is rather like one of Mr. Shakespeare's plays."

"Indeed, it is." Beth nodded, moving a bit closer to David. "It is a comedy of errors with a tragic result."

Marcie sighed deeply. "But all is not lost. We shall simply have to rewrite the ending."

"How?" Paul leaned forward. "Simply offering an explanation to your mama will not suffice. If she has thought ill of me all these years, she will not suddenly change her mind. And do not forget that I nearly proved her correct by failing in my duties at Midvale Park."

Stewart waved away his concerns. "All that is past. You have righted the situation at Midvale Park. All that is left to correct is Lady Bentworth's initial impression of you."

"I think that Miss Elizabeth and Miss Marcella have the proper plan." David nodded quickly. "You must go back to the beginning to correct what went awry. Will you dress as a pirate for the costume ball, Uncle Paul?"

Paul smiled. "Of course I will. I have kept my original costume."

"Once you have arrived at the ball, you must request a dance with Mama." Beth spoke up. "And you must not allow her to refuse you. If it is necessary, simply take her arm and march her onto the dance floor."

Stewart grinned, clearly enjoying his part in this conspiracy. "And once you have waltzed with Lady Bentworth, you must ask her to meet you in the park."

"No." Paul shook his head.

"No?" Beth's eyes widened. "But why?"

Paul grinned as he studied the girls' determined faces. He would be proud to have them in his family. "Because I am not willing to take a chance that fate might intervene once again. I plan to take your stepmother up in my arms and carry her to the park!"

Twenty-three

It was the night of the costume ball and Holly paced the floor of her sitting room anxiously, waiting for Beth and Marcie to be ready. She was wearing the costume of a gypsy princess, but she was not pleased with the fit. The waist seemed much tighter than it had just yesterday, when Madame Beauchamp had come for her final fitting, and she could scarcely breathe.

Holly glanced at the clock and sighed. The girls were taking a very long time and the hour was fast approaching when they must take their leave. Just as she was about to go to their chambers to discover the reason for the delay, she heard footsteps approaching in the hall.

"We're ready, Mama." Beth stopped in the open doorway, dressed as an Indian princess with a beaded leather dress and fringed moccasins. Her hair was arranged in two long braids, which were decorated with colorful feathers, and a beaded headband completed the costume.

"You look lovely, dear." Holly smiled at her elder stepdaughter. "Where is Marcie?"

"I'm here, Mama." Marcie arrived at that instant, out of breath, and dressed as Cleopatra. "You are truly beautiful, Mama."

Holly laughed, shaking her head. "Not nearly as beautiful as you are, my dear."

"Turn around, Mama." Beth cocked her head to the side, a thoughtful expression on her face.

Holly turned in a circle, and when she had returned to her

original position, she noticed that Beth was frowning. "Is there something wrong, dear?"

"Yes." Beth walked a bit closer. "Your skirt does not hang properly in the back. Perhaps Dorri has fastened it wrong."

Marcie nodded. "You are right, Beth. It is crooked on one side. Hold still, Mama, and I will try to fix it."

"Perhaps no one will notice?" Holly stood very still as Marcie inspected the back of her skirt.

"But they will, Mama!" Marcie sounded quite concerned. "You are to take the floor with the duke and all eyes will be upon you. I do believe the material is caught up in the stitching at the waist. Perhaps I can pull it . . ."

Holly gasped as she heard the sound of fabric tearing. "Oh, dear! What has happened?"

"Your skirt has torn loose from the bodice!" Marcie gave a little cry of distress and came round to face her. "I cannot believe that Madame Beauchamp has stitched it so carelessly."

Beth nodded. "You cannot appear at the ball like this, Mama. It will have to be repaired."

"But there is no time. We must leave in less than a quarter hour. Perhaps you girls should go without me and I will join you when my costume has been mended."

Marcie shook her head. "But you are to dance the first waltz with the duke, Mama. It will be considered an insult if you do not arrive in time."

"You must wear something else." Beth took her arm and led her through the door and into her dressing room. "Is there another gown in your wardrobe that will serve as a costume?"

Holly gazed at the contents of her clothespress and shook her head. "No. I do not believe I have any gown that . . ."

"How about this?" Beth reached to the very back of the clothespress and pulled out an angel costume.

Holly stared at the costume in disbelief, and then she shivered slightly. "That looks like the very same costume I wore during my First Season!"

"No doubt it is." Beth smiled happily. "When you asked me

to go through the trunks and choose what we should bring with us, I found this angel costume. You instructed me to bring anything I thought might be of value, and I packed it with the rest of our belongings."

Marcie smoothed her hand over the soft white material and smiled. "It is not even wrinkled, Mama, and it will do perfectly. Your hairstyle is fine, just as it is, and I'll fetch Dorri to help you change."

"Don't worry, Mama." Beth moved behind her and began to unfasten her gypsy costume. "It should not take more than a few minutes, and the moment you are ready, we shall leave. You shall arrive in time for your dance with the duke. You will see."

"You were a vision of beauty, my dear. I declare, you nearly floated in Edgar's arms." Lady Warton smiled as Holly returned from her dance with the Duke of Elmwood and took her chair once again.

"Thank you, Lady Warton." Holly returned her smile. "It was very kind of the duke to partner me."

"Nonsense, dear Holly. Edgar preened like a peacock to have such a lovely young lady in his arms."

Holly decided to change the subject, before Lady Warton attempted to pair her off with another gentleman. "Look, Lady Warton. Is that not Lady Maitland?"

Lady Warton followed Holly's glance and gave a decisive nod. "I fear it is. And if anyone should *not* wear a shepherdess costume, it is dear Amelia! She has far too much flesh for the style."

"There are Beth and Marcie." Holly smiled as she caught sight of her stepdaughters.

"Ah, yes." Lady Warton nodded. "The Indian princess and Cleopatra. Their costumes suit them well. Who are their partners, dear?"

Holly studied Beth's partner, a Spanish bullfighter, and the centaur, who had Marcie on his arm. "I am not certain, but I believe the bullfighter to be Lord Redfield. The centaur must be his brother, Mr. Averill."

"The centaur costume is very clever." Lady Warton laughed. "Look how he drapes the tail over his arm."

"Yes, indeed." Holly nodded, her eyes searching the room for Lord Roxbury and hoping, desperately, that he was not in attendance.

Lady Warton favored her with a knowing smile. "And where is their uncle this evening? Surely he did not send them alone."

"I have not seen him as yet, Lady Warton." Holly attempted to keep the smile on her face. "No doubt he is somewhere in this crush."

Lady Warton gazed round the room again, and then she gestured toward the far end of the dance floor. "I do believe he is there, dancing with Miss Kingston. He is dressed as an Arabian sheik."

"Yes, indeed." Holly's heart pounded rapidly as she caught sight of the gentleman Lady Warton had indicated. He had the build and the height of Lord Roxbury, but his hair was cropped a bit too short. Of course it was possible that Lord Roxbury had altered the style during the fortnight since she had last seen him.

"You have promised him the second waltz, have you not?" Lady Warton raised her brows.

Holly nodded, her heart sinking down to her toes. Surely Lord Roxbury would not presume to hold her to her word. "You were a party to that promise, Lady Warton. Have you forgotten the condition I set?"

"Ah, yes." Lady Warton Smiled. "Lord Roxbury must recognize you. But surely you have let slip a bit about your costume to . . . oh, my! He has come, once again!"

Holly gazed toward the door of the ballroom and gave a small gasp. It was her pirate, she was certain of it! "Who . . . who is he, Lady Warton?"

"No one knows." Lady Warton gave a girlish giggle. "He

appears at every one of my sister's costume balls and he has done so for the past five years."

"But surely the duchess knows who he is?"

"She does not." Lady Warton pronounced it emphatically. "Presumably, he receives an invitation, or he has one made that will pass inspection at the door. Dear Violet says her ball would not be complete without him, as he is really quite charming and he provides a delightful mystery for her guests."

"Then he does not stay for the unmasking?" Holly stared at the pirate and drew in her breath sharply. She was almost certain that he was the gentleman who had broken her heart and she desired to know his identity.

"He slips out without a trace." Lady Warton's eyes sparkled. "Last year, Edgar posted footmen around the perimeter to detain him, but he managed to elude them."

Holly nodded, intrigued. "Does he dance?"

"Of course. And even his partners do not know who he is. He engages them for one dance and then he goes on to the next. There is great speculation about which gentleman he might be, but no one knows for certain. Watch him, dear. He is about to choose his first partner."

Holly watched as the pirate gazed round the room, his glance lingering on one young lady and then another. She trembled slightly as he turned in her direction, feeling a bit like a rabbit, frozen in the glare of a lantern.

"Oh, my! I do believe he intends to dance with you!"

Holly heard Lady Warton's words through a fog as the pirate moved across the floor in her direction. She found she could not move, or even speak. His eyes pinned her to her chair.

"Lord Roxbury is also coming your way." Lady Warton motioned toward the Arabian sheik, who was approaching from the opposite direction. "It appears they both wish to dance with you."

Holly shivered, caught on the horns of a dilemma. She did not wish to dance with Lord Roxbury, but neither did she wish to dance with her pirate. Before she could decide which of the two should be more dreadful, her pirate arrived, bowed low before her, and offered her his arm.

She allowed herself one glance, to make certain that the Arabian sheik was still headed her way, and came to a decision. She would rather dance with the pirate who had stolen her heart than be forced into Lord Roxbury's arms. They were both rakes and bounders who had played fast and loose with her affections, but there was far less danger from an old love than there was from a new love.

Holly rose to her feet and accepted the pirate's arm, allowing him to escort her to the dance floor. And then she was in his strong arms, gliding across the floor to the melodic strains of the very same waltz they had danced five Seasons ago and reliving the memory that she had suppressed for so long.

Paul held his angel a bit more closely than propriety allowed, but she did not resist him as they whirled across the floor. He knew that she was caught up in the memory of that time long ago, before the fates had conspired against them, and he intended to use that memory to his advantage. Her lips were parted slightly and Paul fought the urge to kiss them. He had kissed them that night, five Seasons ago, and found them sweetly passionate and giving. Was it possible for them to renew their first taste of love and forget the delusions of the intervening years? Paul was not certain, but his future happiness, and Holly's as well, demanded that he make the attempt.

It seemed as if they had been waltzing for only the space of a heartbeat, but the melody was drawing to an end. They were approaching the balcony and the doors were open, just as Stewart and Marcie had promised that they would be. This was the moment Paul had longed for through four insufferable Seasons, and he did not hesitate. Before his angel could gather herself enough to resist, he whirled her out, onto the balcony, and claimed her lips with his own.

* * *

Holly gasped as the pirate kissed her. She thought to draw back, to struggle for her freedom, perhaps even to scream. But her traitorous lips betrayed her good sense and she found herself moving even more closely into his embrace. Time stood still, their kiss frozen against the starry skies of an eternity, as cold as ice and as blazing as embers, equally comforting and discomfiting.

His fingers were warm against her face, his other arm a band of steel clamping them together in a vise that brooked no escape. She could not breathe, nor was there any need, as he was her sustenance and her life. She wished to be carried off, in this timeless moment of perfection, and leave the petty cares and concerns of her existence behind her. There was a renewal in his arms, a rising of her awareness, and a sense that life should be a never-ending joy if he would only stay with her.

But he would not stay. He had not stayed before. Tears filled Holly's eyes. This was a fleeting moment, one that would be over all too soon, and she would be left to rue the moment that she had gone into his arms once again.

He sensed the change in her, the first moment that she became aware of their unfortunate past, and he cursed the wry twist of circumstance that had torn them apart. There was no time to lose and he lost not a second, lifting her quickly into his arms and rushing down the steps to the duke's pleasure gardens.

He sped down the winding path, not caring that the thorns of the rose bushes tugged at his costume or the low branches of the trees nearly swept the pirate's hat from his head. He was in pursuit of happiness and he trod swiftly over the stones in the path until he arrived at the gate that led to the street.

The gate was ajar. David and Beth had done their work well.

Paul slipped through, his love nearly insensible in his arms, and crossed the deserted roadway to the park.

She was as light as a feather. He would have thought that he held a wraith, or perhaps even a figment of his own dream of love, but he could hear the rapid beating of her heart and feel the sweet warmth of her.

He had to make her his; there was no life for him without her. The unbearably empty years that had passed since their first meeting had proven it without a doubt. He wanted her as wife, as lover, as mother for the children that they would have. He would go to any lengths to win her heart, even if it meant abducting her from under the very noses of the *ton*.

If she refused to marry him, there was no question of what he intended to do. He would compromise her most thoroughly on the stone bench by the rose garden, where he had waited for her five years ago. And if that would not suffice to convince her to marry him, he would carry her to the lily garden and compromise her there, as well!

Holly felt as if she were dreaming, borne away on the wings of darkness. Her mind spun with useless bits of information. His silk shirt felt soft against her cheek. Jasmine gave up a sweet perfume when it crushed beneath his boots. Moonlight turned the willow leaves to glistening silver.

She was being abducted by her first fickle love. Holly blinked to clear her mind, but the delicious lethargy of being in his arms once more left her incapable of rational thought. Her head was filled with disjointed images that whisked by so quickly, she could not retain them. A bush. A flowering tree. A fountain that trickled musically. The open garden gate.

And then he was through the gate without breaking his stride, and across the street to the lush grass that bordered the park. He crossed the strip of sweet-smelling grass and entered the park, the very same park where he had failed to meet her five

Seasons ago! Was he planning to ravish her here? She must resist at all costs and make her escape!

Holly trembled as he carried her into the shadows of the trees. In only a few moments, they had arrived at the rose garden, and he took a seat on a stone bench, still holding her firmly.

"This is where I waited for you, my angel. Why did you fail to meet me?"

Holly's mind spun with his question. He was her pirate. There was no longer any doubt. His voice was familiar, but she could not place it, perhaps because she was so shocked by his words.

"Answer me, my angel. Why did you fail to meet me? I waited for hours upon this very bench."

Holly felt a great wave of relief wash over her. He meant her no harm. He merely wanted to know why she had not met him and her voice trembled slightly as she answered him. "But I did meet you. I waited for hours at the lily garden."

"So we both kept our meeting in separate places, just as we have been separated these four long years."

There was such sadness in his voice, Holly's eyes filled with tears. "You asked me to meet you at the flower garden. You . . . you did not say which flower."

"Then I was a fool for not saying." He laughed, but there was pain in his laughter. "I have searched for you these past four years, hoping to find you again. I love you, my dearest angel."

Holly shivered despite the fact that he was holding her tightly. "And I . . . I loved you."

"Loved?"

His arms tightened about her, as if he were afraid of losing her again, and Holly felt tears of remorse slip down her cheeks. "Yes. Perhaps I still love you. It is all so confusing that I am not certain. Is it possible that I could love two gentlemen at once?"

"No." His voice was sad. "You must prefer one over the other. That is the way of love. If I may ask, is the Earl of Roxbury my rival?"

Holly did not think to deny it. She admitted what was in her heart. "Yes, I love him. But he does not love me. And . . . and when you kissed me, I began to doubt that my love for him was true."

"That is understandable." The pirate chuckled softly. "Perhaps I should kiss you again to make certain. Take off your mask, Holly, so that I may kiss you properly."

With trembling fingers, Holly reached up to take off her mask. But it dropped from her hand as she realized what he had said. "You . . . you know my name! And I do not know yours."

"But you do." He smiled as he removed his mask.

"You!" Holly's eyes widened as she recognized the earl. "You . . . you cad! You are a rogue and a scoundrel, a dastardly villain who does not deserve the . . ."

"Mrs. Poole sends her greetings, Holly." He interrupted her angry tirade against him.

"What?"

"I said, Serena sends her greetings, as does her husband and Mother Poole. She asks that you hurry back to visit her in the agent's cottage."

"The . . . the agent's cottage?"

"Yes. Mr. Poole's brother is my new agent and the entire Poole family has been installed there."

Holly felt her mind spin. "But what of Mr. McPherson?"

"He is in jail awaiting trial. When I got to Midvale, I realized immediately what had happened. McPherson and my housekeeper conspired to line their pockets with the funds that I sent for repairs."

Holly was so shocked, she could not seem to think. "You . . . you traveled to Midvale?"

"Yes, indeed. That is where we have been for the past fortnight. You were right, Holly. The conditions were shameful when we arrived, but the boys and I have seen to the repairs."

Holly felt her anger at him evaporate, leaving only confusion in its wake, "But . . . but I thought that you truly did not care, that you were simply concerned for the profits."

"Never. But I am at fault for not traveling to Midvale earlier and I plan to return at the end of the Season and take up residence in the manor house for a time. Will you and your girls agree to accompany me?"

"I cannot." Holly sighed with real regret. "I am a widow and you are a bachelor. Even with Beth and Holly in attendance, it would be scandalous for us to travel such a distance together."

He smiled, reaching out to touch her cheek. "But there will be no scandal, Holly . . . unless you refuse to marry me."

"*Marry* you?" Holly's eyes widened. "You are . . . are truly offering for me, Lord Roxbury?"

"You must call me Paul, and of course I am. I love you and I know that you love me. You could open your school at the manor house, Holly, and the girls and I would help you. And after it is established, perhaps Mrs. Poole would agree to assume the position of headmistress so that you and I would be free to travel. Is there any reason why we cannot be wed before we leave?"

Holly thought about it for the space of a heartbeat and then a delighted smile spread across her face. "But . . . are you certain that you truly—"

He pulled her into his arms and kissed her again, silencing her words. As their kiss deepened, Holly's mind cleared and her arms stole up to wrap round his neck. Perhaps it was not so confusing, after all, now that the two men she loved were one and the same.

Their kiss continued until Holly heard a faint sound in the distance. It sounded a bit like applause at the conclusion of a play. There were several shouts of approval that grew louder and louder and she pulled away from Lord Roxbury's embrace with great reluctance.

"Scamps!" Lord Roxbury regarded the two couples who were standing near the park bench, applauding and cheering them on. "How long have you been standing here?"

"We just came upon you this very instant." Beth blushed prettily as the lie passed her lips. "And we think it's a marvelous plan. Please say yes, Mama! We would so love to live at Midvale Park."

Marcie nodded. "Truly we would, Mama, and there is no reason why you should not marry Lord Roxbury. We all know that you love him and it is very clear that he loves you."

Holly laughed and turned to Lord Roxbury with a wink. "Perhaps they are right, Paul. We must combine forces to teach my dear stepdaughters some much-needed discretion. I do not understand how it has occurred, but they have failed to learn that it is not polite to interrupt a lady when she is about to agree to marry her perfect match."

ABOUT THE AUTHOR

Kathryn Kirkwood lives with her family in Granada Hills, California, She is currently working on her fourth Zebra Regency romance, *A Valentine for Vanessa,* which will be published in February, 2000. Kathryn loves to hear from her readers and you may write to her c/o Zebra Books. Please include a self-addressed stamped envelope if you wish a response. You may also contact her at her e-mail address: OnDit@aol.com.

<u>BOOK YOUR PLACE ON OUR WEBSITE</u>
<u>AND MAKE THE</u>
<u>READING CONNECTION!</u>

We've created a customized website just for our very
special readers, where you can get the inside scoop on
everything that's going on with Zebra, Pinnacle and
Kensington books.

When you come online, you'll have the exciting
opportunity to:

- View covers of upcoming books
- Read sample chapters
- Learn about our future publishing schedule
  (listed by publication month *and author*)
- Find out when your favorite authors will be visiting
  a city near you
- Search for and order backlist books from our
  online catalog
- Check out author bios and background information
- Send e-mail to your favorite authors
- Meet the Kensington staff online
- Join us in weekly chats with authors, readers and
  other guests
- Get writing guidelines
- AND MUCH MORE!

Visit our website at
http://www.zebrabooks.com

LOOK FOR THESE REGENCY ROMANCES

SCANDAL'S DAUGHTER   (0-8217-5273-1, $4.50)
by Carola Dunn

A DANGEROUS AFFAIR   (0-8217-5294-4, $4.50)
by Mona Gedney

A SUMMER COURTSHIP   (0-8217-5358-4, $4.50)
by Valerie King

TIME'S TAPESTRY   (0-8217-5381-9, $4.99)
by Joan Overfield

LADY STEPHANIE   (0-8217-5341-X, $4.50)
by Jeanne Savery

ROMANCE FROM FERN MICHAELS

DEAR EMILY   (0-8217-4952-8, $5.99)

WISH LIST   (0-8217-5228-6, $6.99)

AND IN HARDCOVER:

VEGAS RICH   (1-57566-057-1, $25.00)